T0006959

THE ICEMAN'S CURSE

GARY F. JONES

North Carolina

Published in the United States by BQB Publishing
(an imprint of Boutique of Quality Books Publishing, Inc.)
www.bqbpublishing.com

Printed in the United States

ISBN 978-1-952782-78-7 (p)
ISBN 978-1-952782-79-4 (e)

Library of Congress Control Number: 2022942158

Book design by Robin Krauss, www.bookformatters.com
Cover design by Rebecca Lown, www.rebeccalowndesign.com
First editor: Caleb Guard
Second editor: Andrea Vande Vorde

PRAISE FOR THE ICEMAN'S CURSE AND AUTHOR GARY F. JONES

"Author Gary Jones delivers a fast-paced, well-written, and entertaining satirical suspense story in *The Iceman's Curse*. Jones's writing is in the same league as Carl Hiaasen's humorous crime novels that take on current events, politics, and local customs. In *The Iceman's Curse* the mismanagement of a vial containing a deadly virus creates havoc for officials at all governmental levels including the military during a winter blizzard in Wisconsin. Dealing with impossible snow-covered roads adds to the hilarity caused by the desperate criminals and officials alike. A truth-seeking scientist with a pregnant wife due any day provides a warm thread throughout this story. This cinematic-style caper is perfect for readers who have also loved movies such as *Fargo* and *Weekend at Bernies*. Gary Jones's novel is a triumph. If you haven't read his work yet, put *The Iceman's Curse* on your list. Highly recommended.

— Christine DeSmet, mystery novelist, writing coach, member of Mystery Writers of America and Sisters in Crime

CHAPTER 1

THE PROJECT

Monday, January 8, 2018
St. Paul, Minnesota
9:00 a.m. CST

Grant Farnsworth entered the old PathoBiology building of Minnesota's College of Veterinary Medicine and took the stairs two at a time to the second floor. He headed down the main hallway, removing his winter gloves and unzipping his heavy parka. He power walked past the first door on the right, avoiding an open area where a secretary's desk once guarded the entrance to three offices. Years ago, computers had made secretaries unnecessary for mere professors, so the room became an open area with no practical use.

A quick glance across the empty space was a mistake. Grant made eye contact with sixty-three-year-old Ron Schmidt, his faculty adviser, who was standing in the doorway of his office.

A hiker and winter camper, Ron was in good shape for his age. He could look impressive dressed in a suit and tie to meet visiting dignitaries, but today he wore the working uniform worn by professors of basic sciences in the Veterinary College: khaki pants and a rumpled dress shirt open at the collar. He smiled and waved the sheaf of papers in his hand, gesturing to his office.

Grant recognized the smile. *Fuck, another idea for a project,* he thought. He tried to get by with a wave and move on, but there was a fat chance that would work. "Grant," Ron called to him. "Come here. I have something we need to discuss."

Ron took a seat behind his desk, leaned back in his chair, and interlaced his fingers behind his head. His grin was even broader. "How would you like to take a crack at sequencing ancient DNA?"

Grant swore under his breath and pasted a phony smile on his face. An overworked and underpaid postdoctoral student, he was already working seven days a week. His wife Sarah was eight months pregnant and complained that she felt like a single parent. Last night, two-year-old Jimmy had treated him like a stranger. There might be a way out of this, though.

"Sounds interesting, but wouldn't it be faster to send it to a commercial lab?"

"Nah. Ancient DNA is fussy to work with and requires special procedures. A commercial lab would charge too much."

Sure. That would make sense for Ron. Why should he pay an outside company when Grant was working for peanuts and table scraps?

"Besides," Ron continued, "it'll give you a chance to work on something new, expand your résumé. This project will produce a covey of important papers. *Science, Nature,* or *Cell* are bound to accept a few of them. It'll jump-start your career."

Grant's shoulders slumped. Ron was right. Papers published in any of those journals would be a terrific boost to his career—if that's what happened. He'd been through this before, though. Ron would get excited about an oddball project, dive into it without adequate background information, and Grant was stuck with extra work and little to show for it.

Grant steeled himself. "What's the DNA from?"

"Another Iceman. It's a twelve-hundred-year-old corpse a skier found in the Alps. Professor Louis Antoine at the Federal

Technical Institute in Zürich owes me a favor and promised to provide tissue samples from the corpse."

Grant bit his tongue to avoid saying what he thought. What Ron described didn't mesh with any of their other research projects. Grant would have to develop lab techniques from scratch. Worse, what they learned about the human DNA from the Middle Ages was unlikely to help them in their other work.

Ron sat up and spread his hands in an expansive gesture. "Do this, and we'll get invitations to speak at international conferences." When Grant didn't respond, he added, "It'll give you a chance to travel and network."

Grant remembered the last "international conference" Ron had sent him to. It was international, all right. Speakers from Europe, Asia, and South America presented papers—in Ames, Iowa. That was unlikely to happen this time, though, since they'd found the Iceman in the Alps. Even the less prestigious meetings— where Ron would let Grant present their papers—would be in Switzerland, Italy, or Austria.

He might wangle another postdoc or assistant professorship in Europe if the research went well. He hadn't used his German in years, but it could come back quickly, maybe. And anyway, English was the language of science. Sarah might think of it as an extended vacation. Maybe his luck had changed. "I'll get started on a literature search. When will the samples arrive?"

"Louis is one of the speakers at next week's conference on RNA viruses. He's promised to bring us samples from the corpse."

"We have to get approval from the Department of Transportation for that, don't we? Will there be time to get it?"

"I've already applied for the approval."

"Does Professor Antoine have the special shipping containers required by the CDC and the DOT?"

"I hope so, but these samples are small." Ron glanced at his doorway. Grant looked too. No one was there, but Ron lowered his voice anyway. "If he doesn't have the right shipping container, I wouldn't be surprised if he stuffs the samples in his luggage to bring them in. Two samples will be the size of a travel tube of toothpaste. They'll be easy to hide, and European airport boarding exams aren't as fussy as ours. Besides, there can't be anything infectious in the samples after all this time. Most bacteria and any viruses would have died hundreds of years ago."

Grant froze. If the professor was caught smuggling potentially infectious contraband on an airliner, the Department of Transportation, the Center for Disease Control, and the FBI would take turns hanging everyone involved by their balls. "Doesn't he have to ship by FedEx or UPS?"

"Yeah, that's what the regs say, but don't worry. How Professor Antoine ships them is his responsibility, not ours. If he gets caught bringing them in illegally, that's his problem."

Grant had little faith that any of those assumptions were correct, but Ron was the boss. "Let me know when the samples arrive, and I'll store them in liquid nitrogen." He shuddered. Ron had never worked with a tough virus like canine parvovirus, and the Iceman samples weren't just frozen. If this corpse was like the last Iceman, he'd been mummified while frozen. That was basically freeze-dried. Pathogens survived much longer that way.

Ron leaned forward, put his elbows on his desk, and merrily continued. "Professor Antoine is filling out the import applications. He's calling the tissues 'diagnostic samples.' That gets them past the most onerous regulations, and everything will be completely legal, if he can get the required shipping containers in time."

Grant put a hand to his forehead. His mind raced. Ron was a hardcore biochemist with little experience in pathogenic microbiology. The Iceman corpse was freeze-dried. Anything living in the samples would only have been reduced by four or five logarithms. That would drop the viral count by tens of thousands to several hundreds of thousands. If they were supremely unlucky, the tissue could have up to four logs—ten thousand viable infectious pathogens *per gram* remaining. That was three hundred thousand per ounce.

"Look on the bright side," Ron said expansively. "We won't have to get permission from Iceman's next of kin. We can run any study we want."

Grant's stomach churned as his hope for a European academic position dissolved. He thought he was going to be sick. There still might be a way out of this mess. "Do we have grant money for this? Some of the reagents will cost a couple hundred bucks per microliter."

"This is a chance to collaborate with a famous Swiss lab and a well-known German lab. The Germans are using stable isotope analysis on the corpse's teeth to determine where the Iceman grew up. I'll get a grant if I have to type it standing on my head. I'm sure we can get funding for sequencing the bacteria in the guy's gut. There's a lot of interest in how the modern diet has altered our intestinal flora. Seed money is available through the department. We'll use that to produce preliminary data to spruce up the grant application, but we've got to get on it before others beat us to it."

Grant couldn't think of anything else to dissuade Ron. He excused himself and headed down the hallway to his tiny office.

As he dug his office key out of his pocket, he considered what Ron meant by "we." They both knew darn well it would be Grant who'd be stuck with the work. Identifying the bacteria in the gut by sequencing their DNA and comparing them to bacteria in modern intestines was interesting, though. It was a new field, with implications for the normal development of the gut in humans and even for susceptibility to disease. The whole idea of probiotics was built on it.

Grant tossed his book bag on his desk and hung his coat behind the door. Damn Ron! He'd come up with a great idea for a project, but Grant could end up divorced and in jail. He was caught in the slow, dark waltz of possibilities and consequences, of hope and fear.

Grant wondered if he'd been insane to leave his Wisconsin veterinary practice after five years of working with dairy cattle. He'd had a blast learning everything he could while earning his PhD in virology, and his postdoc in molecular biology in Ron's lab was intellectually stimulating. Although academia had been a prolonged intellectual banquet for him, it paid little.

With another baby due in a month, he and Sarah were in a precarious financial position. Next year, *if* he managed to convince a selection committee he was doing world-class research, he might get a job as an assistant professor.

Big whoop. Sixteen years of college, and he'd make less money than a bus driver. He hadn't gone into science for the money, but his family had to eat. His salary would be exponentially larger had he gone into marketing, accounting, or law. That was hard to forget. And talking heads on television wondered why Americans didn't go into the sciences.

As the reality of work in science pressed in, his goals had become more modest. Right now, he'd settle for being able to take Sarah out for a decent dinner and spend a Saturday morning playing with their son.

Grant's apartment
6:15 p.m. CST

Grant had barely pulled off his boots and hung up his coat at home that night when Jimmy yelled, "Daddy," rushed to him, and threw his arms around Grant's legs. He gently broke Jimmy's death grip on his knees, picked him up, and tossed him into the air.

"How's my boy?" Grant caught Jimmy and carried him to the sink where Sarah was chopping onions and celery. "Toddler" wasn't accurate anymore, the way Jimmy raced around. "Have you helped Mommy today like I asked you to?"

Jimmy nodded somberly and wrapped his arms around Grant's neck. To get loose, Grant pursed his lips, pressed them against Jimmy's neck, and blew. Jimmy squealed happily. Grant set Jimmy down, gently put his arms around Sarah's swollen waist, and kissed her on the cheek. "And what does Mommy say?"

Sarah turned, set the knife on the cutting board, put her arms around Grant's neck, and kissed him. "Jimmy has been good today. He wanted to help me chop the onions for the tomato beef tonight, but I told him I preferred little boys who have all of their fingers."

"Good call." Grant tightened his arms around her waist and brought her close against him.

She kissed him again. "And Daddy washed up thoroughly before he left the lab this afternoon?"

He kissed her harder and longer. "Of course. Daddy always comes home clean." He relaxed his hold on her waist. "I've got some bad news, though."

Sarah turned back to the cutting board and sliced a tomato, but it was more squashing than slicing. "Ron has more work for you, and you accepted it?"

"There wasn't much I could do. I'll have to wait—"

She slammed the knife into another tomato with the same

results, swore, and threw both the tomato and the knife in the sink. Red-faced, she put her hands on the edge of the sink and leaned away from Grant. "Tell me, when do Jimmy and I get to ask for some of your time? Huh? When do we get to count?" Hands on her hips, she turned to face Grant.

Grant wrapped his arms around her. He discarded all thoughts of sharing his concerns about the work Ron had lined up for him. This wasn't the time; maybe there'd never be a right time for that. "It's been hard on me, too. I'll tell Ron I can't continue working like this. From now on, Saturday evenings and Sunday afternoons must be for you and Jimmy. No exceptions."

He felt her body stiffen. "You've said that before."

"And I meant it, but something crucial always came up. I'll tell him I can't work on this project unless he agrees to those limits." He hugged her more tightly but gently, careful of her swollen belly.

She pushed him away. "That'd better be a promise."

"It is."

"Okay, then," she said and hugged him tightly.

CHAPTER 2

THE COURIER

Friday, January 12, 2018
Zürich, Switzerland
5:00 p.m., local time

Professor Louis Antoine brushed a piece of lint from his silk tie as he dressed in his bedroom. He paid too much attention to his clothing, but it was better than being like some of the US academics he'd met. Why brilliant and well-educated men, especially from agricultural states, would deliberately project the appearance of "good old boys" mystified him. He'd once sat in on a lecture for microbiology graduate students at a major US medical school. The lecturer wore a T-shirt, gym shorts, and flip-flops.

It was, he'd been told, because American universities couldn't afford to hire lab techs to work in their research labs. The grad students and professors did the work themselves, and nobody wanted to wear good clothes in a lab. "Scientists aren't judged by their clothes, anyway," an American professor said.

The phone on his nightstand rang. It was the shipping office at the Technical Institute.

"Professor Antoine, I've searched our stock room, and we don't have the US Department of Transportation's approved packaging for shipping biological samples. I can order them tonight, but they may take ten days to get here. We have similar packages, but they won't have the required information printed on the outside."

Rats. His plane tickets and speaking engagement at the University of Minnesota were for early next week. Louis wanted to be there when the samples arrived in Minnesota. There were points he wanted to clarify with Ron about this collaboration, points best handled in a face-to-face discussion. Time for Plan B.

"Don't bother," Louis told the clerk. "Thanks for checking for me."

The samples destined for Ron Schmidt's lab were small: three sealed five-milliliter test tubes. Together they contained almost half an ounce of the Iceman's remains. Louis had gotten away with carrying one-milliliter samples of rabbit serum to the US in a coat pocket two years ago. It hadn't been a problem to sneak them past the relaxed boarding exam at the Zürich airport, although the search going through customs in the US had given him a scare.

These samples were only marginally larger than those. If he rolled them up in his underwear and socks when he packed, they'd be difficult to detect by x-ray or casual exam.

Three days later, in a taxi on his way to the airport, Louis received a phone call from Paul Wolfe, a member of the team who had collected "Freddy," so nicknamed by the team that had extracted the corpse from the glacier. At the end of a technical conversation, Paul mentioned that José Bonderas, a team member and grad student from Spain, was hospitalized. He'd gone to the emergency room that morning with a cough, fever, and headache.

Louis briefly considered an infection connected with Freddy, but that wasn't realistic. The team had used reasonable biosafety procedures when working with Freddy. True, they weren't as exacting as the protocols of the *Médecins Sans Frontières* for Ebola, but diseases that required those were extraordinarily rare, and none involved twelve-hundred-year-old corpses.

"Sorry to hear that, Paul. Give José my regards. Is he coming down with the flu?"

"Probably. Darn fool forgot to get vaccinated this year."

Monday, January 15, 2018
Airliner, over Lake Michigan
9:30 p.m. CST

The pilot announced a blizzard was raging through the Midwest. The Minneapolis airport was closed, and all flights were diverted to the Chicago O'Hare airport. The attendants would assist passengers in arranging connecting flights if they wished, or they could make other arrangements when they arrived at O'Hare.

Louis rubbed the sleep from his eyes. *Damn it. Nothing about this trip is going right.* He hadn't slept well on the flight, and he was dog-tired, but he wasn't the sort to dwell on the inconvenience. The Minnesota conference was already underway. Most attendees would already have arrived, so it was unlikely they'd postpone the scheduled talks. He had to get to Minneapolis by noon tomorrow.

A map in an airline magazine indicated there were flights from O'Hare to the La Crosse, Eau Claire, and Wausau airports in Wisconsin, but the storm would soon engulf all of them. Flying to Madison, Wisconsin would save two hours of driving, but it would take him longer than that to get tickets and wait for the flight. Passenger train service in the US wasn't worth considering. It sucked. He'd have to rent a car.

It was snowing in Chicago when his plane landed. Louis counted himself fortunate that O'Hare wasn't closed—yet. He picked up his suitcase at the baggage claim in Terminal 5, the international terminal, and stood in line to go through customs. Lord, he hated lines. Every international airport on the planet bragged about its terminals. All were airy structures of steel and glass, all were crowded when he got there, and all were a pain in the ass when you had to stand in long lines. Flights from Europe to several states had been diverted to O'Hare. The customs people were swamped, lines were backed up almost out of the building, and luggage exams were cursory. That, at least, would help him.

Louis kept his eyes on his suitcase. After two hours of standing in line, the suitcase and samples it carried skated through with a minimal search. He was glad that was over. Between exhaustion and the crowds, he'd had a hard time keeping track of his bag.

The wind off Lake Michigan howled and buffeted the glass walls of the terminal. It was the only indication there was a blizzard out there, as everything was peaceful and warm on the ATS train connecting Terminal 5 to the domestic terminals. Louis congratulated himself on bringing his topcoat, but his gloves were for dress rather than keeping his hands dry and warm in a blizzard. That wouldn't be a hardship once he got to the conference hotel. He could stay all week there and never have to step outside.

He pulled out his cell phone and called Ron Schmidt. It took five rings before Ron answered. His speech was slow and halting at first.

"Ron? This is Louis. I'm at O'Hare."

Ron's response sounded like a loud yawn. Louis grabbed his bag and climbed the stairs from the train to the terminal. Damn, the bag seemed even heavier than when he'd checked it. He blamed it on his exhaustion.

It took a moment to get used to the bright lighting inside the terminal. A clock on the wall indicated it was midnight, local time.

"Plane diverted?" Ron yawned again.

"Yes. How far is Minneapolis from Chicago?"

"About four hundred miles."

Louis heard "miles," but he was tired and accustomed to thinking in kilometers. *Four hundred kilometers, 240 miles.* "That's doable. If I can't get there tonight, I'll stop at a motel and be there by noon. It can't be worse than driving in the Alps during a snowstorm. I'll let you know if I get lost or stuck."

Ron asked for his cell phone number. "Your route is simple. Get on I-94 and stay on it. Don't leave your car if you get stuck. Snowplows may not be out until the storm has passed. Call and leave a message for me if you stop for the night."

Louis ended the call and looked over the lines at the rental car agencies. All were long and slow moving. "Shit! Another bloody line. Can anything else go wrong on this trip?" he mumbled to himself.

CHAPTER 3

THE BLIZZARD

Monday, January 15, 2018
Chicago O'Hare Airport
10:00 p.m. CST

Frank got off the flight from Zürich and picked up his bag. It was nearly midnight when he got to the front of the line for the customs exam. Sweat beaded on his forehead while his suitcase was searched. His sweat smelled rank. He associated the smell with fear. It always smelled like that going through customs on these trips. He stuffed his hands in his pockets, faked a yawn, hummed an off-key tune, and looked around the terminal like a tourist. It took a Herculean effort for him to keep his cool.

He closed his eyes and breathed a sigh of relief when the harried and overworked customs agent made a few cursory passes through the bag with his hand, closed the bag, and handed it back to Frank. Putting the heroin between the outer wall of the bag and the interior lining had worked again. The agent hadn't even searched his dirty underwear, or they'd have found the half kilo bags of fentanyl he'd stuffed there. Thank God for the blizzard.

When he'd packed his dirty laundry in a plastic bag for the trip home, he'd made sure the bag smelled like a plugged sewer.

Nothing like skivvies with racing stripes to discourage customs. He could have saved himself the trouble. Now he'd have to listen to his wife complain when she washed them.

This was his fourth trip as a mule. The packets in his suitcase contained pure fentanyl and heroin worth millions. They'd be worth twenty times that when cut and distributed by Big Freddy in Minneapolis. On the walk to the car rentals, he noticed that the guy who went through customs just before him had a bag identical to his. The guy was tall, thin, and well dressed, with dark hair. He'd sat near him on the train to the domestic terminal. Ended up standing behind him again at the car rental counter. Neither spoke. The guy looked tired. Frank was beat, too. He didn't think about it again until he got into his rental car and opened his suitcase to find clean clothing, carefully folded, and looked expensive. The sides of the suitcase felt smooth from the inside. There was no evidence of the hidden drugs he'd carefully placed there. *What the fuck?* Stunned, it took him a moment to realize it wasn't his suitcase. A tag on the handle had the name "Prof. Louis Antoine" and a Zürich address.

Nerves tied his stomach in a knot. He was a dead man if he didn't recover those drugs. Fear-induced sweat rolled down his back and forehead. As he closed his bag, he saw that Louis guy in a car two stalls from him. *There's the son of a bitch who has my bag.* Frank remembered setting his bag on the floor and pushing it ahead with his foot when he'd stood in line at the rental counter. *Shit.* He could have grabbed Frank's when they got off the train or standing in line at the car rental.

Frank drove out behind Louis and followed him onto the freeway. He fished his cell phone from a pocket, and when Louis headed north on I-90, he called an old associate, an enforcer whom he'd worked with a couple of times.

"Tony, this is Frank. Blizzard got me rerouted to Chicago.

Some asswipe grabbed my bag. I've got his. I'm following him. We're at the junction of I-90 and I-94, headed north toward Wisconsin."

Tony yawned. "Jesus, Frank. What am I supposed to do about it? I'm in bed."

"Well, get the hell out of bed. My balls are on the line here. Take I-94 north. I'll call you when the guy stops or turns off the road. We'll get together and, ah, swap bags when he stops for food or gas. Bring your Glock and one for me."

Tuesday, January 16, 2018
Atlanta, Georgia
2:00 a.m. EST

Sybil Erypet fumbled for her phone, opened one eye, and checked the time. She yawned and swore. "This is Dr. Erypet. Whoever you are, you'd better have a damned good reason for calling at this godforsaken hour."

"And a good day to you too, doctor."

Sybil recognized her boss's voice. If someone had rousted him, it was unlikely she could talk her way out of whatever work he'd lined up. She'd never figured out how the hell he always sounded so blasted chipper. On nights like tonight, she suspected he did it just to irritate her.

"Two o'clock. What could be this important, Sam?" She swung her legs out of bed, flipped on a light, and caught sight of herself in a mirror by the door. Her mousey brown hair looked like a rat's nest.

"Remember that Iceman they pulled out of the glacier in Switzerland last week?"

"Yeah." She yawned. "I read about it. So?"

"When they examined the corpse in the lab, they found he'd bled from his nose, mouth, eyes, and ears before he died. On necropsy, there was evidence of massive internal bleeding. Sound familiar?"

Sybil's slouch left her abruptly. "A viral hemorrhagic disease?"

"You got it. Several American labs were clamoring for tissue samples from the corpse before anyone suspected the guy was infected. It's the kind of academic free-for-all likely to encourage shortcuts. Some idiot might ignore regulations and try to sneak samples out of Switzerland and into the States."

"Yeah, but this corpse is, what, twelve hundred years old? There can't be anything infectious left in the tissue."

"I wouldn't put money on it. The Swiss sent out a confidential warning to the CDC minutes ago. A member of the team that recovered the corpse died with symptoms consistent with hemorrhagic fever, and three more look like they may be in the early stages. They've quarantined everyone who had contact with the deceased or the Iceman. The administrator wants you to fly to Zürich this evening. You're to learn what you can about the virus and make certain everyone on the Iceman project remembers our regulations for transport of infectious material."

"Oh, for Christ's sake. Sam, I'm beat. I only got back from the Congo this morning. I'm not the only person working at the CDC. Can't somebody else go?"

"You love chocolate. Bring some back for me. Grab your passport and be ready to go by the end of business today."

"Can you at least arrange a business class ticket for me? I can't sleep in those cramped coach seats with bawling kids around me."

Sam said he'd try. Sybil hung up and dove back under the covers, swearing. But she was already digging through her memory for information on hemorrhagic fevers. She loved the thrill of knotty problems, problems that, if not solved, could mean the deaths of hundreds or thousands of people. Analyzing and solving those problems was what she'd spent a lifetime training for. The challenge gave her life excitement and meaning.

But concentrating on the rational and scientific had left her life unbalanced. Underneath her irritation with Sam was an emptiness she didn't want to face. She'd been Sam's personal fireman for two years, sent to Syria, Yemen, the Congo, and now Switzerland. It was the most exciting time of her life, but it'd had a terrific price.

A year ago, her fiancé, Mike, had purchased tickets for a romantic getaway in the Bahamas. It was to be a week they could spend with food, drink, and each other without phone calls from Sam, emergencies in developing countries, or politicians to educate.

An emergency in Yemen blew up three days before their flight to the Bahamas. She'd gone to the Middle East, and Mike had ended the engagement. Being dumped by text had stung, but as he'd said, she was rarely around to talk to, and she didn't have time to chat on the phone.

She tried not to blame the bastard. In the year they'd been engaged, he said he'd had more sex with porn sites than he'd had with her, and twice his computer had gotten a virus. *Why would any guy stick with a woman whose profession was more important to her than he was?* he'd asked.

Were the viruses his computer caught from the porn sites technically STDs? God, she'd gotten to the point where even her jokes were about disease.

This CDC appointment had been her dream job, but it was getting old. She had no one to talk to unless the topic was infectious medicine or budgets. There wasn't a hand to hold, a shoulder to rest her head on, or arms to enfold her. She didn't have the energy or guts to think about her life tonight, but at least the food would be better in Switzerland than it had been in the Congo.

Tuesday, January 16, 2018
I-94, central Wisconsin
4:00 a.m. CST

Louis could go no farther. He hadn't slept well on the plane, and he'd driven for four hours through the blizzard. The snowfall and wind had increased when he was an hour north of the last exit for Madison. The wind blew snow horizontally across the freeway. His headlights reflected off it, creating a wall of bright white that obscured the road ahead. It was worse than driving in thick fog with his high beams on. Signs announced that I-90 and I-94 would split up ahead. He didn't want to chance taking the wrong road in this blizzard. It was long past time to look for a motel.

A green sign read, TOMAH, NEXT EXIT. He watched for the turnoff. Accustomed to the left lane, driving in the United States confused him. Signs and oncoming traffic weren't where he expected them to be. In the blowing snow, he feared he'd miss or fail to recognize the signs he needed. Five minutes later, he admitted to himself that he'd missed the exit. Twelve miles past the Tomah sign, he slowed to read another green sign partially obscured by snow.

Louis checked his rearview mirror. The only headlights behind him were distant. He pulled onto the shoulder, got out of the car, and wiped the snow off the sign. There wasn't mention of a town, but food and lodging were available at the next exit—if he could find it through the whiteout.

As he got back in his car, he noticed the headlights behind him were no closer than when he'd parked. *Odd.* Perhaps they'd pulled over to change drivers or relieve themselves. He drove forward at thirty miles per hour. That was as fast as he dared to go, or risk missing the exit to the motel. Three minutes later, he saw fresh tracks in the snow leading off the freeway. *It must be the exit ramp.* He turned and followed the tracks, signaling his turn by force of habit—no one was close enough behind him to need the warning. The distance to the headlights in his rearview mirror hadn't changed. They must have been looking for a safe place to stop too.

Visibility was so bad he feared he might have followed a drunk's tracks off the road and into a ditch. At the end of a long descending ramp, he came to a sign, again obscured by snow. He repeated the drill he'd used to read the previous sign. Lodging was to the left. The lights from the car behind him swung across his path. That car had also turned off at the exit.

He drove under I-94 and passed a sign that read, KIRBY, UNINCORPORATED. Snow blew across the road, but trees along the right of way, like a snow fence, had piled the snow on the road in deep drifts. Nothing indicated the snowplows were out yet. He got past the worst drifts by putting his rented Blazer into four-wheel drive and staying in the tracks of the cars or trucks that had managed to get through. It was a relief when he arrived at the motel on his right. The well-lit sign and lights at the motel entrance were barely visible through the blowing snow, but he couldn't see the driveway entrance. Everything looked like a flat carpet of white.

A post with a reflector nailed to it looked like it marked the driveway. Louis gunned the Chevy Blazer to get through the snow and turned in toward the motel. The nose of the Blazer fell, and he came to a sudden halt. He'd driven into a ditch. The driveway was on the other side of the post.

Snow came up to the door handles of his car. *Damn it.* Once again, four-wheel drive had just gotten him into deeper crap. Louis looked around. It could have been worse. The motel entrance was two hundred feet in front of him. He swiveled in his seat and shoved his door open with both feet. It took several pushes before the door opened enough for him to squeeze out of his car. He kicked and pawed snow away from the SUV's back door, and fought the snow to open it. Grabbing his suitcase, he climbed out of the ditch. He skirted four-foot mounds of snow and floundered through two- and three-foot drifts toward the motel's entrance.

His feet and fingers were soaked and freezing before he was halfway to the motel. He pushed forward, stumbled against snow-covered parked cars, and fell on his face twice. The shock of it only darkened his mood. He brushed ice from his eyelashes.

When he reached the door, he found it locked. He pressed a doorbell to the left. The response was slow in coming, and by then he'd pushed the button several times.

The door was finally opened by a heavyset, bearded man in pajamas. He looked to be in his mid-thirties. An ample beer gut rolled out below his T-shirt and over the cord holding the pajama bottoms up. "We ain't got no vacancies," the guy said, yawned, and turned to go back to bed.

"I'll take anything," Louis said. "Do you have a room that isn't supposed to be rented—one with a broken television, a stained carpet, a leaky faucet? I'll take it if you have one." That approach had worked well for him before when motel rooms were scarce, and he was desperate.

The guy motioned him in and walked to the front desk where he flipped through pages in a notebook. "Yeah," he said. He gave Louis a calculating look. "We got one. You can have it for the night, half price." He ran Louis's credit card and handed it back with a key card. "Room 221." He raised a cautionary finger. "Hold on a sec," he said and disappeared through a doorway behind the counter.

The chubby motel operator reappeared a moment later, holding a toilet plunger. "Here. You'll need this," he said with a grin.

Oh, for God's sake. What have I gotten myself into? Louis accepted the plunger and looked for an elevator. "Where is the—"

"We don't have an elevator," Chubby said, and pointed toward the stairway.

Louis climbed the stairs to the second floor, toilet plunger in one hand, suitcase in the other. He glanced at the plunger. *This would make a great picture for* Infection and Immunity. "The distinguished Professor Antoine walks to the podium with his latest molecular tools." Thank God no one here knew him. He really was in the hinterlands.

The room fit what he'd expected after being handed the plunger. Its carpet was worn, seams between panels of wallpaper were opening, and the bedspread looked like it would benefit from a trip to the laundry. He stripped off his wet clothes and took a hot shower. The towels were threadbare.

He felt better after the shower, but the room was chilly. With a towel around his waist and one over his shoulders, he turned up the heat and opened his suitcase. Front and center in the suitcase was a plastic bag with dirty clothes. Everything that wasn't in the bag was wrinkled and cheap. *Mon Dieu!* This wasn't his bag. He'd picked up the wrong bag. How could that have happened? He looked through the suitcase. It smelled awful—the bag holding dirty underwear hadn't been closed properly, perhaps by the customs agent. As he tried to cinch the cord to close the bag, he noticed two packages of a cream-colored powder among the filthy underwear. He removed them and set them in the suitcase, so they wouldn't interfere with closing the plastic bag.

He checked his ticket stub for a telephone number. After six rings, he was connected to Baggage Claims in Minneapolis and was put on hold for fifteen minutes. He waited, frustrated and shivering. An operator explained that he had the wrong airport and gave him the number for baggage claims at O'Hare. Calling O'Hare every five minutes got him nothing but busy signals and a headache.

He remembered what Ron Schmidt had said and gave him a call. It rolled over to voicemail. Louis left a message, his voice shaky. "I'm in a motel in Kirby, Wisconsin, a town on I-94. I'm safe, but I must have grabbed the wrong suitcase at O'Hare. Somebody else has my bag and your samples. I'm trying to reach the baggage claims office at O'Hare." That done, he returned to calling O'Hare until there was a knock on the door. Still wearing only two towels, he opened the door.

"You Louie Anthony?" a short, beefy-looking man asked. A taller, thinner man in the shadows stood behind him.

"Antoine," Louis corrected the pronunciation.

"Louie, I think we got each other's bags at O'Hare. Is this yours?" He held Louis's bag out.

He could have hugged the man. "Oh, thank you. I just discovered I had the wrong bag. Please come in, come in." Louis stepped aside. Cold air flooded in from the hallway with the men. Louis coughed and shivered.

"You was lucky to get this room. Dipshit at the desk called other motels for us. Seems this room was the last vacancy within twenty miles. Name's Frank, by the way." He turned and gestured toward the tall man. "This is my associate, Tony."

Frank and Tony walked into the room. Still coughing, Louis closed the door and showed them the open suitcase on the bed. He felt hot, which seemed weird in the chilly room. Now that the initial relief at finding his bag had faded, there was something about these men that made Louis apprehensive. Why were there two of them?

He pointed to the open bag. "I assume this is yours, yes?"

"Looks like it," Frank said. "Mind if I make sure?"

The man held up the packages of powder Louis had found, opened the laundry bag, and pulled a third package from the foul-smelling sack. Louis retreated from the disgusting smell. "Yup, this is it. I see you found these packages?"

"Yes. Your laundry bag had opened. What on earth are they?"

An instant later, he could have kicked himself for asking. He'd been so worried about his samples that he hadn't considered the obvious.

Frank looked at the bag of fentanyl in his hand, the one that Louis had found. *Jesus.* Nobody was so dumb they wouldn't recognize this as illicit drugs. All it would take to send him up for ten years would be a couple of words to the cops. The drugs would be confiscated, his boss would put a hit on him, and he wouldn't survive a month in prison.

That was it, then. If he was going to live, Louis wasn't. He nodded to Tony. "Go ahead, Tony."

Louis watched Tony pull out his Glock and screw on a sound suppressor. The bozo just stood there with a stunned expression until Tony gave him a double tap, one in the chest and one in the head.

Frank felt sick. He'd never killed anyone or ordered anyone's death before. *It was him or me*, he told himself. The guy probably didn't feel the second shot. That made him feel a little better.

Louis fell back against the wall and slowly slid to a sitting position, dead before his butt hit the floor. Frank looked out the motel window. He couldn't see anything but snow coming down.

Tony looked over his shoulder. "It was bad enough driving here, and it's getting worse. We won't get far through that shit, and the guy who let us in said there weren't no rooms within twenty miles. We got two beds here. Which one is mine?" he asked as he unscrewed the silencer.

Keeping his stomach and expression under control, Frank pointed to the bed farthest from the bathroom. He nodded at a streak of blood on the wall and a pool of blood on the carpet. "Better clean that up. Use the towels he's wearing."

While Tony cleaned up the bloody mess, Frank got out his phone and called his wife in Minneapolis to tell her about his plane being diverted to Chicago. "I tried to drive home and got snowed in. Don't know when they'll dig us out," he said. She wasn't happy about it, but she was used to inexplicable changes in his itineraries. She objected less after he told her how much he missed her and promised to get home as soon as he could.

He'd been tempted to use the room phone and let the call be billed to Louis, but that would connect him to the corpse. Not a good idea.

CHAPTER 4

COMPLICATIONS

Tuesday, January 16, 2018
Minneapolis, Minnesota
10:00 a.m. CST

Ron Schmidt called Louis Antoine every fifteen minutes from eight o'clock to ten. It took a while to find the number, but Ron finally got through to the Kirby Motel. No one had seen Professor Antoine this morning, but his Blazer was still in the ditch in front of the motel. He couldn't have gone far. The roads out of town and to the interstate were closed by snowdrifts. Ron tried to reach Louis's room. No answer there, either. *Where the hell could he be?*

Grant walked into Ron's office, unzipping his parka and removing his gloves. "Hear about your Iceman this morning?"

"No. What's up?" Ron asked warily.

"They believe the Iceman had a viral hemorrhagic disease like Marburg virus, yellow fever, or Ebola. NPR said the authorities have clammed up, but word is a number of people are quarantined at a Swiss military hospital."

Ron put down his phone and gave Grant his full attention. "I can't locate Louis Antoine, and he was a member of the team that dug up the corpse. He wouldn't have had time to get really sick, would he?"

"I have no idea, but we'll be lucky if he checks into a hospital before he gets here. That will save us from being exposed to this bug. The report said one of his coworkers is in the hospital in critical condition. Rumor has it he may have died."

Grant seemed to relax after Ron said that Louis hadn't been in touch.

"Hemorrhagic fevers are RNA viruses, aren't they?" Ron said.

Grant flopped in a chair opposite to Ron's desk. "They haven't identified the virus yet, but all the hemorrhagic fevers I know of are caused by RNA viruses. The authorities aren't letting much information out."

"What the devil would a hemorrhagic fever case be doing in Dark Ages Europe? The only cases of viral hemorrhagic fevers on record there were modern, caused by the importation of monkeys from Africa, right?"

"Yeah, at least in modern times. This virus might be one we haven't encountered in a lab before—something that died out a thousand years ago. A friend at Yale is a postdoc. He heard the serology on the sick guy was negative for all known hemorrhagic viruses."

Ron leaned forward on his desk and buried his head in his hands. *Oh, my God. This could get ugly.* He looked up at Grant. "Could it be too early to get anything but a negative serological test?"

Grant shook his head. "Unlikely. They dug the Iceman up about a week ago. That's plenty of time for those exposed to make early antibodies like IgM. My source said the Swiss are fishing in the viral genome using the Polymerase Chain Reaction. They hope to amplify sequences from even distantly related viruses by dropping the temperature of the reaction and increasing magnesium concentrations in the buffer. They'll have those results tomorrow. It should only take a couple of days to have the whole virus sequenced." He leaned forward in his chair. "At any rate, I assume this means we won't be doing anything with the samples, even if Louis delivers them."

"You got that right." Ron closed his eyes and gathered his courage to make the phone call. The samples Louis had with him were no longer a misdemeanor infraction. They threatened to start an epidemic if they weren't controlled. If Sam Barker blamed him for Louis's smuggling, the next time he heard a toilet flush it would be his career headed to the sewer. It could take a while to muster the balls to make this call.

"Early medieval records describe something similar to hemorrhagic diseases in Europe," Grant said. "Nothing like them exists today. It's believed the viruses died out because they were too virulent. They couldn't survive in a world of small villages and lousy transportation."

Ron's stomach and breakfast hit free fall. "How do you mean, 'too virulent to survive'?"

"Populations were small and widely dispersed. As long as the diseases didn't reach the few cities, the virus died out when it killed all the people in a village." Grant placed a couple of pencil stubs and a pen on Ron's desk, ten inches apart from each other. "Imagine these are villages ten miles apart. People back then rarely traveled more than four miles from home. A virus infecting one village would be like Ebola when it was confined to small villages. Once the people of a village died, the virus did too. It wasn't until African transportation improved that Ebola got to the cities."

"You're saying a virus from the Iceman might be more virulent, more deadly, than any virus we have today?"

Grant shrugged. "It's possible, even likely. Periodic famines, primitive housing, and brutally hard work left medieval populations stressed. Evolutionary pressure in a population like that favors the most virulent strains of a virus. With air travel and our dense populations today, a virus like that wouldn't die out. It would roar across the world, killing hundreds of millions."

Ron cringed as Grant chattered on. Evolution of virulence was Grant's favorite topic and finding a reason not to work on the Iceman samples seemed to have loosened his tongue.

A stab in his gut let Ron know his ulcer was back. He groaned as Grant went into hyperdrive.

"We were lucky with Ebola. It spreads only by physical contact. If this new virus were to spread through the air or water, it could make the Spanish flu of 1918 look like a minor digestive upset. In the cities, they'll have to use carts to collect the dead off the streets, like they did during the plague in the fourteenth century."

Ron shuddered. *How clueless can this kid be? I could go down in history as the Bluebeard of microbiology.* "Sit tight," he said, his heart pounding. "I have to call the CDC and tell them about Louis." He hit a few keys on his computer and brought up a phone number. His cell phone was in his hand before he changed his mind. For security, he decided he'd better make this call on his landline.

He asked to speak to the director of the CDC, was given a runaround, and asked for the head of the emerging infectious diseases group. The CDC receptionist said Dr. Barker wasn't available, either. "Get a message into Sam's meeting," Ron said. "Tell him Professor Ron Schmidt from Minnesota said that samples from the recently discovered Iceman are already in the United States, and they are not secured. He'll agree that this is more important than his meeting." He gave the woman his phone number and ended the call.

He turned to Grant. "Ever heard of Kirby, Wisconsin?"

Grant shook his head. Ron did a search on his computer,

but they'd only had time to bring up a map of I-94's path across Wisconsin when the phone rang. Ron picked it up. "Ron Schmidt here."

"This is Sam Barker. Did you tell my receptionist that some jerk brought samples from the Iceman into the US?"

"Louis Antoine, a Swiss scientist—"

"Yeah. I know him," Sam cut in. "Arrogant jackass. Thinks he's above rules."

That gave Ron hope. *Sam might blame it all on Louis.* "Anyway, he's on the agenda to speak at a conference in Minneapolis this week. He was shipping samples of the Iceman to the US for a research project, but he said he might bring them in his luggage if he couldn't get the approved DOT packaging in time."

"That fucking son of a bitch," Sam roared. "I'll have him . . ."

Ron held the phone away from his ear and gave Sam time to calm down. When the cursing stopped on the phone, he tried to explain. "Antoine said he hadn't been able to get the proper shipping containers in time."

"So he smuggles them in his luggage? Goddamned Louis! That's just the kind of thing he'd pull. It's the dumbest goddamned stunt I've heard of," Sam growled. "There'll be a hefty fine, and he might be banned from ever entering the US again. That's if I can't talk a judge into giving him a jail term."

"I've been trying to reach him, but he isn't answering his cell or the phone in his room. The motel staff said his rental car was still in a ditch in front of the motel in Kirby, Wisconsin."

Ron searched his desk, found his notepad, and gave Antoine's cell phone number and the number for the motel to Sam. He stared at the floor, considering his options after Sam hung up. The CDC was a vast organization. It could take days for a big bureaucracy to get someone into Kirby. Grant was still rattling on about evolution of virulence. Ron had a faster option than the CDC. It would put Grant and his lectures on the evolution of virulence miles away, too.

Ron looked across the desk at his colleague and smiled. "Grant, you enjoy cross-country skiing and winter sports. How'd you like to take a week off with pay?"

Grant turned pale. "No!" he said. "Don't even think that. What could I do in Kirby?"

"You can be there in two hours. The CDC will take days to get someone there. It's imperative that you get those samples under control, maybe even get Antoine quarantined. Millions of lives could depend on it."

Grant was out of his chair and pacing in front of Ron's desk. "I have no authority. I'll just be in the way when the CDC shows up."

"Stick what you'll need from the lab in your car, toss in your winter camping gear in case you can't get a room, and take off for Kirby. Better toss your skis in too, in case you get stuck or the roads aren't open. Find Antoine and get those samples under control. I'll pick up the tab for gas, food, and lodging."

Grant spread out his arms and let them drop to his sides. "But jeez, Ron, this is insane. I've been working seventy hours a week. Last night I promised Sarah I'd make more—"

"No excuses. Millions of lives and both of our careers could be at stake. Take lots of biosecurity gear with you, at least a couple cases of, ah, what do you call 'em? The sterile plastic coveralls?"

"Tyveks?"

"Yeah. That's it." Ron paused a moment. This could be expensive. "And keep your receipts. I might be able to talk the department into covering our costs."

CDC, Atlanta, Georgia
11:15 a.m. EST

Dr. Sybil Erypet was on the phone to a kennel, asking them to board her dog for another couple of weeks when Sam walked in. She held up one finger and pointed to the chair in front of her desk. Sam sat, listened to her conversation for a few seconds, then reached over and broke her phone connection.

"What the hell, Sam?"

"Plans are changed. Some moron has already imported samples of the Iceman. A storm diverted Louis Antoine, the courier, from Minneapolis to O'Hare, and from there to Kirby, Wisconsin. Pack your boots, warm gloves, and thermal underwear. It's twenty degrees and snowing in Kirby, but likely to hit thirty below after the blizzard moves through. Fort McCoy, the army's base for winter training, is a few miles southwest of Kirby. You'll fly into Fort McCoy this afternoon where a tracked snow vehicle will be waiting for you."

Sybil glared at Sam. Last week she'd put up with a hundred degrees in the shade. Tomorrow she'd be north of the army's winter training base. Were they trying to kill her? "What kind of snow vehicle? Am I going to freeze my ass off riding a snowmobile?"

"For God's sake, Sybil, let me finish. The tracked vehicle will have an enclosed and heated cab. It may not be as comfortable as your car, but you won't freeze."

"Will I have help, and will the roads be open?"

"Yes about the help, no about the roads. I've pulled strings to make sure Kirby stays snowed in. The road crews have been told to ignore the roads in and out of town. They will remain closed until we have those samples under control and anyone exposed to them or Antoine has been quarantined. Nobody but you and your crew will get in or out until then."

"How big a town is Kirby?"

"It isn't."

Sybil did a double take and stared at Sam. "What do you mean, 'it isn't'?"

"It isn't incorporated. It sounds like a crossroads in the woods with a few houses, a gas station, and a motel. If it's like other villages I've seen in that area, the main industries will be milking cows in the summer and poaching deer in the winter. I'd guess the population is between fifteen and fifty, but there may be a couple hundred people living within a two-mile radius. The town is three miles off the freeway."

Once, just once, Sybil would like to have an assignment in which she'd sit in front of a computer in a room with central heat and air conditioning. Ideally, she'd only have to talk to people a few times a day, and then only to fellow scientists. Others would have to deal with stubborn and ignorant civilians. "You must stay up late at night thinking of godforsaken holes to send me to."

Sam smiled and shook his head. "That's the price of being the best we got, kiddo. Another of the Iceman extraction team died last night. The Swiss authorities are frantic. So far, they haven't made the deaths public. They have an epidemic of a fatal disease starting in their largest city." Sam pointed at Sybil. "And *you* are going to make sure we don't have that problem."

"You said you've pulled strings?"

"I called the local sheriff. I didn't give him much information. He was reluctant to take orders from me until we got the governor and the head of Homeland Security to call him. That shook him up. He fell all over himself to cooperate after that. His deputies will blockade the snowmobile trails. The State Patrol will handle the roads."

Sybil slumped back in her chair. She could kiss her dreams of another day's rest goodbye. No rest, no free time, no time for a personal life, and an ex-fiancé who'd broken their engagement by text because there wasn't any other way to reach her. She'd had no time for a social life and no real prospects since. That was just fine some days. Who needed or wanted a man who couldn't respect what she did? She really did love her work.

Her dreams of a life in science and medicine had concentrated on just that: science and medicine. She hadn't thought to plan for a social life—or, if she'd thought to, it was simply too much to juggle. The studies and then the practice of medicine and science at her level sucked up all the mental energy she had. But maybe that had been a mistake. Now she was so busy, so overworked, she rarely had time to cuddle her dog, let alone go on a date. What she needed was to recalibrate what she expected from life, but she wasn't getting time to do it. "How long will it take them to blockade the snowmobile trails and roads?" she asked.

Brows furrowed, Sam stood and paced in front of her desk, looking at the floor. He seemed to be thinking through his answer as he spoke. "Businesses are closed in the area, and the snowed-in roads will keep people at home today. There'll be guards on the roads by late afternoon. The army has blocked snowmobile access to Kirby until the sheriff's deputies get in place."

It was Sybil's turn to furrow her brows and lean back in her chair. "The army is helping?" she asked. That didn't fit with what little she knew of US law.

Sam stopped his pacing and looked at her. "The National Guard. The camp commander will assist you, at least as far as he legally can. I've asked that they be ready to provide food, fuel, and hospital facilities for the Kirby population."

"Any chance the medications used to treat AIDS will work on this virus?" Sybil asked.

"You mean the anti-reverse transcriptase medications?"

Sybil shrugged. "Yeah, those and the others."

"The Swiss are trying several of the AIDS drug combinations," Sam said. "They've included the anti-reverse transcriptase, anti-integrase, and the anti-RNA protease drugs."

Sybil shook her head. "Sam, I'm not a molecular biologist. Translate that into English."

Sam nodded. "The reverse transcriptase of the virus allows its RNA to be transcribed to DNA, the integrase puts the viral DNA into our chromosomes, and the RNA protease makes the viral-specific proteins. The drugs block those enzymes. The enzymes are unique to RNA viruses, so blocking them doesn't harm the patient."

"What are the odds one or more of the AIDS treatment combinations will work on the Zürich Virus?"

"Nobody knows. Better get out your rosary beads, 'cause we're screwed if they don't."

CHAPTER 5

DEPUTY KRUEGER

Tuesday, January 16, 2018
Kirby, Wisconsin
10:00 a.m. CST

Tony prodded Frank awake. "Get up or we'll miss breakfast."

The curtains opened and light poured into the room. The clock read eight o'clock. Damned thing probably hadn't worked for years. Tony shook him again. "Hey! That guy Louis was smuggling dope just like you."

Frank rolled out of bed and lurched for the toilet. He left the door open and spoke as he peed. "What makes you think that?"

Tony sat on Frank's bed and tied his shoes. "His suitcase. I found three tubes of brown stuff hidden in his rolled-up socks."

"What is it?"

"How the hell would I know? It's kind of stringy, but it turned to powder when I rubbed it between my fingers. Doesn't smell or taste like anything we've handled. Kinda tasted sweet, like pork. He only had a little, so he couldn't have been selling. He was using."

Frank scratched his ass as he walked back into the room. "Let me see it."

Tony whipped out a test tube and handed it to Frank. He took it, inspected it with the top on, removed the top, and sniffed.

"Smells like a burger you left in the back of the refrigerator too long. With a name like 'Louis Antoine,' the guy must be French. Who knows what he would be carrying around?" He recapped the tube, handed it back to Tony, and raised his eyebrows. "Maybe it's a new high-powered date-rape drug. We can try it out tonight."

Tony looked out the window. "You can try it. I ain't never needed one. I'm more worried about getting out of town. The street out front is only plowed up to the motel entrance, and it must have snowed another six inches since we got here."

Frank looked grudgingly at Tony. Six-foot-three, chiseled jaw, luxuriant black hair, blue eyes, and built like a heavy-weight boxer. *Christ!* No wonder the jerk never had a hard time getting laid. He just wished Tony didn't talk about it.

They stopped to check on the weather and highway conditions on their way back from the complimentary breakfast in the lobby. The news was as bad as the motel's tasteless scrambled eggs. Betty, according to her name tag, relaxed behind the desk, looking Tony over.

"Ah, Betty," Tony said. "Any chance we'll be able to get out of here today?"

Her height, about five-foot-eight, and tight blouse became evident as she stood up straight and moved closer to where Tony leaned on the counter. Frank checked her out. She looked like a caricature of a beautiful woman drawn by a cartoonist with cataracts. Everything was where it was supposed to be, but somehow not quite right.

She leaned on the counter near Tony and looked him over. "Not a chance anyone will get out of here today. I'd have to stay here tonight if I didn't have a snowmobile. You're stuck here for the night, maybe longer. Highway 12 will be plowed in town, but only in town, and County Road O hasn't been plowed at all. Those are the only two roads in or out of Kirby."

Frank elbowed Tony in the side. "Why's the street in town open but nothing else?"

She shrugged. "It's Ed, the owner of the tavern. He has a plow on the front of his jeep. The plow is new, and he likes to play around with it. Nobody complains if he knocks over a mailbox or two because at least we can get around town. The roads are supposed to be the county's job, but Kirby don't rate high on their list of priorities. It might be two or three days before they get around to clearing the roads." She wrapped a finger in her long black hair, snapped her gum, and quickly shifted her gaze back to Tony. "Not much to do here 'cept catch up on your sleep. But if you bought a couple of bottles down at Ed's, we could have a party tonight."

Frank was used to women fawning over Tony and ignoring him. "Won't this guy, Ed, want to clear the road into town to get business?" Frank asked.

She answered but didn't take her eyes off Tony. "Nah, the snowmobile crowd will keep the tavern full. Nobody can get to work today with the roads like they are. I'm surprised there isn't a crowd at Ed's now, three sheets to the wind already."

She leaned forward on the counter toward Tony until Frank thought her breasts were going to fall out of her blouse. "TV reception here sucks. In the winter the only entertainments are snowmobiling, drinking, and sex. Ed carries all my favorites: Jägermeister, Irish Cream, and Amaretto. Bring back a couple tonight, and you can try everything Kirby has to offer."

Frank glanced at Betty—female, but not beautiful by any stretch—and then at Tony. The fool needed to have his eyes checked before he handled a gun again. His tongue was damned near hanging out, and he looked like he might start drooling.

"So, we're stuck here tonight, maybe all day tomorrow?" Tony asked her left breast.

"You'll be lucky if you're not stranded through the weekend," she said. "You don't have to worry about eating. Ed serves pizza, bratwurst, steaks, and hamburgers at the tavern every day. He hikes the price a little on days like today—says it's blizzards that keep his books in the black."

Unless Ed had a sadistic streak, his meals would have to be better than the motel's breakfast, Frank reasoned.

Back in Louie's room, Tony groused, "We gotta get Louie out before I can bring Betty up here. Any ideas?"

Frank sat in the only chair in the room, looked at Tony, and decided there was no hope for him, but the corpse did have to go. "Yeah. And he'll be kind of ripe by tomorrow. I bet the staff will be in bed by eleven, earlier if the party is any good. People get tired fast in cold weather."

Tony nudged the corpse with his toe. "So, you going to carry him out?"

"*We* are going to carry him out late tonight," Frank said and nodded toward the corpse. "We'll carry him to the stairwell, haul his ass outside, and dump him in a snowbank."

Tony looked at the body and shivered. "Handling corpses gives me the creeps. He's skinny. You can carry him by yourself. I'll act as a lookout in case Betty and a friend come up. I'll keep 'em entertained until you get back."

"Screw that shit. We each take an arm around our neck and carry him out."

Tony sulked. "Then I want him out of here early in case Betty shows up. I ain't never had a beautiful woman throw herself at me like that." Tony sat on the bed and crossed his arms over his chest. "How about we dress Louie and drag him out about eight. If we bump into anybody, we tell 'em Louie's dead drunk, and we're taking him for a walk in the cold."

Frank pictured Betty. *Beautiful? Nobody can be that blind and still sober.* "You don't have a bottle hidden around here, do you?"

Tony shook his head.

Frank paused for a moment and considered critiquing Betty's looks, but Tony was hopeless. It would be safest just to keep him happy. "Okay. We'll get him dressed, and if the halls are clear, we'll take him out at eight. But you've got to help. I'm not doing it myself."

"What about Fatso at the desk?" Tony asked. "He knows we didn't check in."

"Nobody else knows that. We stay out of Fatso's sight and sneak out the side doors for lunch and dinner. If he catches us, we tell him we're staying with Louie and slip him a C-note for the extra people in the room."

Frank and Tony walked to Ed's at noon, passing the gas station on the way. The station was emptier than a church during Mardi Gras. They had to walk on the street because the sidewalks, if Kirby had any, were under three feet of snow, and in many places, four or five feet, where Ed's plowing had dumped extra snow. There wasn't any traffic, anyway.

Frank started out walking with his hands thrust in the pockets of his coat. A few steps on ice cured him of that. He would have landed on his ass if Tony hadn't caught him. After that, he kept his hands free to adjust his balance, even if his hands ached from the cold. By the time they neared the tavern, his fingers and toes were numb, his ears smarted from the cold, and even his legs felt frigid. *Next time I travel in January, I'm packing long underwear.*

Five snowmobiles sat in front of Ed's Tavern, a log cabin that seemed like an extension of the forest that abutted the parking lot. Frank had expected more snowmobiles, the way Betty had talked. The entrance to the tavern amounted to a small air lock, large enough to hold several people. Moisture frozen to the inside of the outer glass door rendered it opaque. A wreath of pine boughs was attached to the tavern's entrance door.

Warm air tinged with sweat and stale beer and the noise of multiple conversations greeted them as Frank and Tony entered the tavern. Empty bottles on tables and loud voices suggested the locals had gotten an early start on celebrating the blizzard.

The building wasn't large. Frank made his way to the bar, past tables shoehorned between the outer log wall and the bar. On his guard, he scanned the room and patrons. All of them—there were only nine—were sitting near a potbellied wood stove at the far-right wall. One of the patrons was in a corner, obscured by the others. Frank could only see the top of his head.

Melting snow from boots soaked into sawdust scattered on the floor. It was January, but Christmas lights still hung around the windows.

A door at the end of the bar looked like it led to restrooms and a kitchen. Frank didn't expect much from the kitchen, but at least nobody could screw up heating a frozen pizza. He headed to the men's room. As he left the toilet, he glanced through a window on an exit door at the end of the hallway and saw two dilapidated outhouses behind the tavern. *I hope those are from years ago. A guy would freeze his dick off out there.* He took a stool at the bar next to Tony.

"Stranded by the blizzard?" the bartender asked.

"Yeah," Frank said before Tony could answer. He'd told Tony to let him do the talking. "Barely made it here from the freeway." He ordered a tap beer for himself and Tony. When the bartender set the beer before him, he asked, "You got Christmas lights around all your windows yet. What gives with that?"

"Name's Ed. Windows are triple paned, but we'd have half an inch of ice on the inside of them if it weren't for the lights."

Frank looked around. The nine customers filled a third of the chairs in the tavern. "You're kind of busy for noon, aren't you?"

"There'd normally be twice as many snowmobilers here on a snow day. Somebody said the cops closed the snowmobile trails into town."

"Why'd they do that?" Frank asked.

"Damned if I know. Maybe Gordy knows why." He turned and called to a corner of the room near the wood stove. "Hey, Gordy. A guy has a question for you."

A tall, powerfully built man in a uniform tossed his playing cards on the table and walked toward them. Frank nearly choked on his beer.

"Guys, this is Deputy Gordy Krueger. He's stuck here too."

Every sphincter in Frank's body clamped down. It took him a minute to collect his wits, force himself to relax, and look up at Gordy. "We . . . I was, ah, wondering why the snowmobile trails are closed."

Muscles in his arms, chest, and shoulders filled out Krueger's uniform as he towered over them. He scratched his chin and shook his head. "Can't help you there. I'm as much in the dark as you guys. I heard the army closed the trails, although the army isn't supposed to get involved in law enforcement problems."

"And what," Frank gulped, "what's the law enforcement problem?"

"I have no idea."

"Hey Gordy, ya gonna yak all day?" someone called from his table.

Gordy looked up, waved to them, and turned back to Frank and Tony. "I have to get back to my card game, but it was nice meeting you boys. Stay warm," he said and returned to his table in the corner.

Tony looked pale. He leaned close to Frank and whispered. "Where the hell did he come from?"

"I don't know, but he scared the shit out of me. Jesus, I ask an innocent question, and I get a muscle-bound cop sitting in my lap." Frank thought for a moment. "I never heard of the army blocking off trails and roads that weren't in an army reserve, except maybe in national disasters."

He caught the bartender's eye. "Refills?" Ed asked.

"No, we're fine, but can we get a pepperoni and mushroom Tombstone pizza to go, and a six-pack of Pabst?"

While they waited, Tony reared back and honked out a sneeze that blew two napkins off the bar.

"Cripes! Watch it," Frank said. He grabbed a small damp napkin somebody'd left under their beer and wiped the side of his face. "Aim somewhere else next time."

"Sorry. Didn't have a warning on that one."

The waitress brought their order, took their money, and glared at them over the snot on the bar. She grabbed a rag and wiped off the bar.

Frank relaxed after they left Ed's and headed back toward the motel. An old guy entered the gas station as they passed. Frank put an arm in front of Tony to stop him. "Look at these gas pumps. They're antiques. None of them take credit cards. That means an attendant has to pump your gas for you."

"Who does that anymore?"

"I get a kick out of these small-town gas stations. Let's go in and take a look. It'll be warm inside."

A bell above the door tinkled as Frank opened the door. The small room was poorly lit. Wood burning in a potbellied stove sizzled and popped in a corner, and a short counter with a cash register on top with candy bars and cigarettes under it bisected the room. Quart cans of oil and transmission fluid filled shelves on the wall behind the counter. An old *Playboy* calendar covered the only spot on the wall not covered by shelves. The floor and other flat surfaces were covered with a thin film of dirt mixed with oil. But the room was warm and comfortable.

The attendant looked like he needed a shave. He was at least seventy years old, wore darkly stained overalls, and relaxed in an office chair with stuffing sticking out of tears in the vinyl seat. He ignored Frank and Tony and concentrated on the fold-out from a copy of *Hustler*.

Frank nudged Tony in the ribs with his elbow and raised his eyebrows, indicating, "See. I told you." He shifted his gaze to the calendar. "A good year." He nodded toward it. "June 1995, right? Miss December that year looked like she was going to give Santa a ride. I had a copy hidden under my mattress until Mom changed my sheets. Jesus, did I catch hell."

"Deserved it," the elderly attendant said without putting down the fold-out. "Had any sense, you would have stuck with Miss April. There was a piece worth drooling over."

Frank snorted, looked over the candy selection, and picked the candy bars farthest from the old guy. "I'll have a couple of those Kit Kats." He dropped a $10 bill on the counter.

"Name's George." The attendant stood and got the candy bars. He looked at the ten but didn't touch it. "Haven't ya got a couple of ones?"

Frank didn't look in his wallet. "No. That's all I got."

"Fuck ya, then," the old guy said. He tossed the candy bars back under the counter and returned to reading *Hustler*.

Tony sneezed again, but this time he tucked his nose in the crook of his elbow and turned away from Frank. Droplets covered the counter.

"Oh, for . . . Get the hell out of here," George snarled as he popped out of his chair. He grabbed a dirty rag and wiped the counter down. Tony and Frank left the station, laughing.

"See," Frank said. "I told ya these places were something. God, you shoulda seen his expression when you let fly." They continued to the motel. A tow truck sat in the parking lot. In the lobby, a guy in a heavy coat, a cap with ear flaps, and dirty jeans talked to the chubby manager behind the counter. Frank slowed to a stroll and listened.

"Do you think the guy with that car in the ditch out front wants a tow?" the driver asked.

"He hasn't asked for one. Want me to call his room?"

Frank prodded Tony toward the stairs. As his heart thundered in his chest, he whispered, "Don't look back, and don't answer the phone when we get to the room."

Frank pulled out the key card at the door to Louie's room. He put it in the slot the wrong way the first two times he tried it. The phone in the room was ringing, and his hand shook by the time they got into the room. Tony pulled the chair up to a small table in the room, opened a beer, and started in on the pizza. The jangling phone made Frank nervous. Too nervous to sit, he picked up a slice of pizza and paced back and forth across the room. Between bites, he said, "We got to get Louie outta sight." He pointed at the corpse with the slice of pizza. "We can't leave him sitting there. We're toast if somebody comes up to bring fresh towels or gets suspicious why nobody's seen him."

"Under the bed?" asked Tony.

Frank pulled up low-hanging blankets and looked under the bed. "No room at all here. Maybe the bathtub. Put your damned pizza down and give me a hand."

Frank seized Louie's feet. Tony grabbed his hands, shifting

to Louie's head when the arms wouldn't bend. "Damn, he's stiff," Tony complained.

They half dragged, half carried the corpse to the bathroom. There, they swung it over the tub and let go. It landed with a reverberating *thunk*. Tony went back to his pizza and Frank pulled the bathtub's curtain closed. Two minutes later there was a knock on the door. Frank looked at Tony. Tony shrugged and nodded toward the door; his eyebrows raised in question.

"Maybe they'll go away if we're quiet," Frank whispered. "Toss a towel over that bloodstain Louie left, just in case."

"Anything wrong in there?" a male voice called from the hallway. Frank heard a key card slide in the slot.

Frank raised his voice. It came out as a loud squeak. "We're okay."

The door opened. Chubby from the front desk stood in the doorway, looking suspicious. "There was a loud noise. Sounded like something fell."

"No problems. I, ah, I tripped. Nobody's hurt. Thanks for your concern," Frank babbled and tried to close the door.

Chubby put a hand on the door and held it open. "I'm Bill, the manager. Who are you? I don't remember checking you in. Where is Mr. Antoine?"

Frank's gut contracted and shoved gas and maybe something more out. He was going to need a nice hot shower when he got rid of this yokel, but he held his ground at the door, his eyes wide and his mouth hanging open, desperately thinking up an answer to the question. "Oh, Louis is, ah, Louis is having a pizza down at the tavern. We're old friends. Met him in the parking lot late last night. He, ah, he said we could use the other bed." Frank extracted a $100 bill from his wallet. "Will this cover the fee for extra people in the room?"

Bill's face took on a calculating look. "It'll cover the cost for the first two nights, but I'll need another hundred for the next two."

"We don't plan on staying that—"

"Doesn't matter what you've planned. I hear there's a problem getting snowplows to Kirby. We're going to be snowed in for at least four days."

Frank's face fell. Four days in this frozen excuse for a town? That wasn't going to happen. "Ah, okay. How about if I drop by and pay you in a couple of days, if we're still here."

Bill blocked the door with his foot. "Since you didn't check in, that'll be paid in advance," he said and held out his hand. Frank laid another $100 bill in the outstretched palm. Bill's hand transferred the note to his front pocket so fast Frank's eye couldn't follow it. "You and your friend should come down to the desk when you get a chance and sign in."

Bill left, and Frank headed for the bathroom. He looked at Louis in the bathtub and decided there'd be room for him to take a shower. It wasn't as though he would be sitting on him.

During his shower, Frank stepped on Louis's fingers a couple of times. It didn't interfere with his shower, but it felt creepy as hell. He toweled off, walked to his bed, and lay down. Tony asked him if he wanted more pizza.

"I can't think of food now. Fatso didn't believe a word I said, but he'll bleed us for all the money he can before he calls the cops. Until then, we avoid him. We avoid the lobby during the day and exit and enter the motel by the side door when he's at the desk."

"And Louie?"

"It'll be dark by six. We get him dressed, and as soon as the hall clears for a while, we stick him in a snowbank. After that, you can play with Betty for the rest of the night."

CHAPTER 6

THE GATHERING STORM

Tuesday, January 16, 2018
St. Paul, Minnesota
11:00 a.m. CST

Grant opened the door to his first-floor apartment in Como Student Housing. He and Sarah had what the university optimistically called a "garden-level flat." It was that, if a couple of scraggly shrubs, now devoid of leaves, could be called a garden.

As he opened the door and let cold air into their tiny living room, Sarah poked her head around the corner from the kitchen. At five-foot-eight, she'd always been trim and athletic, but at eight months pregnant, her belly was swollen, her legs and feet were swollen, and her blonde ponytail was usually in disarray. "What are you doing home at this time of day?" she asked.

"Ron's sending me to a little town in central Wisconsin," Grant said.

"Why? I thought you were buried in lab work here?"

"Ron and a buddy of his in Switzerland imported some tissue samples and screwed up." Grant told her the story of the Iceman, the samples, and the missing Professor Antoine.

"That sounds dangerous," Sarah said. She hugged Grant and rested her head on his shoulder. He put his arms around her and kissed her forehead. She looked up at him. "Do you have to hop to it every time Ron comes up with an idea? You could become infected. You could drag something back and infect Jimmy and me."

"Ron insisted I take a boatload of protective gear, and I'll be careful. I don't plan on handling the samples. I'm just going to find Antoine."

Sarah rubbed her swollen belly. "You'd darn well better be careful. I don't want Jimmy and the baby to be orphans before she's born." She put her arms around Grant's neck and nuzzled him. "Jimmy and I wouldn't know what to do if something happened to you." She pushed herself away from Grant and frowned. "Is this trip even legal?"

"Of course it is," Grant said without conviction. At least, he thought it was legal. There hadn't been anything on the news of an official quarantine of Kirby, and if there was, it shouldn't include him. He was a virologist, and unfortunately an associate of the guy who arranged for the samples to be brought to the United States. "Look, I'll take it slow getting ready and loading up at the lab. Maybe Ron will change his mind if I give him time to think about it."

"Promise you'll be careful?"

"Absolutely."

They embraced and he kissed her deeply. He felt the baby kick as Sarah pressed against him. He chuckled, bent down, and kissed her belly. "And I promise Baby I'll make it back in one piece too."

Grant drove back to the lab and dillydallied as he loaded the Tyvek plastic coveralls, latex gloves, boots, plastic boot covers, surgical masks, and other biosecurity personal protective equipment into his old Ford Explorer. He grabbed a couple cases of each, as all were made to be used only once.

He waited for his cell phone to ring, an indication Ron had come to his senses and canceled this stupid trip. When that didn't happen, he drove home and spent another fifteen minutes packing his tent and winter camping gear. He might not be able to find lodging, and the more time he wasted now, the more time he gave Ron to call this trip off. He tossed in his cross-country skis, too, in case the Explorer couldn't get through to Kirby.

Grant hadn't found a way to balance work and family, nor did he know any other graduate student or scientist who had. His work in the lab and the reading he had to do to stay current consumed most of his time and energy. He'd met people who had run businesses before graduate school but, as scientists, seemed to have lost the ability to do the simplest bookkeeping and stay within their budgets. Many were full-time professors, and all were focused on the science, not the money.

Grant found that he and other scientists didn't just study a subject. They were enthralled by it. It occupied their minds while they ate, while they watched movies, even while they made love. The thrill of learning, of discovery, of applying new knowledge captivated them. Stumbling across a continual supply of new questions to answer was addictive. Sarah was eight months pregnant. Grant had tried with limited success to spend more time with her and pull back on the energy and time he allocated to virology and molecular biology. Even that hadn't been easy.

It wasn't the pointless trip that bothered Grant the most. It was the extra time away from Sarah and Jimmy. He hadn't minded working long hours when he was a doctoral candidate. Sarah visited him in the lab, even helped him a little before she became pregnant with Jimmy. The pregnancy changed that, and this pregnancy had tied her down even more. His typical work schedule included evenings and weekends, which was bad enough. Now he'd be gone for several nights, and he wasn't sure when he'd be able to return.

If the samples had been opened, or if Antoine had become ill,

Grant feared he'd be quarantined in Kirby. If that happened, he'd be unable to see his family for weeks after the trip. He pushed that possibility out of his mind.

It was twelve thirty, and Ron hadn't called off the trip. Grant couldn't delay any longer. He was in Wisconsin on I-94 by one thirty, headed southeast toward Kirby. Snowplows had cleared the freeway, salted and sanded, and driving was normal for winter. He reached the exit for Highway 12 and Kirby by mid-afternoon. It was clear of snow, as was Highway 12 headed south, but the highway headed north toward Kirby was covered with snow and drifted shut. The snow depth appeared to vary from none, where the wind had scoured the road, to drifts three to four feet high where trees or brush had partially blocked the wind.

Grant sat at the foot of the exit, uncertain what to do when a milk truck with a plow mounted on the front came through headed north. With three axles, ten tires, and thousands of pounds of milk on board, the truck blasted through the tallest drifts as though they weren't there.

The road was clear to the first dairy farm, maybe farther. Grant shifted into four-wheel drive and followed the truck. It pulled into a farm driveway a mile later, and Grant was again left in a quandary. He could give up and tell Ron that he hadn't been able to get to Kirby. It would stretch the truth a little, but not a lot. Looking at the road in front of him, he estimated his odds of getting through to Kirby without getting out his skis at no better than fifty-fifty.

His Explorer had four-wheel drive and higher road clearance than a car. Although the shovel he kept in the back might not get him to Kirby, it would get him a lot closer than he was. If he got stuck and couldn't dig his way out, carting in his equipment on skis would be physically possible but a lot of work. That could take the rest of today and all day tomorrow.

He couldn't be blamed if he called it quits and went home, but he'd always had a hard time admitting he couldn't complete a task. And if the samples were mishandled by anyone in Kirby, hundreds—maybe thousands—of people might become infected. The CDC would have someone here to prevent or contain that, but not for a day or so. Nasty things could happen before that.

He backed up the Explorer and took a run at the first drift. The SUV bulled its way through, fishtailed a little, and kept going.

Grant made it half a mile before hitting a drift that was halfway up the Explorer's grill. It stopped him cold. He tried to rock the SUV back and forth only to hear his tires spin. It took ten minutes of hard work to shovel enough snow from under the Explorer to free his axles and drivetrain from the snow, and another ten minutes to clear the snow from behind the tires. Out of breath and sweating, he sat in the SUV and rested before backing up and smashing into the drift again. This time he broke through.

The rest of the way to Kirby was a series of repetitions of the same procedure made worse by visual problems. The white surface of the road, ditches, and fields blended into a vast, unbroken blanket of white. Under those conditions, he couldn't see where the road was. He managed to stay on it only by keeping equal distance from the fence posts on his left and telephone poles on his right. Tall weeds in the ditches helped delineate where the road had to be. It took over an hour to go two miles.

He pulled into the Kirby gas station at 3:30 and filled up on gas and junk food. The old man behind the counter asked how the devil he'd made it into town. Grant told him of the milk truck and asked about the motel. The guy grunted and pointed north, fifty yards up the road. Grant called Antoine's cell phone and motel room. No answer. He pulled into the motel's parking lot, went to the check-in counter, and asked if anyone had seen Professor Antoine recently.

"I wouldn't know Professor Antoine from Adam," said a woman whose name tag identified her as Betty.

Grant asked for Antoine's room number, which Betty refused to provide. Ron had given him the room's phone number. He looked at the last three digits of the number: 221. Maybe 221 was also the room number. He found Room 221 and knocked. No one answered. He banged on the door again, and a bald, tubby guy opened the door.

"What do you want?" the man asked.

Grant gawked at the guy for a moment, surprised that it wasn't Louis. "Could I . . . could I speak to Professor Antoine?"

The guy shrugged. "Never heard of him."

"Professor Louis Antoine?"

"Oh, Louie," the guy said. "Yeah, he isn't here right now. He stepped out for a bite to eat."

"When do you expect him back?"

"No idea. You can wait for him in the lobby," the guy said and tried to close the door.

Grant blocked it. "Okay. If you see Antoine, would you tell him Dr. Grant Farnsworth, an associate of Professor Ron Schmidt's, needs to talk to him?"

"Yeah, sure."

"And your name is?" Grant asked.

"I'm Frank, an old friend of Louie's. You can catch him on his way back from Ed's if you wait in the lobby." The door slammed shut.

Stunned, Grant looked blankly at the door. Nothing about this exchange seemed right. He didn't have enough to complain to the police, if there were any in town. It seemed as though all he could do about it was wait for Professor Antoine to return. Grant sat in the lobby until 4:30. He tried to rent a room, but there were no vacancies. Betty said there was a motel ten miles north of Kirby on Highway 12, although it didn't look like the highway to the north was plowed. Grant remembered the work it had taken to travel two miles on the unplowed highway. He wouldn't survive working like that for ten miles. "Can I sleep in your lobby on one of the chairs?"

"That'll be okay. Just don't leave a mess for me to clean up." She told him he could have breakfast tomorrow for ten bucks. If he didn't want that, he'd have to clear out before breakfast was set up.

Grant paid the ten dollars and watched her put it in a pocket of her jeans. He was pretty sure the motel management wasn't going to see that money.

He went back to Room 221. Frank answered on the first knock.

"Professor Antoine hasn't shown up," Grant said, "and what I have to tell him could be a matter of life and death."

Frank's mouth looked as though he were ready to sneer. His forehead furrowed and his eyes narrowed for a moment. The furrows disappeared and his sneer transformed into a smile. "Yeah, yeah. Tell me and I'll give him the message when he gets back."

Grant didn't believe a word of Frank's and his previous misgivings gelled. Frank looked like a slob. Antoine had a reputation for being a picky dresser, proud of his appearance, and something of a wine snob. Frank hadn't recognized Antoine's title when Grant had asked for the professor, and it stretched probability to the breaking point to believe Antoine would socialize with a jerk like Frank.

But maybe Antoine had met this guy at O'Hare or on the road north and had felt sorry for him. The only option Grant could think of was to proceed as though Frank were telling the truth and see if there were any cops in town. "Tell Antoine the news about the Iceman is worse than what's in the papers and on TV. Several of his team were hospitalized, and one has died." He wrote his name, and Ron's, on a sticky note with his cell phone number and gave it to Frank. "Ask Antoine to call me as soon as he gets in. He *must not* move or open the samples until he has talked to me. People have died from exposure to those."

"Okay." Frank nodded. "Say, what's in these samples?"

"Dehydrated muscle and guts from a body. They're tissue samples from the Iceman, a guy who was frozen in a glacier for a thousand years."

Frank looked a bit queasy as he listened to the description, but he didn't ask anything further. As he spoke, Grant noticed the remains of reddish-brown stains on the wall and carpet. They looked as though someone had tried to clean up blood stains. A hole in the wall almost six feet off the floor and a couple of inches wide was encircled by the stains. To Grant, it looked like the aftermath from a bullet exiting the skull.

Grant glanced briefly at Frank and tried to hide his interest in the stains and hole in the wall. If his fears were right, this guy had a gun and would use it. "Thanks for giving him the message," he said nervously. "Ah, a friend is waiting for me. I'd better be going." Grant turned and trotted to the stairway. He took the stairs two at a time and didn't slow down until he came to the lobby. A backward glance verified Frank wasn't following him.

By the desk, he waited until he'd stopped shaking before he asked how to get in touch with the local police. Betty told him the sheriff's department took care of Kirby. "Gordy, one of the deputies, is stranded in town. He's probably playing cards at Ed's until the roads are opened."

Frank turned from the door to look at Tony and the bloody wall. "We gotta do a better job on that bloodstain. Maybe try some cold water and soap from the bathroom."

Tony gave the wall a passing glance, but he had other things on his mind. "What did that character say about a deadly disease?"

"Aw, don't believe that shit. He's just some punk trying to act important, throw his weight around, and scare us. You ever see a real doctor running around in jeans and a sweatshirt like him?

Tony shrugged. "You got a point. When do you want to go to Ed's to eat?"

CHAPTER 7

FROZEN

Tuesday, January 16, 2018
Fort McCoy, Wisconsin
5:00 p.m. CST

The plane was small enough that Sybil could watch their approach through the cockpit windows. It made her stomach queasy. To handle the crosswinds, the pilots aimed the aircraft several degrees to the right of the runway. It looked as though they were coming in sideways. As an undergrad, she'd sailed on Lake Mendota as a crew member on twenty-foot class C sailing scows and was used to the idea that you aimed a boat one way, but the wind and waves pushed it another. That was on water. It was emotionally different when the only thing supporting her was air. She closed her eyes and didn't open them until the plane came to a stop.

The starboard engine sputtered, went silent, and its propeller swung to a halt. At last Sybil had silence. She hated the continuous drone heard on propeller-driven planes, but jets couldn't land at McCoy. Glancing through the window, she saw only white: white on the ground, white in the sky, and white blowing about in between. She struggled into her parka, heavy gloves, and insulated boots, grabbed her bag and her briefcase, and waddled to the exit door. *I feel like a goddamned penguin.*

The plane's door opened, and subzero air hit her in the face. She staggered backward from the shock. It took a moment to collect herself before she clambered down the short staircase to the tarmac. Blowing snow swirled around her as she hiked toward what she would have called the terminal, had it been larger. The building wasn't imposing, but at least it looked warmer than where she was.

Two days ago, she'd been sweltering in an isolation suit in hundred-degree heat collecting samples from Ebola patients. Now she was freezing her toes, fingers, ears, and nose on a bright and sunny day with a wind chill factor of minus fifty degrees. *Goddamn Sam.* As she lumbered over the tarmac, she plotted scenarios that would lure Sam to Fort McCoy. *Let him take a leak in the woods and get frostbite. Would serve him right.* A gust of wind sent her staggering off her course toward warmth and safety. *I feel like a frozen extra in a documentary about Antartica.*

Sybil tried to hold her bag and briefcase with one gloved hand while she opened the terminal door with the other. She dropped both bags. Before she could catch them, the wind blew them over the ice and snow until they hit a snowbank. A man in his late twenties or early thirties opened the door for her from the inside. At least six-foot-four, dressed in a sweatshirt and ski cap, without gloves or coat, he glanced at her bags and smirked. She felt ten degrees colder just looking at him. Sybil looked the soldier in the eye and pointed to her luggage before hustling into the building. *Rank has its privileges.*

The soldier ambled out and retrieved her bags. Still smirking, he walked slowly back to the door. Watching him made her feel old as well as cold, even though he had to be about her age, and she was in the warm terminal. *The cheeky bastard is doing it deliberately.*

He led her to a room with an oblong conference table in the center and put her luggage on the floor. She removed her gloves and cap and took off her coat. The gloves were a clumsy nuisance, but they'd kept her hands from freezing.

"Welcome to Fort McCoy," said a voice behind her. She turned and shook hands with an officer. Over six feet, lean, and muscular, he appeared to be in his midforties. "I'm Colonel Williams. This is Captain Stevens and Doctor Wickert," he said, introducing the men standing on his right. "Given our normal winter temperatures, how did they happen to stick you with this job?"

Sybil recognized the implied sexism and decided to squelch it. "McCoy isn't that cold compared to some areas I've been. I had an assignment in Antarctica three years ago, Colonel." No need to admit it was only three days long. She shook hands with each of the men as they took seats around the end of the table. Colonel Williams explained that he'd been told there was a biological threat in or near the village of Kirby. He hadn't been given any specifics. Sybil gave him a summary of the Iceman story, the sickness and fatalities in the recovery team, and the Swiss efforts to identify the virus.

Then she gave him the bad news. "A Swiss professor smuggled three samples of the Iceman into the United States on his way to a conference in Minneapolis. He landed in Chicago during the blizzard, somehow got through customs, and made it as far north as the Kirby Motel. He called his contact at the University of Minnesota last night around midnight. They haven't been able to reach him since."

"So, samples containing a deadly virus are loose in Kirby?" the colonel asked.

"That's what we fear," Sybil said. "With luck, they'll still be packed in his luggage."

The doctor asked, "Do you know how the virus is spread?"

"No."

"Isn't it unusual for a virus to survive for so long at the temperatures in the glacier, without additives to protect it?"

"Absolutely, for most viruses, but not for all," Sybil explained. "Don't think of this in binary, die-or-survive terms. Bad conditions for the virus reduce the time required to inactivate half of the virus particles. Do the math, and you end up with a death curve for the virus that flattens out as time rolls on. By the time 80 percent of the virus particles are inactivated, the die-off rate, although constant as a percentage, is much slower in actual numbers killed, hence the flatter curve with time. Our problem is that if you start with eight or nine logs of virus per gram of tissue, there will still be enough viable virions to cause infections after 99.9 percent of the virus particles have been destroyed."

The doctor nodded and scribbled on a tablet. "Eight logs of virus per gram would be about seven times ten to the eleventh power in a 150-pound man."

"What's that for the non-scientist, Doc?" The colonel asked.

"It's 720 billion viral particles per pound, marginally less if bone isn't infected." The colonel and captain looked at each other, eyebrows raised.

"Do we know the ID50?" the doctor asked.

The colonel looked from Sybil to the doctor and back. "What's an ID50?"

"An ID50," Sybil said, "is the dose of virus that will cause infection in half of the people exposed to it. And no, we have no idea what that number is, although we suspect it's comparatively low, perhaps a few hundred to a few thousand virus particles. Much would depend on the health of the person and amount of stress they were under."

A knock came at the door. An enlisted man entered the room

and saluted. "Sir, a Dr. Barker from the CDC called. He said CNN will carry news from Zürich soon."

Williams turned on a flat screen TV on the wall and tuned to CNN in time to sit through five minutes of ads for adult diapers, nutritional supplements for prostate health, and medications for erectile dysfunction. Sybil hated those ads. The actors always looked tanned, fit, and fifteen years younger than anyone who had the problems.

Wolf Blitzer connected with a reporter at a press conference in Zürich. A distinguished figure at a podium speaking in German gave the story of the Iceman. Fortunately, there were French and English subtitles. All people in close contact with the corpse, he said, had become ill, and two had died. He listed the early symptoms and said authorities had quarantined people known to have been exposed to the infected patients or the corpse. Schools, theaters, and churches in Zürich were closed for the next ten days. Anyone developing a headache and fever should stay in their home and call an emergency room or hospital. Under no circumstances should they leave their home to seek medical care. Medical personnel would come to them. For the next ten days, the Zürich airport and train stations were closed to civilian traffic. Civilian auto and bus travel into or out of Zürich was banned.

Pandemonium broke out among the reporters. Questions were shouted in English, German, French, and Italian. A French reporter asked if the ban included shipments of swiss cheeses, and an English reporter asked if it was true that the Iceman was German. The speaker said the identity of the virus, fatality rates, how the virus was spread, and whether treatments were available were all "unknown at this time." In the most unnecessary warning of the decade, the speaker stressed that the virus was not a threat to take lightly.

The reporters referred back to Wolf, who said that all flights from Switzerland to the United States were canceled, and passengers on planes now en route would be quarantined. The colonel turned the television off when Wolf turned his attention to a video of a singing porpoise.

"Man, it took guts to talk to reporters with so little known about the virus," Sybil said. "We should do everything they're doing in Zürich on a smaller scale for Kirby. Since there are few households in Kirby, everyone will be quarantined in their homes. Food, fuel, and medical care will be brought to them as needed."

"How long will the quarantine be maintained?" the colonel asked.

"Ten days if no one becomes infected, or two weeks after the last diagnosed infection. That's a guess for now. We might have to add a week to each of those figures once we learn more."

The colonel fiddled with a pencil, frowned, looked at the doctor, and then back at Sybil. "Why is the military being dragged into this? I don't want my troops exposed to a fatal and untreatable disease. They didn't sign up for that." He slammed his pencil on the conference table.

"Our needs are not negotiable, Colonel," Sybil said firmly. "This is a potential national emergency. We need your troops to block traffic in and out of Kirby until the sheriff's department and State Patrol can take over." She stood and paced back and forth along the table. "We will need your help in setting up a field hospital for any cases we have in Kirby. You'll need a cluster of small units with double entry air locks, HEPA filters on the air vents, and a gas or propane heater for each unit."

"That will put my medical staff at risk, won't it?" the colonel countered.

Sybil gathered her thoughts before speaking. She stared at the colonel. "Look. We will have the same biosafety procedures in place that proved effective in combating and treating Ebola.

That's why I was sent here and put in charge by Sam Barker of the CDC. I spent six months in the Congo."

The colonel started. "That's good, but—"

Sybil raised a firm palm. "We can treat cases we get in a field hospital in Kirby, or we can bring them to your base hospital. It's your choice. If you find both options unacceptable, you may ask to be relieved." Sybil didn't give the colonel a chance to answer. She turned to Dr. Wickert. "Can you set up a field hospital with isolation facilities in Kirby?"

The colonel and doctor conferred before the doctor answered. "We can set up a hospital, but we don't have sufficient staff or equipment for biosecurity if we're to treat this like Ebola."

Sybil slid a note to the doctor. "The University of Wisconsin hospital and other Wisconsin National Guard units have promised assistance and supplies. Call this number to get the ball rolling. Because of their experience with Ebola, Doctors Without Borders will send an adviser. He'll be here in two days. I hope we don't have any patients, but build flexibility into your plans."

"How much do we tell the people of Kirby?" the doctor asked.

"Kirby must be isolated before we make any announcements," Sybil said. "We don't want families bolting for Madison, Milwaukee, or the Twin Cities. That would be a disaster. We'd have a mess like Zürich on our hands all through the upper Midwest. We should be ready to quarantine Tomah and surrounding villages if we must. If it comes to that, we will have to close all nearby exits and entrances from I-90 and I-94 and seal off other highways."

The mood in the room turned somber. Everyone around the table nodded. Sybil relaxed. *At least they understood that.* She continued, "Nobody goes in or out of the area without our knowledge and permission. We must have control of communications—landlines and cell phones. If word about this gets out before we have a quarantine lockdown, I can guarantee you some jerks will pack up the kids and hightail it to other cities, or another country."

Williams looked crestfallen. *Good,* she thought. *Threatening to relieve him worked. Now I'll have to soothe ruffled feathers.*

"You're asking two questions," Williams said. "The first is, 'When can we control physical movement?' That's the easiest. The State Patrol is moving to blockade the roads. They should be in place late this afternoon. My men have blocked the snowmobile trails in and out of Kirby. They'll be relieved by the Monroe County Sheriff's Office in a day or two. A sheriff's deputy was stranded in Kirby. He has been ordered to assist when we enter the town."

"Can you legally take army personnel into Kirby and use them to control travel?" Sybil asked.

"The troops on base are in the Wisconsin National Guard. They can help, but I don't want to do it the way you've described." Williams looked at Sybil and paused a moment before continuing, as though waiting for her to object. "Let law enforcement officials blockade the roads and control travel. Properly trained medical personnel should take care of exams and treatments. I'd rather have the residents see the guardsmen as helpers. They can be used to deliver food and supplies, but they'll leave them at the front doors. They should not be exposed to anyone who's possibly infected."

Sybil put down her pen and looked at the colonel. The guy had a point. Here's where she could make nice. "Excellent points, Colonel. Can your people legally do that?"

"The National Guardsmen on base can do that as soon as the governor calls them up. I trust he will do that quietly."

She asked about restricting telephone communications.

"I can't do anything about phone lines or cell phone towers,"

Williams said. "The politicians and bureaucrats will have to handle cutting communications."

"Blast it. That could take a week, maybe longer. Can you have a crew dig some holes when we get to Kirby and 'accidentally' hit the telephone lines and do the same for power to the cell phone towers in the area?"

Colonel Williams paused before answering. "No. Your eagerness to keep everything quiet is going to cause more problems than it prevents. People resent being ordered around without adequate explanations. I don't want my men associated with telling lies. It'll be better, in the long run, to be honest and announce that Kirby and the area around it are quarantined because someone has a rare disease. You should have auto and snowmobile traffic under control in twenty-four hours, long before we'd be able to do anything about communications."

Sybil considered how she'd explain that to Sam Barker. He'd probably agree. "That makes sense. When can your people move into Kirby with the hospital?" she asked.

The colonel and captain conferred and agreed they'd be ready to enter the village with food to distribute and the basics for a field hospital tomorrow afternoon.

Sybil never felt comfortable when things seemed to easily fall into order. Experience told her that was when things were most likely going wrong. The colonel was confident no one was getting into Kirby. His men and the sheriff's department controlled the snowmobile trails, and the roads weren't passable. That seemed like an assumption dying to be proven wrong.

"Colonel?" she asked. "Can I have a vehicle and a driver to check the roadblocks?"

"The sun is going down. Are you sure you want to do that tonight?"

"Yes. Can I get something to eat first?"

The colonel agreed and the captain stepped out of the room. He returned shortly with the soldier who'd chased down Sybil's luggage. "This is Corporal Jones," Williams said. "He'll escort you to the commissary and be your driver this evening."

The soldier still wore a smile. She thought of it as a smirk. It gave her the irritating impression he knew something she didn't. His expression and eyes belied intelligence; his face was rugged but not unduly so. He didn't look anything like her former fiancé, which gave him a leg up in her estimation.

Damn. Why couldn't he have been an ugly, middle-aged jerk? No doubt about it. She found him attractive, but it was an attraction she'd have to hide. She'd have to watch herself around him if he really was smart, had a sense of humor, and was willing to take orders from a woman. She was still on the rebound, and that was dangerous. The last thing she needed was a bright hunk as an assistant. She was here to work, and people could die if she got distracted.

As the group dispersed and she walked out the door, she heard the colonel say softly to the doctor, "I don't understand why an academic is in charge and not army physicians and scientists."

With her jaws clenched, Sybil pretended she hadn't heard the colonel. Let him complain and she'd refer him to Sam Barker. Straightening out who was in charge was part of Sam's job.

CHAPTER 8

THE GATHERING

Tuesday, January 16, 2018
Kirby Motel, Kirby, Wisconsin
6:00 p.m. CST

Frank felt a nudge, ignored it, rolled over, and returned to his dream about what it would be like to be young and tall, like Tony, and have women throw themselves at him. Betty wasn't any prize, but it was a hard dream to give up. The nudge came again. He opened his eyes and blearily looked around. Tony stood over him. Fantasizing about women had infinitely more appeal than talking to Tony.

"Whatcha want?" Frank mumbled.

"Get out of bed. Time to buy some booze, maybe a sandwich or pizza at Ed's."

"Oh, for Christ's sake. Betty can wait an hour." Frank struggled out of the sheet wrapped around his legs. "Do you think she might be a pro?"

"Who cares? Out of bed. We still have to move Louie." Tony thought a moment. "You're sure it's safe to carry Louie around? What that skinny guy said . . ."

Frank dragged himself out of bed and headed to the bathroom. "Oh, for Christ's sake. Enough with that guy. I told ya, he can't be a real doctor. He's some jerk trying to push us around." He closed the door and sat on the toilet in thought. Telling Tony not to worry had been reflexive. *What did that character mean about life and death? He sure was persistent, pounding on the fucking door and jabbering about infection.* Frank shook his head as he reached for the toilet paper. *Ah, hell. That guy wasn't old enough to be a doctor at a university. He's just making up stories to scare us.* Since Frank routinely lied to authority and often to those he worked with, it was easier for him to assume that Grant was lying than to sort out a conundrum he couldn't understand.

Frank dressed, and the two of them walked across the motel's parking lot. At least the lanes between the parked cars and in front of the entrance were free of snow, or mostly so. Somebody, maybe Ed, had plowed the lot and heaped three feet of well-packed snow behind their cars. "Look at that, will you?" Frank said. "Now we're really stuck. I'll bet Ed and Fatso at the motel worked this out so nobody can leave even if the roads get cleared. Bastards will probably sell us the shovels to dig our way out."

"Quit your griping and get moving," Tony snapped. "It's cold enough to freeze our balls off out here."

The snow had stopped, but the temperature had fallen from twenty degrees last night to minus twenty. It took them five minutes to walk to Ed's, and Frank whined about his cold ears, frozen fingers, and icy toes every step of the way. He wondered where he could buy a knitted ski cap, one that would cover his bald spot and be loose enough to pull down over his ears.

Damn. There were no stores in Kirby.

The crowd at Ed's was larger than it had been at noon. Some of the patrons looked like they'd been there all day. Frank and Tony grabbed a couple of bar stools nearest the wood stove and asked for menus. "Look at this," Frank whined. "Everything that ain't pizza is fried. I'll have a coronary if I have to eat this crap."

As Frank complained, Tony looked around. He leaned close to Frank and spoke softly. "Turn around, and you'll have that coronary quicker. The asshole who came looking for Louie is sitting with his back to us, talking to the deputy sheriff."

Frank's heart pounded and his back stiffened. He didn't look up from the menu. "We order and get the hell back to our room. Louie goes as soon as we're back."

"We go now," Tony whispered. "We can't wait."

"Go now? It'll look suspicious, and we'll be hungry as hell when we need to concentrate. The asshole doesn't have anything on us yet. Let's get something to go. It won't take much time, it won't look suspicious. and we'll have something to eat."

A tired-looking middle-aged waitress approached "What's the fastest food you've got?" Frank asked. "We've got to get back to, ah, to a sick friend in our motel room."

The waitress sighed, put her notepad to her chin, and told them what they could get in a voice that suggested she'd given others the same information a hundred times that evening. "Cold hamburgers and frozen fries. You can reheat both in the microwave back at your motel."

"We'll have two fries, four burgers, and a six-pack of Bud Light," Frank said. When the waitress left, he turned to Tony. "When she comes back with our order, get your booze for Betty, and we head back to take care of Louie."

Fifteen minutes later, they hoisted Louie out of the bathtub. Frank grunted as he lifted. "At least he ain't so stiff now."

"Yeah," Tony nodded. "Rigor mortis goes away a day or so after you plug a guy. I picked that up from a hitman I met. Sure makes it easier to move him."

When they had Louie out of the bathroom, they gently and quietly laid him on the floor. "Get his clothes," Frank said.

"Why are you whispering?"

"I don't know how thin the goddamned walls are, or who the people are in the next room. Just get his damned clothes off the dresser where he left 'em."

Tony returned and dumped Louie's slacks, shoes, shirt, sports coat, and underwear in a pile next to the corpse. "Pants first?"

Frank nodded. "You do the pants. I'll get him into his shirt."

Tony slipped a foot of Louie's through a leg hole of the boxers. Frank looked up from struggling to put an arm through a shirt sleeve. "What the fuck are you doing? He doesn't need underwear. Christ, we only need him to look alive and drunk in case we run into somebody as we haul his ass to a snowbank. Chances are, we're only going to meet drunks anyway."

"That don't seem right. It's cold out there."

"Shit! He's dead. He won't care," Frank almost shouted. When Tony looked like he might object, Frank added, "Hell, maybe he'd like going commando. He's French, ain't he?"

Tony glared at Frank. "Not so loud. I got a headache, and remember the walls."

"Okay, okay. Just get his pants and shoes on. Do that before I try to get further with the shirt."

It was a struggle, but they managed to get his pants, shirt, and jacket on. They picked him up and tossed him on the bed. Frank sat down, opened the bottle of brandy Tony had purchased, and took a pull. "I'm not sure my heart is gonna survive this. We still got to get his shoes on, get him down the hall, down the stairs, and out to a snowbank."

There was a knock at the door. Frank and Tony stared at each other. Frank yelled, "Just a minute," and whispered for Tony to see who was there. "Look through the peephole before ya open the door."

Tony went to the door and peered through the peephole.

When he turned around, his face had gone white. "It's the sheriff's deputy and the asshole."

"Give me a second and let 'em in." Frank grabbed the bottle and splashed brandy over Louie's face and chest. "Okay, let 'em in. Tell 'em to be quiet 'cause Louie's asleep." He rolled the corpse onto its stomach. The face looked to the right—its unmarked side up, the entry wound buried in the pillow. The jacket hid the exit wound in Louie's back, and a pillow tossed over part of Louie's head hid the chunk of scalp where the bullet left his skull. "Damn it, Tony," Frank muttered. "You always use too big a caliber. The pros say a .22 is big enough. It rattles around in the skull, tears the brain to shit, but it doesn't leave an exit wound. You don't take any pride in your work." "Shut the fuck up, for Christ's sake," Tony hissed. "You got us into this shitstorm." He went to open the door.

Frank pretended to be putting the burgers in the microwave when Grant and Officer Krueger entered the room. He turned to Krueger. "Shh. Louie's finally asleep. Don't wake him. He's drunk as a skunk and a pain in the ass when he's awake."

Krueger sniffed and backed away from the corpse. "He must have tied on a good one, but I don't remember seeing him at Ed's." He turned to Grant. "Did you see him when you were there?"

Grant shook his head.

Frank's pulse rate headed into the stratosphere. "Ah, he ... he didn't start drinking hard until he got back to the room. I was just heating up some hamburgers in case he wakes up."

"He doesn't look good," Krueger said. "His skin looks ..."

Krueger bent over the body. "Man, it looks ashen, almost like he was dead. I'll call headquarters to see if we can get a doctor to look at him."

Frank clutched the handle of the microwave door to keep his hand from shaking. "That ... that would be, ah, very kind of you. Any idea when the doc might be here?"

"Nope. From the chatter I heard on my radio, the military and State Patrol are limiting access to Kirby. They mentioned something about an infection. If he's still bad tomorrow, maybe the army can get a physician here in the morning."

Frank glanced at Tony, standing behind Krueger and Grant. Tony's face was pale, and he was moving his hand toward the gun he carried in a holster low on his back. Frank rolled his eyes to the ceiling and tried to be subtle as he shook his head. "We'll, ah, we'll be on the lookout for the doc. Louie should be awake and sober by the time he gets here. Maybe all he'll have is the world's worst hangover."

Tony snickered. "Yeah. He had a bad headache when we first got here."

Frank glared at Tony. "We'll be sure to call you if he isn't better tomorrow."

Krueger led the way out of the room. Frank closed the door. He wanted to throttle Tony, the stupid ass, but he caught a glimpse of Grant and Krueger conferring as they walked toward the stairs. *Rats. The deputy would believe anything, but the young guy didn't swallow any of it.*

Frank collapsed on the empty bed and covered his face with his hands. His heart thundered in his chest. Tony seemed determined to give him a heart attack. He couldn't handle this much stress. "We can't move Louie until Dudley-Do-Right and Bullwinkle are out of the way. We'll move him as soon as those guys bed down for the night."

The microwave dinged and Tony grabbed two of the reheated burgers. "Whew, we got through that okay. I thought I'd have to shoot those two. Think they'll be asleep by the time Betty is off duty?"

Frank ignored the question. After a moment's rest, he sat up in bed. "We need to find another place to stay, someplace nobody will look for us, but how do you do that in a town that's so damned tiny?"

Tony sat in the chair and held his head in his hands. "All of this is making my headache worse. How about we leave Louie where he is and try to get a couple of broads to invite us in?"

"You're dreaming," Frank said as he rose and got the remaining burgers out of the microwave and put the fries in to reheat. "We gotta dig our cars out yet. Let's eat, then you can take a couple of aspirin and lie down for a few hours. You'll feel like a new man. We'll dump Louie, and you can bring Betty up here. God, but I'm hungry." He opened a beer and took a long swallow. For the next ten minutes, the only sound in the room was chewing, gulping, and belching.

Kirby Motel Hallway

"None of that looked right," Grant whispered as he and Krueger descended the stairs. "Professor Antoine wouldn't ever get that drunk, and certainly not with those guys. He has a reputation as a wine snob who buys expensive clothes. He'd never sleep in a six-hundred-dollar sport coat."

Grant doubted whether Krueger had ever investigated any-thing more serious than shoplifting. A whiff of Krueger's breath indicated the officer had downed his share of beer while playing cards that afternoon.

"Nothing I could do," Krueger said. "He looked dead to the world and smelled as though he'd swum laps in brandy. The doc can look at him tomorrow. No matter what, those two thugs aren't going anywhere tonight." At the bottom of the stairs, Krueger asked Grant where he was sleeping.

Grant pointed to a chair in the corner of the lobby. "Over there. Best I could do."

"You've got my phone number. Call me if you see Tony or Frank doing something suspicious." Krueger put his hand on Grant's arm. "Don't try to handle anything by yourself. Got that?"

That was what Grant wanted to hear. He'd happily turn the whole mess over to Krueger. "I got it. I'll call you if anything comes up."

CHAPTER 9

US ARMY WINTER TRAINING GROUNDS

Tuesday, January 16, 2018
Fort McCoy
6:30 p.m. CST

Sybil took a quick glance. Corporal Jones hadn't lost his smirk. *What's with this guy? Does he think I look like a penguin or something?* Fully dressed in her parka and insulated pants, she felt like an overstuffed bird while the corporal looked sharp. Maybe it was the uniform. Over a brief dinner, she asked him, "Do you find something amusing, Corporal?"

"No, ma'am. Your luggage has been taken to a guest room for you. I'll take you to the roads leading into Kirby. Happy to do that. Do you mind if I ask what this is all about? We haven't been told anything."

Sybil considered how much she could share with him. They planned to announce the search for the virus-infected samples tomorrow morning. Williams had made it clear that secrecy would work against them. "I'll explain on the way to the first roadblock."

The JLTV, or Joint Light Tactical Vehicle, was the replacement for the Humvee, Jones explained. It looked taller and heavier than a Humvee. Sybil had to stretch to step up to the running board and get into the cabin. The darn thing was loud, too. Almost shouting to be heard over the engine noise, she gave Jones the short version of the Iceman story and Antoine's samples as they drove a backroad to Highway 12 a mile south of Kirby.

Jones caught on fast. There was a brain beneath that smirk. He was about her age and physically fit—that was obvious, even under the layers of winter clothing. It didn't hurt that he was darkly good looking, and the smirk indicated a sense of humor. But he didn't say much.

Sybil kicked herself for letting her mind wander. It was hard to keep it in check. No one had embraced her or even given her a hug since long before Mike's text a year ago. There were days and long nights when she needed one.

The JLTV's four-wheel drive, chains on the tires, and high clearance took them through four-foot drifts on the backroad. The lights mounted above the cab lit up the night, but Jones turned them off when they hit the highway. Highway 12 was plowed to the entrance ramp to I-94, as Sybil had been told. A single lane was open toward the north. A state patrol car sat in a bare spot next to the cleared lane.

"This is the road to Kirby?" Sybil asked.

"Yes, ma'am."

"I was told it was drifted shut. I could drive my car over this. What's going on?"

"Only one lane is clear. That's how milk trucks open a road."

Sybil pictured the old door-to-door milk delivery trucks. "You're kidding me. A milk truck can get through and open the road?"

"A milk tanker," Jones explained, "with up to forty thousand pounds of milk on board. The trucks gather milk from dairy farms. The cows can't wait for the snowplows to open the roads, so some of the trucks mount plows during the winter."

"And this trooper let the truck through?"

"The trucks were on the road early. It could have been here this morning or early afternoon. The State Patrol wasn't going to set up their roadblocks until late afternoon."

"Goddamned son of a bitch," Sybil swore. "So much for the quarantine." She told Jones to stop next to the squad car, which should have been blocking the road. He pulled up to the driver's side, and she rolled down her window. "How much traffic have you had, Officer?"

"Not much. I've been here since five this afternoon," the officer said. "The milk truck came through earlier. He must have gone all the way to Kirby, because three cars and a bus went into Kirby and returned. Other cars may have gone through before I got here, but I didn't hear that anyone had problems getting through."

"Are you out of your mind?" Sybil barked. "What in the hell possessed you to let them pass? This is supposed to be a roadblock. Nobody, absolutely nobody is supposed to go into Kirby, and no one is supposed to leave."

"Yeah, but the cars were locals who needed to gas up. The nearest gas station is twelve miles away if they can't get to Kirby."

"What about the goddamned bus?" Sybil roared.

The officer looked perplexed at all the fuss. "The bus was picking up old folks for an evening of card games at the civic center in Tomah. It's their regular night, and they really look forward to it. If the road is open, on what legal authority are we supposed to close it?"

Sybil ignored his question. "Is the road north of Kirby open?"

"I don't know. The cars and bus returned this way, so it might be closed to the north."

Sybil asked the officer his name, rank, and badge number. She told him that *no* civilians were to pass his roadblock under any conditions. For medical emergencies, he was to call Fort McCoy.

A helicopter would pick patients up. She turned to Jones. "Do you have a radio or telephone connection to Fort McCoy?"

Jones lifted a handset for the radio, called McCoy, and handed the set to Sybil. The radio operator said the colonel was out of the office, but she could take a message for him.

Sybil had difficulty keeping her voice at a normal level as she spoke into the microphone. "Tell Colonel Williams that we've had buses, goddamned buses, drive through the roadblocks. Have him call me ASAP." She hung up the handset and told Jones to drive to Kirby. "We might as well find out how many roads are open and what kind of circus we have."

They drove to the Kirby gas station while she waited for Williams to call. Sybil thought of cars and buses loaded with infected patients leaving Kirby for nearby towns. Her stomach ached, and an imp banged out a raucous drum solo between her ears.

Williams returned her call as they drove into Kirby's gas station. Sybil controlled her voice as she told him what had happened. "Colonel, a milk truck opened Highway 12 to Kirby from the south. The state patrol officer let local people and a darn bus through his roadblock." She gave him the patrolman's name and badge number. "If the State Patrol can't run a roadblock properly, the National Guard will have to do it."

There was a little radio static before the colonel responded. "The best way to get compliance would be to tell them why Kirby is under quarantine. The governor will have to impose martial law to make your quarantine legal if the National Guard is to blockade the roads."

"I'll contact the CDC," Sybil said. "Sam Barker will call the governor and let him know we need a declaration of martial law."

Sybil handed the radio set back to Jones. He'd parked at the gas station. She exited the JLTV and went inside. The elderly attendant, a guy who looked like he hadn't shaved for days, leaned back in an office chair, snoring quietly in the small, grimy office. Sybil woke him, introduced herself, and asked for a list of people who'd purchased gas that afternoon.

The old guy scratched the stubble on his chin. "On whose authority?"

Sybil looked at him closely and saw a grumpy old man who lived to be disagreeable. Her father had been like that. She'd learned that further talk was generally useless with this type. They loved to argue. "Your name?"

"George Pecker."

"I'll have a warrant tomorrow morning," she said and stomped back to the JLTV. "Drive north, Jones. We need to see if Highway 12 is open there. We'll check the county road after that."

As she typed a text requesting a warrant, she told Jones the old guy's name. "Any guy who had to grow up with that name would have an attitude problem."

Highway 12 was drifted shut on the north end of town. North of the motel, Jones switched on the lights over the roof of the JLTV to see farther down the road. Snow effectively closed the road until it curved out of sight behind trees a hundred yards away.

Jones turned to her. "Do you want me to bull through the drifts for a way to make sure another milk truck hasn't opened the road ahead?"

Sybil looked at the snowbanks. Shadows cast by the spotlights on top of the JLTV played across the snowy mounds. She knew the shadows made them look bigger, but the effect put a damper on any urge to explore farther. Importantly, there were no tire tracks visible in the snow. If the JLTV drove through, it would provide a path for other vehicles. "I have no wish to take turns shoveling to get back to Kirby," she said. "Let's check County O."

"Whatever you'd like," Jones said. He backed into an entrance to a small field, turned the JLTV around, and headed back into Kirby.

It surprised Sybil how much Jones's answer pleased her. She'd had to fight to get men to agree with the simplest things she'd asked them to do in Syria, Yemen, and the Congo. And it wasn't just in developing countries. Even Colonel Williams seemed to get his hackles up, either because she had no military rank or he didn't like taking orders from a woman. True, she outranked Jones, sort of, but he'd done as she asked without questioning her, and he was agreeable about it.

County O headed east was open for a block after it left Highway 12, probably because there were two houses there. The road had been plowed shut only twenty feet after the last house.

The county road didn't go straight across the highway. It made a three-block dogleg before heading west from the highway. It was open for two blocks to the west, but it hadn't been plowed beyond the last house. Sybil shook her head. The houses were small, but judging from the barbed wire fence between them, the lots were at least an acre, maybe larger. She checked her map to make sure they'd checked all roads out of town before telling Jones to head back to the base.

The drive back took ten minutes. Sybil was tired, but Jones seemed wide awake. She appreciated that as they drove the last four miles over snow-choked roads. Jones surprised her. They'd talked about sports, but he'd also carried on intelligent discussions about wine, classical music, politics, anthropology, evolution, and global warming. He refused to admit to an education beyond high school, saying that it wasn't the degrees a man had that mattered, but the age at which he stopped learning. Nice. She'd probed for knowledge and found wisdom.

The conversation had been so pleasant that when they reached the base, she'd been tempted to ask him if he'd like to come up for a drink. But a scientist and a corporal assigned as her driver? That wouldn't fly on a military base. She thanked him and said good night.

Room 221, Kirby Motel
7:00 p.m. CST

The reheated french fries were soggy and the hamburgers tasteless, but Frank managed to bolt his down. Tony ate his but with little appetite. He hit the sack and Frank watched television until ten o'clock. He turned the lights on and woke Tony up. "I'm going to look around, see if that buddy of Louie's is around. If it's quiet, we'll take Louie out."

Tony mumbled something that sounded like, "yeah," waved a hand, and went back to sleep.

The hallway was empty when Frank stepped out of the room. He walked the length of the motel, listening as he went. He heard music and grumbling from televisions in a couple of rooms, but there weren't any conversations or party sounds. Cold and boredom had kept the evening quiet.

He listened at the head of the stairs, heard nothing, and quietly descended to the lobby. Betty sat at the desk reading a cheesy romance novel. The television was off, and Dr. Grant snored in a chair in the corner. Betty waved. Frank waved back and tiptoed up the stairs. Grant was the only person he'd been worried about. Frank was sure he could bamboozle anyone else. It was time to move Louie.

Back in the room, he woke Tony. "Come on. Time to get sleeping beauty to his ice castle. Help me get his shoes on him."

That was harder than he'd anticipated, partly because Tony

was half asleep. Once the shoes were on, Frank looped Louie's right arm over his shoulder and around his neck, and Tony did the same with the left arm. They half carried, half dragged Louie out into the hallway and headed to the stairs at the end of the motel. Frank almost dropped his half when Louie's coat sleeve shifted, and Frank felt cold, dead skin against his neck.

Tony whined and complained about having to carry the corpse all the way to the exit door at the end of the hallway. Frank took the bellyaching as long as he could before telling him to shut up and carry his share. Hell, Louie wasn't heavy, just cumbersome.

Frank had his hand on the crash bar of the door to the stairway when they heard someone call their names.

"Tony, Frank, there you are," Betty called from their room. "I'm off work. What are you guys up to?"

Tony turned toward her with a dumb grin. "Ah, helping a drunken friend to his room. I'll be back in a minute."

Betty came down the hall toward them. "How bad off is he? I've got two girlfriends who'd like to party. Think your friend would like to join us?"

"Get rid of her," Frank told Tony in a sing-song whisper.

"What's your buddy look like?" Betty asked as she caught up with them. She stepped in front of them to look at Louie.

Frank thought he'd have a stroke. He looked at Louie's face. Thank God, a hank of hair had fallen forward and covered most of the head wound.

"He ain't half bad," Betty said, steadying herself with a hand on the doorframe.

From what Frank could tell, she'd started partying early, very early.

"Is he really out of it?" she asked.

Tony tried to step between Louie and Betty. "You wouldn't believe how out of it this dumbass is."

"He's kinda cute. Would some coffee help?" she asked.

"Not for this guy," Tony said. "He, ah, he found out he caught the clap and spent the day trying to drink his worries away. Kept saying he didn't know how to tell his wife."

"Ooh. Disgusting. I'll wait for you in your room with one of my friends. Take showers when you come back."

Frank turned away so Betty wouldn't see his face if he snickered. He rolled his eyes and told Tony, "Clap, huh? Come on. Let's get lover boy tucked in."

He opened the door, and they got Louie down the stairs. At least they had gravity working with them. Neither of them had worn coats or gloves, something Frank didn't think of until they were on the first floor, going out the door. Shivering, they tossed Louie off the sidewalk and into the nearest snowbank, only three feet away. The snow had developed a crust, and Louie only sank in a few inches.

Frank wrapped his arms around himself, trying to warm up. "Wade out there and stomp him under."

Tony stamped his feet trying to get warm. "Why me? This was your idea."

"Okay, we'll both do it. You stomp him under, and I'll throw snow over him."

In the poor light from a weak bulb over the door, Frank saw that they'd missed covering part of Louie's coat sleeves and the heel of one shoe. "Piss on it. I'm freezing. Nobody's going to examine snowbanks in this weather."

Kirby Motel Lobby
11:00 p.m. CST

Loud and angry voices woke Grant in the darkened lobby. Betty had turned the lights off, except those over the desk. From his chair in the corner, he saw Frank and Tony enter the motel. They stomped snow off their shoes and waved their arms. Neither wore coats or gloves.

"How the hell could I have known our key cards wouldn't work on a side door, and we'd be locked out?" Frank said.

"It was your brilliant idea," said Tony. "You should have checked."

"Listen, Brain Trust, it was partly your idea. You wanted him out of the bed so you could slip it to Betty."

The men disappeared up the stairway, still arguing and complaining of headaches. Grant couldn't make out anything else they said. What he'd heard intrigued him. He thought of calling Officer Krueger but decided against it until he knew more. When he could no longer hear Frank and Tony bickering, he tossed off his blankets and put on his coat and boots.

Frank and his buddy hadn't worn coats or gloves. As loud as they were, he couldn't believe they'd snuck past him on the way out. That meant they left the building through one of the exit doors at the ends of the main hallway. Grant didn't have a key card and wasn't sure if one was necessary to enter through the front door. He dug his flashlight out of his bag and quietly walked to the end of the hallway closest to Professor Antoine's room.

The light from the stairwell reflected off the glass door, limiting what Grant could see outside. He opened the door and stepped out, maintaining his hold on the open door. He hadn't zipped up his coat, and the cold air cut through his sweatshirt and jeans. The beam of his flashlight picked out an area of trampled snow a few feet from the sidewalk. Dark blotches above the snow looked like cloth and possibly part of a shoe. That was enough for Grant. *They didn't even bother to carry him out of sight. Talk about lazy.* He stepped inside, let the door close, and dialed Officer Krueger.

No answer. It rolled over into voicemail. Grant left a message and walked back to the check-in counter. He hit the bell on the counter several times before the manager staggered through a doorway behind the desk, his eyes half closed.

"No vacancies," the manager said, yawned, and turned to leave.

"I don't need a room. Can I get back in if I go out? I think Professor Antoine in Room 221 has been murdered and dumped in a snowbank."

The manager woke up fast. "My God, murdered? Here?"

"Yeah. Room 221." Grant saw the manager's expression change from disbelief to concern when he mentioned the room.

"Those two guys looked pretty rough, but you can't be serious about murder."

"The last time I talked to them they let me in the room. They claimed Antoine was eating at Ed's every time I asked to speak to him. There are bloodstains on the wall and carpet and what looks like a bullet hole in the wall."

"Good Lord. I knew there was something strange when they offered me a hundred bucks. I should never have taken their money. Have you called Officer Krueger?"

"He's not answering."

The manager gave Grant an odd look. "Name's Bill," he said. "I suspect the deputy is busy at the moment." He handed Grant a key card and promised to stand by while Grant took a closer look at the snowbank. Grant put on his coat, and together they hustled to the side exit where Grant found the partially frozen corpse of Professor Antoine.

CHAPTER 10

TYVEK GHOSTS

Wednesday, January 17, 2018
Kirby Motel
12:10 a.m. CST

Grant called Officer Krueger from the lobby after he verified it was Professor Antoine's body in the snowbank. Krueger didn't answer repeated calls over the next half hour. Grant gave up and called Professor Ron Schmidt.

"Ron, I've got a body on my hands."

Ron yawned loudly and asked Grant to repeat.

"I said I've got a body on my hands. Professor Antoine has been shot, once in the head and once in the chest."

"What?" Ron yelled. "Holy crap, you said Antoine is dead?"

"Yes. He's been murdered. Two thugs are in his room. I assume they have the samples, although I can't imagine what they'd want with them."

"Jesus Christ. Have you told the local police?"

"The officer isn't answering the phone. The only cop around is a sheriff's deputy stranded in Kirby by the snowstorm. He spent the day in a tavern, playing cards. I suspect he's sleeping it off or he's lost his phone. Maybe both."

There was silence on the line.

"You still there, Ron?"

Ron sighed. "Yeah, I'm here. I assume Antoine was incubating the virus since he was a member of the team that excavated the Iceman. Don't handle him without adequate biosecurity. At the very least, wear two sets of Tyvek coveralls, boots, two pairs of gloves, a face plate, and a respirator. You said he was in a snowbank?"

"Yup. Somebody tried to hide the body."

"I'll call Sam Barker. When he gets somebody there, they'll have to disinfect all that snow. My God, this is getting complex. Sit tight. Don't do anything until I get back to you."

"But Ron—Ron?" Ron had hung up.

Grant looked at Bill. "He hung up! Told me to sit tight and hung up. I'll try the sheriff's deputy again." He dialed the deputy. Still no answer.

Leaning against the counter at the check-in desk, Bill looked at the ceiling, looked at the counter, and then back at Grant. He sighed and said, "Deputy Krueger won't be answering his phone. He's banging one of the guests. They're in Room 206. I'm pretty sure he doesn't want to be disturbed. He's had too much to drink too."

"I don't care if he doesn't want to be disturbed," Grant said. "I need to get him."

"Ah, you don't understand. Deputy Krueger is married, and he's with . . ." Bill checked the signature log on the desk. "He's with Randy Johnson. At least that's what the guy in 206 calls himself tonight. They're, ah . . . I'm not sure how to put this. They're old friends."

"Huh?"

"What I'm saying is, you can go up and pound on the door to 206 till your fist is bloody. Randy Johnson, or whatever his real name is, might answer, but no way in hell will he admit that Officer Krueger is in his bed. Krueger will hide if you go in after him."

"What?" Grant was vaguely aware his jaw was hanging open.

"Randy has a thing about guys in uniform, and Krueger is happy to please him. Randy really gets off on it when his, ah, partner handcuffs him, or handcuffs him to the bed, sometimes to a chair."

Grant covered his eyes with his hands and turned away as if to avoid looking at a picture. After a moment, he turned to face Bill and asked, "How, ah, how do you know all of this?"

"Not that I do it, of course, but some of my staff listen at doors, and they tell me there are peepholes with a good view between 204 and 206." Bill avoided Grant's eyes. "I've heard rumors that somebody has filmed things. That's just a rumor, so I hope you won't repeat it." Bill looked embarrassed. "There's not a lot else for entertainment around here. Nobody gets hurt as long as everyone keeps their mouths shut."

Grant sat down. This was a lot of information to absorb. He'd always thought of rural villages as innocent and devout. Apparently there were exceptions, or maybe his picture of isolated hamlets and rural life was simplistic. Although Andy Griffith and Mayberry were powerful images, boredom, human nature, and the sexual revolution were a strong combination.

Bill was looking at him from the corner of his eyes, and he changed the subject. "We do have a church in town. Sunday services are at eleven if you'd like to go. We share a minister with two other little congregations in the county. Pastor Ruth preaches at a Baptist, a Presbyterian, and a Methodist church. Father Dan steps in to help when Ruth is on vacation, so our services are kind of ecumenical."

There went another image of life, but it was a hell of an improvement over the religious wars of previous centuries. He had to focus on what his priorities were. He reasoned that Antoine had almost certainly been infected, as were several other members of his team. That meant the infection was easily spread, so the guys who had murdered him, carried his body out, and were staying in his room were probably also infected. They certainly were, if they'd found and opened the samples. He couldn't arrest the murderers without Krueger, but he could keep them in the room, maybe scare them, and contain the virus in Antoine's body.

"I need to limit everyone's exposure to a virus that infected Professor Antoine," he told Bill as he headed for the door. "Bio-security suits and equipment are in my SUV. Will you help me?"

Bill wasn't eager but relaxed a bit when Grant brought in Tyvek coveralls, latex surgical gloves, faceplates, surgical masks, safety glasses, and other equipment. The white woven plastic Tyvek with booties and hoods were enough to assuage most of Bill's worries. He was won over when Grant insisted he wear two pairs of latex gloves and showed him the faceplates that would block anything from splashing on their faces. They suited up and headed for Louie. In their full garb, they looked like chubby ghosts or the Pillsbury Doughboy.

They were careful not to move snow close to Louie, as all the snow near him would have to be disinfected. After digging Louie out, they moved him to the sidewalk and put two Tyvek suits on him.

Professor Antoine was partially frozen, and there was still some rigor mortis left in his muscles, making it a challenge to bend legs and arms to get him into the suit. "What keeps the virus away from us will keep it with Antoine," Grant explained to Bill. Instead of a faceplate and respirator, Grant put two transparent garbage bags over Antoine's head and cinched them around his neck.

"Are we going to leave him outside to keep him cold?" Bill asked.

"Nope. Too great a chance dogs, coyotes, and raccoons will chew him up and drag parts of him around."

They moved Antoine's corpse into the stairwell, and Grant brought a pump sprayer filled with disinfectant from his vehicle. The sealed concrete-block walls and concrete steps of the stairwell made it a good place to spray disinfectant on their suits and on Antoine's. Between the residual rigor mortis and the cold, they were able to stand Antoine up and lean him against a wall. That simplified getting good coverage with the disinfectant.

"That stuff smells like bleach," Bill said.

"It is. It's more concentrated than how we use it in the wash, but bleach will kill almost anything except spores and some parasites."

"Well, I'll be damned," Bill said. "What do we do with him now?"

"Put him back in his room where he belongs. Everyone in that room has been exposed to the virus. We can't leave the corpse outside. If we left him in the stairwell, he'd be a potential source of infection for anyone walking past, as we can't be certain that we've sealed the virus inside the Tyveks. Storing the corpse in a room that's already contaminated is our safest bet."

"But those guys have guns. What do we do if they . . . if they start shooting?" Bill's voice rose half an octave as he spoke.

"I don't think they will. We'll lean Antoine's corpse against the door. I'll knock on the door while you run for the stairs." Grant smiled under his respirator and faceplate. "I overheard Betty tell another woman there'd be party tonight in Room 221. Between women and booze, I'm hoping they'll be slow to answer, and too horny or drunk to look for us."

Grant taped a note to Antoine's outer Tyvek to explain about the virus. He wanted Frank, Tony, and the women to understand the danger they faced. He had truly never been in a situation like this before, yet here he was taping a note to a dead man he was about to drag back to the motel room where the murder had taken place. It was a desperate gamble with deadly risks, but it bordered on comical.

Antoine was a deadweight, but he wasn't heavy. Grant and Bill put the corpse between them and carried it up the stairs. Their Tyveks made a swishing sound with every step as the plastic material of one leg slid against the other. It was 2:00 a.m. when the little group stopped at the top of the stairway and waited for condensed moisture to clear from their faceplates. It didn't. Grant pulled a couple of disinfectant wipes from his pocket, handed one to Bill, and showed him how to wipe off the condensate from the inside of his faceplate.

There was a tiny risk of exposure to the virus in doing this, but Grant depended on the disinfectant to kill any stray virus. They needed to see where they were going.

"Silent as a tomb," Bill said as they carried Antoine between them down the hallway. Grant glanced at Bill, but through the faceplates he couldn't tell if Bill had loosened up enough to make jokes.

At the door of Room 221, they listened for voices. There were enough moans, groans, and sighs to confirm there was heavy activity going on. Grant smiled to himself. Their timing was perfect to ruin Frank's evening. They propped Antoine against the door to 221. The combination of slight rigor mortis, cold, and support from the door was enough to keep Antoine upright. Grant motioned to Bill to take the stairway to the lobby. He knocked on the door when Bill reached the head of the stairs.

He waited a minute—the men wouldn't give up their sex for just one knock. They might not have even noticed it with the other pounding going on in the room. Grant banged the crap out of the door a second time and ran for the stairs. He turned the corner to descend and waited, just out of sight of Room 221.

A moment later he heard a muffled, "All right, all right. Jesus, give me a minute," followed by the sound of the door opening and a loud gasp. Grant peeked around the corner just as the door slammed shut. The corpse was no longer in sight.

Bill took Grant to a shower where they each sprayed the other's outer Tyvek, boot covers, and gloves with disinfectant using Grant's sprayer. They removed their disinfected protective gear and stuffed them in a medical waste bag Grant supplied. They repeated the disinfection with the boots, inner Tyvek, the first layer of gloves, and the faceplates; removed them; and added them to the medical waste. Both men were sweating by the time they'd removed all their protective gear.

"Care to go up to Room 206 with me?" Grant asked.

"Why do you want me?" Bill asked. "I don't know anything about this."

"I got the impression you know Randy and Gordy. Maybe you can help me convince them to help. What we're facing is so serious nobody will ask what they were doing."

Bill thought a moment. "They won't like it, but I'll try giving them a call. We have an agreement: I leave them alone and don't say anything, and they pay a little extra to use my motel. I'll word it so they can pretend they weren't in the same room."

Bill called from his office. "Randy, there's been a murder in Room 221. The victim was a Swiss scientist infected with a deadly virus ... Yeah, that's right. It's the same virus that's loose in Zürich ... The CDC and army will take charge eventually, but Gordy will have to keep an eye on these people until the cavalry arrives." Bill winked at Grant. "If you happen to see Gordy, would you let him know? Thanks. A virologist and I are in the lobby if Gordy would like to talk to us."

Bill hung up and turned to Grant. "They'll be down in five minutes. What do you plan to do about Frank and Tony?"

"Whatever we do, we have to prevent anyone from leaving that room. Romeo Krueger will have to tell us how to do that."

CHAPTER 11

THE PROFESSOR'S RETURN

Wednesday, January 17, 2018
Room 221, Kirby Motel
2:30 a.m. CST

"I'm coming, I'm coming," Frank bellowed and muttered to himself, "Jesus, give me a minute." He found the light switch over the bed, flipped it on, and stumbled toward the door, naked and complaining.

He passed Tony's bed. The damned fool's headboard continued to rhythmically bang against the wall. Between the glare of the lights and exhaustion, Frank's eyes were barely open when he half felt his way to the door and opened it. A white-suited body toppled on top of him, knocking him flat. He gasped, squealed, and pushed it away. As he did, he saw Louie's face through the transparent plastic bags. Only layers of thin plastic had separated those dead lips from his.

"Get this guy off me."

The pungent stench of chlorine bleach burned the membranes of Frank's nose as he squirmed underneath Louie. At that moment, Cindy screamed. She stood over Frank, wrapped in a sheet, her hands at her mouth as she whimpered, "It's a body and it's cold. It's cold."

"Oh God. Oh God. Oooh," Tony moaned. After some hard panting he said, "Damn, Betty. You're the best lay I've ever had."

Betty drunkenly rolled onto her side and turned away from him. "Yeah, whatever." She pulled the sheets over her bare breasts. "At least one of us knew what they were doing." Without bothering to sit up, she called out: "Hey, Frank. What did you say about a body?"

"Nothing for you to worry about. Go to sleep," Frank said, and Betty pulled the covers up to her shoulders and did just that. *How much booze has she had?* Frank thought. He peeked down the hallway. It was empty. Muttering, he dragged the corpse through the doorway. *Who dressed Louie in this weird outfit?* He examined the Tyveks, boots, and gloves covering every inch of Louie and nodded as understanding soaked through his alcoholic haze. *Grant must have done it.* He closed the door and told Cindy, or Sandy, or whatever her name was, to get back in bed. She seemed happy to oblige and crawled under the covers in double time.

"Hey, Tony! Get over here," Frank whispered.

"What? I'm tired," Tony complained and leaned over Betty, hoisted a glass of whiskey off the nightstand, and took a long swig.

"Get your ass over here. Louie's back," Frank whispered, and he propped the body against the wall in a sitting position.

"So?" Tony asked. "What the fuck am I going to do about it?" He rolled over and went to sleep.

I've got a buzz on, and I'm the soberest one here, Frank thought and marched over to the bed to wake Tony. He had to shake him a couple of times before the jerk sat up. "Come on. Get your ass out of bed and give me a hand. Louie's back."

"I heard ya the first time." Tony crawled out of bed, slipped into his pants commando style, and joined Frank by the door. "No wonder he came back. It was cold out there."

Frank whirled around and stared at Tony. Nobody could be that stupid, or that drunk and still walk, but Tony was managing it. Frank watched Tony until the imbecile pointed at the note taped to Louie's white suit. Frank's eyes followed Tony's finger. "What the hell's this?" Frank said quietly. He unfolded the note and read it aloud to Tony.

Hi, guys. Antoine was dying of a virus when you shot him. That was stupid. The virus probably blew all over the room when the bullets hit. The disease starts with headache and fever. An army doctor will treat you and save your sorry lives— if you'll wait for him. Leave before then, and you'll be dead within a few days. Don't damage Louie's outfit. It keeps the virus inside.

Tony leaned against the wall. "Frank, I—I've had a headache for a couple of days and I feel hot."

Frank held up a hand in protest. He chose not to believe the bad news in the note. This was part of some ploy. "Don't let this get to you, Tony. Lots of things can cause a headache. This must be from that busybody, Grant. I told ya before, he's just a blowhard pretending he's a doctor and trying to scare us."

"They went to a lot of trouble to dress Louie like this." Tony staggered back to his bed and collapsed next to Betty. She woke up and looked around.

"What's going on?"

Frank rolled his eyes. Now he'd have to explain this shit to two women as drunk—and almost as dumb—as Tony. "Nothing. That creep Grant is playing a practical joke. Go back to sleep." The interruptions made it hard for Frank to think, but yesterday he'd seen Grant talking with Krueger. Everybody in the room was too soused to take actions against a sober lawman. Maybe the note taped to Louie could prove that Frank and Tony hadn't dressed the corpse and delivered it to the room. If they were in the clear on that, he could claim Louie had been drunk but healthy when they'd last seen him.

"I don't want to die, Frank," Tony said, his voice shaking.

"Jesus H. Christ, Tony. Ain't nobody going to die. Shut the fuck up and go back to sleep. We'll figure this out tomorrow."

"What's this 'dying' stuff about?" Betty asked. "I have to set up for breakfast this morning. Cindy's supposed to help me."

Cindy peeked from beneath the covers of Frank's bed. "I'll help with breakfast, but I'm not going to step over a stiff to do it." She ducked under the covers again.

"What stiff?" Betty asked. She looked at Tony. "You got a dead guy in the room with us? Why would you bring a dead guy in here?"

"I ain't got nothing to do with no dead guy in the room with us," Tony said. He pointed at Frank. "The dead guy belongs to him. Frank's got the dead guy in the room with us."

"Why's he have a dead guy in here? It isn't Halloween."

"The dead guy, he came back," Tony explained. "I shot him, we dumped him in a snowbank, and he came back."

"Why'd you shoot a corpse?"

Tony shrugged. "He wasn't a corpse when I shot him."

Frank looked from Tony to Betty. How drunk could these people be without passing out? Had they pickled every bit of gray matter they had? Streams of sweat ran down Tony's forehead. *Crap.* He did look sick. Maybe he was delirious.

Betty fumbled for a glass on the nightstand, found it, and poured herself an inch of Amaretto. She gave Tony a withering stare and downed the booze in one gulp. "God, the things I put up with to get laid. Someday I hope I find a guy with brains bigger than his balls." Turning toward Frank, she asked, "How did this dead guy come back?"

Tony's head swung around to look at Betty. It looked like he didn't have full control of his muscles. "Maybe he's pissed 'cause I shot him, or maybe he just got cold out there."

Betty wiggled farther under the blankets. "If I could find batteries that really lasted, I'd never date a guy again." She snuggled against Tony, who draped his arm over her. "The least you can do is warm me up."

Tony was snoring before Betty finished her complaint. From what Frank could see, Cindy was the only other person in the room who seemed to think the world was out of whack, and she was hiding under the covers. *What the hell am I doing standing here naked and cold? At least the bed and Cindy are warm.* He joined Cindy under the covers.

They had to do something about Louie and Grant early tomorrow, but the situation was too complex to think about with a buzz on. Grant had become such a pain in the ass it would be a pleasure to blame Louie's death on him if they could get away with it.

CHAPTER 12

THE SIEGE

Wednesday, January 17, 2018
Kirby Motel Lobby
3:30 a.m. CST

Grant greeted Officer Krueger as he came down the stairs. Their greeting seemed outwardly normal, but something in Krueger's eyes told Grant that Krueger knew his activities in Room 206 were no longer a secret, and that they wouldn't be discussed. He was sure he had the same expression. He motioned to a group of chairs in the lobby, and they sat.

"Thanks for joining us, Officer," Grant said. "I believe Bill told you there's been a murder in Room 221. Everyone involved in it has been exposed to a potentially lethal virus. The murderers, and the women in their room, must be kept there until the National Guard arrives with a field hospital and isolation facilities."

Krueger leaned back in his chair and held up his palms. "Whoa. Let's cover this one step at a time. You can start with the murder. Where's the corpse?"

"I returned Professor Antoine's corpse to the room. It's dressed to prevent spread of the virus unless Frank or Tony do something stupid. I left a note explaining that they should leave it alone."

Krueger sat up, tense and alert. "You moved a body at a crime scene? That's a felony, buddy."

"The dead man is almost certainly infected with a hemorrhagic fever virus," Grant explained. A glance at Krueger's expression suggested that Grant had better lay it on a little thicker. "It's the virus from Zürich, the one causing so much trouble in Europe. Some believe it's related to Ebola. We can't afford to have a corpse with an infection like that sitting out where any hungry raccoon, dog, or coyote can dig in, tear it apart, and spread it around. Maybe drag it all over a school playground or parking lot."

Krueger blanched, nodded, and relaxed. "This still sounds like science fiction. Can you substantiate any of this? Hell, can you even prove who you are?"

Bill was sitting between the two men. He raised his hand. "Gordy, I can verify there's a corpse and this kid has lots of medical equipment with him."

Grant pulled out a notebook and found Sam Barker's phone number. "You can call this number at the CDC during business hours. He doesn't know me, but he's familiar with the virus and he knows it's here in Kirby."

Krueger demanded identification from Grant. Grant handed him his Minnesota driver's license and his University of Minnesota ID. The University ID included his academic degrees and his position in Schmidt's lab. Krueger looked them over and handed them back to Grant. He rubbed his forehead with one hand. A moment later, he called his headquarters and asked if anyone there knew why Kirby was quarantined or if they had heard of Dr. Grant Farnsworth.

Grant couldn't hear the answers, but something Krueger heard on the phone made him glare at Grant. "I'll need backup. Two murder suspects are holed up in the motel. They are armed." Krueger listened for a moment. "Yeah . . . the sooner the better.

Don't use a siren or flashing lights near Kirby. I think the perps are asleep, and I'd like them to stay that way."

Krueger put his phone away. Standing over Grant, he put his hands on his hips. "Nobody's heard of you. Why?" he demanded.

"That's because my boss, Professor Schmidt at the U of M, didn't tell the CDC about me," Grant explained. He shrugged and leaned back in his chair. "There isn't much more I can say."

Krueger nodded and relaxed. "I believe you. The officer on duty said the sheriff got reamed so bad by the head of Homeland Security that he hasn't sat down since he hung up the phone. After that, the governor called and reamed him again. Both mentioned a virus so dangerous it's a matter of national security. That fits your story. You said there are two women in Room 221?"

"Yes. They're innocent, as far as I know, but they've been exposed to the virus. We can't let them out of the room without risking exposure of others."

"This scares the hell out of me. It's the damnedest mess I've been involved with. As I see it, it's a world-class clusterfuck on the hunt for scapegoats, and you and I are at the bottom of the hill."

Grant was sure the hill was a metaphor, but he didn't quite get it. "Could you explain the hill you're talking about?"

"The one all the shit rolls down. If we aren't careful, neither of us will ever have a job again. I don't know a virus from a goat turd. What do you recommend doing with Room 221?"

"I don't know. I've never had to deal with guys holding guns before."

Krueger took a deep breath, reached in his pocket, and came up with some change. He shook his head, pulled out his wallet, and handed folded cash to Bill. "Can I get change in nickels and pennies?" he asked.

Bill snorted. "Man, you're not going to try that old trick?"

"Got a better idea?"

Clueless, Grant looked from one man to the other.

Hallway, Kirby Motel
3:45 a.m. CST

Krueger and Grant, dressed in Tyveks and gloves, took places on either side of the door to Room 221. Grant pulled out a stethoscope he'd stashed with his medical equipment, put it to the door, and listened. He thought he heard snoring from a couple of different people. He flipped his faceplate up and nodded to Krueger. "At least a couple of them are asleep."

Krueger pushed against the door. It didn't move. He quietly put his shoulder into it. Small spaces opened between the door and the frame above, and below the doorknob. Grant slid as many nickels and pennies into the spaces as he could fit.

Krueger gently released his pressure on the door and the two men headed to the lobby. "You're sure that will keep them in the room?" Grant asked.

"No, but it always worked in the dorms when I was in school. I pennied my roommate in once. Thought he had his fiancée in bed with him. He had a girl all right, but it wasn't his fiancée. Neither of them could get out of the room before his parents and fiancée visited that afternoon. Boy, there was hell to pay."

"Bad stuff all around, huh?"

"Yup. Anyway, with Room 221, if this doesn't lock them in, it will at least make getting out slow and noisy. You ever handled a gun before?"

"I used to hunt deer and plink at targets," Grant said.

"With long guns, right?"

"Yeah. I've never handled a pistol."

"I'll give you my rifle. Bill will loan us a chair. We'll take turns guarding the door until backup arrives." Krueger looked at the door again and made a wry face. "I hope these idiots don't jump out the window before then."

A squad car with two officers arrived at 5:00 a.m. Grant got them dressed in Tyveks, gloves, and faceplates; and Krueger put one on guard at 221's door and one outside to cover the window. They had orders to keep everyone in the room. Krueger looked like he was hiding a grin when he went back to Room 206. Grant told himself it was none of his business and fell into his lobby chair. With everything contained, he thought he might be able to get some sleep.

Wednesday, January 17, 2018
Fort McCoy, Wisconsin
7:00 a.m. CST

Could there be anything more inconvenient than a phone call when you're brushing your teeth? Sybil dropped her toothbrush, spit in the sink, and quickly wiped her face. She found her phone after the call had rolled into voicemail. The message, "Call me ASAP," was from Sam.

She tapped in his number. "Sam, what's up?"

"I got your message about the roads, and I called the head of Homeland Security. He got the governor out of bed and chewed him out. The governor promised him that the head of the State Patrol understands he's unemployed if one more civilian gets past that roadblock. The officer who let those people through will be guarding piles of cow manure at the state fair this summer. Glad I'm not him. You'll have a warrant to get the gas station's records in an hour."

"Thanks, I—"

"One of the people who got to Kirby before they set up the roadblock was a Dr. Grant Farnsworth. He's a veterinary virologist working with Professor Schmidt at the University of Minnesota. There are two men and two women in Professor Antoine's room. I'm sure they've all been exposed to the Zürich Virus. You'll have to take care of them as soon as you have medical staff in Kirby."

"Take care of them how, Sam?"

"Preliminary reports from Switzerland regarding medicine used to treat the virus should be on my desk soon. I'll call you when they come in."

"So, we've got our first patients already scheduled?"

"In a way."

Sybil looked at her phone. "What do you mean, 'in a way'?"

"The two men in the room murdered Professor Antoine, and they have a gun, or guns. There's a sheriff's deputy in Kirby, and he's called for backup. We hope the felons can be talked out of their room by the time you get the field hospital set up. Oh, and the two women in the room with them are potential hostages."

"Jesus Christ, Sam. How the—?"

"Settle down. You aren't responsible for the murderers, and they're at the motel—along with most of the other people who might have been exposed to the virus. Law enforcement will neutralize the bad guys. You will have to supervise how they're quarantined."

Sybil walked back and forth across her room, waving her phone as though she meant to throw it. It was her way of calming down before she answered Sam. "Have there been more deaths in the extraction team?" she asked.

"None, which suggests at least one of the treatments they've used might be working."

There was a rap on the door.

Sybil ended her call, grabbed a robe, and threw it on. "Come in."

The door opened a foot. It was Jones. "Dr. Erypet, your vehicle is here. They are ready to move the hospital and staff into Kirby."

Sybil felt her face flush. "I'll, ah, I'll be right with you." She closed the door.

What on earth is going on? She'd greeted generals in that old robe without embarrassment. She had a murder, a hostage situation, a potential epidemic staring at her in the face, and she was acting like a lovestruck teenager. Had she lost her mind? She had to admit, the prospect of sharing her meals with Jones and spending another day riding the countryside with him appealed to her.

CHAPTER 13

SURPRISE, BOYS!

Wednesday, January 17, 2018
Room 221, Kirby Motel
7:30 a.m. CST

Frank, already dressed, shook Tony by the shoulder. "Time to get up. We got work to do."

Tony tried to wave him off. "I got an awful headache and I feel like shit. Jesus. I'm sweating just laying here."

Frank had a headache and wasn't feeling so great himself. "If Deputy Krueger nails your ass, you'll be facing life in prison for murder. Now get out of bed and help me."

Tony, still wearing his pants and shirt from the night before, groaned and rolled out of bed. He staggered toward Louie's white-suited corpse. Betty and Cindy continued to snore in the beds. "What're we going to do with Louie?" Tony asked.

"Screw him. Get your shoes on. We gotta get out of here. Grant must have found an open road to get here. We gotta dig one of our cars out of the snow and take that road out of town."

Tony finished dressing, downed a handful of aspirin, and leaned against the wall behind Frank, who was at the door already dressed in a coat and gloves. He tried to turn the doorknob. His gloves slid around the knob, but the knob didn't move. Neither did the door. Frank put some muscle behind pulling on the door. Still nothing. He took off his gloves to get a better grip on the knob. It wouldn't turn. He pushed on the door and tried again. Nothing moved.

"I gotta sit down or I'm gonna fall down," Tony whispered. He left Frank and sat on his bed next to Betty.

She woke up, looked at him, and put the back of her hand against his forehead. "You're burning up, Tony. You need a doctor."

Frank tried the door again and swore.

Betty shifted her gaze to Frank. "What are you doing, Frank?"

Frank held a finger up to his nose to quiet her. "I'm going to get a doctor," he whispered, and again turned and pulled as hard as he could on the knob. Once again, nothing moved.

Someone on the outside knocked on the door. Frank jerked back as though he'd been goosed. He reached in the pocket of his coat for Tony's gun.

"Yo, in the room," said a demanding voice. "This is the sheriff's department. You are surrounded, you're under arrest, and you're infected. Toss your guns out when we open the door or die a painful and prolonged death. We watched films of the Swiss who died with your virus. It wasn't pretty."

Frank heard scratching around the door and what sounded like coins clinking together. The knob turned and the door opened six inches. He couldn't see anyone in the hallway. They must have been standing on either side. An open bag was held out on the other side of the doorway.

"Toss your guns out," a male voice said.

Frank's heart thundered in his chest. *Stand-downs are a hell of a lot easier when I'm the only one holding a gun.* He slammed the door shut.

"Oh my God," Betty gasped. Tony moaned.

Frank looked back at them. Betty had blood on her hands, and Tony was bleeding from the nose, maybe from his eyes too. It was hard to tell from the way he'd smeared the blood around. Looking at Tony and thinking about Grant's note made Frank sick to his stomach. *Maybe Grant's story about the virus wasn't bullshit.*

But why would this virus be any worse than the flu or chicken pox? "Why should I believe you that this bug Tony's got is fatal?" Frank yelled at the door.

"Turn on CNN, MSNBC, or NPR. They'll explain it to you."

The cops sounded confident. That was enough for Frank, but he had the women. "I've got two hostages. I want out of here and a four-wheel drive SUV with a full gas tank. Nobody follows us, and I'll drop the broads off later."

There was silence for a while.

"Did you hear me?" Frank bellowed.

"We heard you. We're checking with the experts."

"What is there to check about? I got a gun and two hostages."

Silence. Frank returned to his bed and pulled Cindy out, naked. He forced her to walk back to the door with him where he put a gun to her chest. "Tell 'em," he said.

She screamed at the door. "He's got a gun. This fucker is nuts. He doesn't care about Tony, and he's pushing a gun in my left tit."

"Frank," came another voice. "This is Grant. Do you have a headache yet? Do you have a fever? I'll bet Tony is sick as hell. Might have a nosebleed, maybe even bleeding from the eyes and ears. If he isn't bleeding yet, he will be by the end of the day. You might not start bleeding until tonight or tomorrow."

Frank's head was pounding, but that was probably from listening to that asshole Grant. He glanced back at Tony. Jesus, there was blood all over his face, dripping off his chin. Tony was sniffling and sucking blood back up his nose. Betty stumbled to the bathroom and washed her hands.

Frank felt a tickle in his own nose and wiped it against the blanket Cindy had wrapped around herself. The snot looked sort of clear. Or was there some blood in it? Damn, this stuff was playing tricks with his mind. He turned back to yell at Grant. "Tony's got a nosebleed. So what?"

"It means the disease is entering its final phase. Tony is shedding virus like wild, in the blood, on his skin, and with every breath he takes. He's going to die if we don't treat him soon. It's a nasty way to go, Frank, and he'll be shedding virus all over you. Tony's virus is attaching to the cells of your lungs right now. Same for the women. You've got another twenty to thirty hours before you're as bad as Tony. The only doctors in the US who know what treatments to use are the army doctors here in Kirby. Toss out your guns and we'll start treatment."

"I still got hostages. Get me a four-wheel-drive SUV."

"We can't give you a car, Frank, and we can't let you and the women out of Kirby. You'll spread the virus all over the state if you run. Millions could die. For the safety of the country, we are prepared to wait here until all of you are dead."

"You're bluffing," Frank said, but he had a sinking feeling Grant was telling the truth.

"Your call, Frank. Just bang on the door when you're ready to give up. Try to break out with hostages, and we'll have to shoot. You won't make it to the stairs. It's a matter of national security. None of you can be allowed to go anywhere but a hospital isolation room."

Frank shoved Cindy away from him, rushed to the window, and moved the curtain to the side. A squad car sat in the parking lot, its driver's door open, an officer crouched behind it with a rifle aimed at the window. Farther out in the parking lot, men in army uniforms were putting up tents of some sort. He wasn't getting out that way.

Tony groaned on the bed. "I need a doctor, Frank." He tried to stand and whimpered from the pain. "Give him my gun. Please, Frank, give him the goddamned gun."

Frank sat on his bed and buried his head in his hands. He'd always been afraid his career would come down to surrendering to the cops or getting executed by his boss. He'd never imagined a screwed-up mess like this. His nose tickled again and he sneezed. It hit the sheet, and there was a drop of blood in it. Maybe the dry air, maybe the virus. Shit. The cops didn't even want his hostages. The only thing he could do was surrender and hope the medicine the army docs had would work—unless the medication they would put him on was nothing but tranquilizers to control him.

Maybe he could set things up for a breakout. Tranquilizers, if they were pills, could be palmed and he could fake being docile, if that was what the docs tried. Give them Tony's gun and hide his. He'd bide his time, see what happened, and hope they would leave him in the motel room for a few days.

He looked around the room. Tony was passed out. Betty was still in the bathroom, scrubbing her hands. Cindy was buried under the covers, maybe still asleep, maybe not, but at least she wasn't looking around. He removed his gun from under his belt and looked for a hiding place in the closet. He found nothing until he noticed a gap between a ceiling tile in a corner of the closet and the wall. It took work, but he pried the tile loose and stashed his gun above it. Quietly, he slid the closet door shut and scanned the room again. Nobody had watched him.

He took off his gloves and coat, walked to the door, and banged on it.

"Ready to give up?" Grant yelled.

"Yeah. But how about some breakfast?"

"Gun first. Breakfast will take a minute. Nobody has set it up yet."

Frank opened the door and tossed Tony's gun into the bag that was held out. The gloved hands holding the bag closed it, and somebody sprayed it with a can of something. It smelled like a disinfectant. Frank closed the door. From behind him the shower kicked on. Betty must have decided washing her hands wasn't good enough.

Frank sat on his bed and held his head in his hands. He felt like crying. Nothing in his life had gone this badly before. Even the hostages weren't doing him any good, and why should they be comfortable? He returned to the door. "Breakfast set up was Betty and Cindy's job," he yelled through the closed door. "Can they come out and do it? I'm hungry."

"Nobody can leave your room. Somebody else will set up breakfast. What do you want from the menu?"

Shit. He couldn't even *give* his hostages away. "The only things on the menu that don't taste like crap are the waffles, sausage, and fried potatoes. And when do we see a doctor?"

"The army is setting up the hospital now. They'll start treatments in your room. I'll let you know when they're ready. You can't leave your room until we can reduce the amount of virus you're shedding."

Frank didn't want to believe Grant, but Tony had something bad, real bad. Frank walked back to his own bed and threw himself onto it.

Cindy screamed from under the covers.

"Oh, shut up," he told her. "I'm not gonna hurt ya. I'm just trying to save my ass, but ain't nothin' working."

Cindy whimpered. "You scared the shit out of me. Watch what you're doing and move your fat ass over. I'm not your pillow."

Even my hostages give me shit. What the hell have things come to? I'm not cut out for this. He couldn't escape. He couldn't get breakfast, he had to keep his hostages, and if he didn't get medical treatment, a virus was going to kill him slowly within the week. There must have been a *True Crime* issue he missed, 'cause this sure as hell didn't fit anything he'd read about.

He turned on the television. It was set to one of the news channels, and some broad was talking about the virus with a guy dressed in a baggy green top and similar pants. An ambulance drove past in the background. The guy's English wasn't great, but there was a scroll across the bottom.

"The virus produces many virions that set off massive reactions in the immune system. Some reactions cause fevers. One of the cascades—"

"Cascades?" asked the reporter.

"Yes. One reaction sets off another, like dominos falling. We call it a cascade. One of the cascades causes tiny clots to form everywhere throughout the body. This leaves the blood having nothing with which to form clots where they are needed."

"Is there a name for the reaction?"

"It's called Disseminated Intravascular Coagulopathy, or DIC. Another reaction causes capillaries to leak. Because of these reactions, the patients have fever, headaches, and nosebleeds. Bleeding in the joints causes severe joint pain. They may also bleed from the anus, the ears, and the eyes. Massive internal bleeding leads to shock and death within one or two days unless treated."

"How are you treating the virus?"

"We use supportive therapy—fluids, IV feeding, and transfusions of platelets. One of the drug combinations used to treat AIDS reduces the viral load, although it doesn't completely cure. It doesn't kill all the viruses, but it has saved patients' lives. Experimental treatments are being developed. You should warn people to take Tylenol instead of aspirin or other nonsteroidal anti-inflammatory agents for fevers or headaches while this virus is on the loose. Those drugs decrease the ability to form clots and make the hemorrhages, the bleeding much worse."

"How many people have died in Zürich since the outbreak began?"

"I don't have the latest figures. The last numbers released by the government were four hundred infected patients, 145 of whom have died."

"But the outbreak is under control, isn't it?"

"We've seen evidence that the virus is spread by coughing and sneezing. This greatly increases the ability of the virus to spread from person to person. There were four new cases in the suburbs—"

The television went to snow for a moment. The woman came back on. "We've lost our connection to Zürich. A spokesman for the Swiss government announced that the outbreak is nearly under control."

Frank felt sick. He turned off the set. *Grant was a bastard, but he knew what he was talking about, and poor Tony. The guy had been eating aspirin by the handfuls for his headache for the last couple of days.*

There was a knock at the door, and it opened before he could move. Two guys dressed in white like Louie's corpse came in with guns drawn. They looked like they were in some kind of space suit. One carried Louie's body out while the other held his gun on Frank. A moment later another one came in, or maybe it was the same one who carried Louie out—Frank couldn't tell with those puffy white suits and masks that they wore. This guy carried folded hospital gowns. He set them on the dresser next to the TV set. He turned to Frank and pointed at the gowns.

"Off with your street clothes. You ladies too. Everybody puts on the gowns, then pack yourself into the bathroom and we'll get

more beds in here and change the bedding on the two you've got."
The speaker backed up to the guy with the gun, looked at Frank
and Tony, and said, "Move it. Now. Breakfast will be here when
you're dressed and the new beds are in place."

Betty and Cindy asked to be put in a different room, but the
cops just shook their heads. "Nobody leaves this room until
they've had several days of treatment. Put on the hospital gowns
and get in the bathroom."

"Why do we have to get in the bathroom?" Cindy asked.

A third guy in the white suits had come into the room. "You've
been exposed to a really nasty virus. Nobody is to be exposed to
you any more than absolutely necessary."

Betty and Cindy wrapped themselves in sheets from the beds
they were in, grabbed the hospital gowns, and changed in the
bathroom. They wouldn't let Frank or Tony in until the men had
dressed in their hospital gowns. Frank and Tony sat on the edge
of the bathtub, Tony leaning against the wall to stay upright. They
heard clanking and voices in the motel room.

After what seemed like forever, there was a knock on the
bathroom door. "You can come out now," a male voice said.

There were four hospital beds with fresh bedding in the room
when Frank and the others came out of the can. Guys in white with
guns directed the women to the two beds nearest the door. "You,"
another white-suited figure said to Frank and Tony. The figure
motioned to the other two beds with his pistol. "Into bed, guys.
Frank, put your left hand up to be handcuffed. Tony, put your right
hand up."

Frank and Tony obeyed. They were cuffed, and the cuffs locked
onto strong metal rails on the hospital bed. Frank saw that Tony
was so weak he had trouble holding his hand up to be cuffed.
Breakfast was brought in. The women dug in with both hands,
but Frank could eat with only one. Tony had to be hand-fed he

was so weak. Tony and Frank were given shots of a sedative. A few minutes later, a nurse gave each of them a shot of a local anesthetic near their collar bones, and some kind of minor surgery was done. Frank heard the doctor say something about a port for intravenous treatments, but none of the doctors or nurses bothered to explain any further.

He found out an hour later when nurses put a pole holding a bag of fluid next to his bed and one next to Tony's. A tube connected the bag to a wicked looking needle, and the needle was put into the "port" that had been inserted under his collarbone. He hardly felt the poke. Betty and Cindy lucked out. They were only treated with pills.

A nurse with an expression that brooked no guff stood over him. "Don't mess with the IV," she growled. "You'll be on this medication for a week. It's your only chance to make it out of this alive."

CHAPTER 14

THE CAVALRY ARRIVES

Wednesday, January 17, 2018
Kirby Motel Parking Lot
9:00 a.m. CST

Sybil clambered down from the JLTV, otherwise known as the Humvee from hell, and watched the tents going up in the motel parking lot. She approached the nearest doctor, introduced herself, and showed him her CDC identification. Neither Sybil nor the doctor were wearing protective gear.

"Can you tell me what biosafety protocols are in place?" Sybil asked.

The doctor nodded and pointed toward the motel. "The building is contaminated, so no one is allowed in unless they're wearing two sets of Tyveks and gloves, boots, boot covers, surgical masks, and faceplates. They are disinfected in stages as they come out."

"Sounds good. Why'd you decide to set the hospital up here?"

"Since the motel is already contaminated, if we set up here, we won't be spreading anything. I suspect the motel will be our main source of patients for the next few days, the parking lot is fairly level, and nobody complained when we offered to dig out and move their cars. Most importantly, drainage from the lot can be controlled and disinfected."

"I guess you were ready for that question. Have our first, ah, patients been treated?"

"We started all four in Room 221 on the three-drug cocktail. Three enzymes unique to RNA viruses should be knocked out, according to the Swiss. The two gunmen are handcuffed to their beds and are on IV fluids and supportive care, as recommended by the Swiss."

Sybil put her hands on her hips, looked at her feet, and back at the doctor. "The Swiss are the experts on treating this, and you'll soon have more experience with it than anyone else in the United States. My expertise is biosecurity. I'd like to watch your procedures for entering and leaving Room 221."

That was arranged. Sybil had to suit up in Tyveks just to watch a nurse enter Room 221. She halted the procedure as the nurse returned from the room.

Hands on her hips, Sybil went into lecture mode. "You have to set up contained spaces for removing contaminated clothing inside and outside Room 221. They'll essentially be air locks. You can make them out of plastic sheeting on each side of the door to Room 221. You'll need an entrance flap or door that seals for the inner air lock and a similar exit for the exterior air lock. People's inner Tyveks will be sprayed with disinfectant in the exterior air lock, but they won't take them off until they leave the building and are sprayed off again. You'll have to check with the engineers to set up air handling for this room. You'll need HEPA filters on the exhaust from the room to trap the virus. Air pressure in the air locks and room must be staged so that the air locks have lower air pressure than the hallway, and the air pressure in the room is lower than the rest of the motel to prevent the virus from being blown out when your people go in. Otherwise, you've got things under control."

She stayed long enough to look at preliminary drawings for

the contained spaces to be built for Tyvek removal to verify they suited her. The main entrance to the motel had been built as an air lock to save heat in the winter. Sybil had it used for disinfecting people again as they exited the motel and removed their inner Tyveks. "A second person *must* watch your people remove their inner Tyveks in the exterior air lock to make sure they don't contaminate themselves," she emphasized.

On her way out of the lobby, Sybil asked the doctor to wait and stopped at the counter. She asked for Dr. Farnsworth's room number. The clerk pointed toward a chair in the corner. The chair had been turned toward the corner for privacy, and drapes over nearby windows kept the corner dark.

"He slept in the chair?" Sybil asked.

"No," the clerk said. "He's sleeping in the chair now. I heard he was up half the night guarding Room 221."

Sybil turned to the army doctor. "That exhausted young man tracked down the Swiss scientist's corpse and trapped the murderers—your patients—in their room." She shook her head. "He saw what had to be done and he did it. We need people like that. Keep him occupied when he wakes up. I'd like to talk to him later."

Sybil turned her attention to her biggest worry—the people who'd gotten through the roadblock. She felt foolish getting a ride to go fifty yards to the gas station, but she wanted to appear as official as possible when confronting that ornery old buzzard behind the counter. The place looked closed when Corporal Jones stopped the JLTV. He checked. The front door was locked.

"Who would know where that grumpy old coot lives?" she asked Jones.

They stopped at Ed's Tavern. It was open—even had a few patrons drinking a late breakfast beer. Ed offered each of them a free beer, but Sybil declined for both.

"How can I help our people in uniform?" Ed asked.

"I need to talk to that crotchety guy who runs the gas station," she said. "He's not there yet. Where can I find him?"

"His house is the second one on the side road behind the station. If you want to talk to old George before noon today, you ought to have that drink first. Maybe two. He can be mean as sin when he's feeling good, and last night he closed the bar. Wake him up with a hangover and he might come out shooting."

Sybil's mouth dropped open. "You *are* kidding, aren't you?"

"Not really. He won't shoot the first time you knock, but if you bang on his door, he'll let you know he means business. Last time we went through this circus, he aimed over their heads and used shotgun shells loaded with lead dust, the kind you'd use on mice, rats, and Jehovah's Witnesses. It's his way of saying 'go away.' He uses one grade heavier shot for Mormons."

Sybil snorted. "Before I forget, did either of the two guys from Chicago staying at the motel come here?"

"What do they look like?"

"One is tall and skinny, the other short, pudgy, with thinning hair. Neither had clothes appropriate for the weather, and they probably didn't mingle with locals."

"Yeah. They came in and bought beer, booze, and food. Why are you asking?"

"Those two are infected with a deadly virus. We'll have to close your tavern until we can disinfect it. I'll have someone drop by and discuss that with you. If you or any of your people develop headaches, fever, or a bloody nose, go to the hospital being set up in the motel parking lot. They'll take care of you at government expense. You can take acetaminophen for headaches or fever, but avoid aspirin or drugs containing it. They'll make everything worse."

She turned to Corporal Jones and asked for the copy of the warrant. She scanned it, thanked Ed, and walked out of the tavern.

"What now?" Jones asked as they got into the JLTV.

"The warrant covers a search of the premises. We go back, look through his records, and hope everybody paid with credit cards. That'll tell us more than George is likely to."

"Do you want me to break in?"

Crap. She hadn't thought that far ahead. *Break glass or the doorframe and he'll be impossible to work with.* "No. Can you pick a lock?"

Jones shook his head. "Never tried. I'm willing to learn, though." He grinned. "Especially if you order me to. Can you look up lock-picking on your smartphone?"

They pulled out of the tavern's parking lot and drove back to the gas station. Sybil had Jones park on the roadside a hundred feet from the station. "George may walk to the station before we get the information you need. He's liable to turn around and go home if we're parked there."

Sybil was still searching for instructions on picking locks when Jones tapped her on the shoulder. "He's at the station, looking right at us." She signaled Jones to drive into the station and put her phone away.

"What do you want now?" George asked. "Have you got me under surveillance?"

Sybil stepped out of the JLTV and handed him the warrant. "We need to know who drove into town to buy gas yesterday. They may have been exposed to a lethal virus brought into Kirby by men who stopped at the motel Monday night."

George spat on the floor and sneered. "Can't ya come up with a better story than that?" he asked.

"Watch the news about Zürich, George. The virus came in on a direct flight from there. Has anyone staying at the motel stopped at the station?"

"A couple of guys did. Wanted a candy bar and tried to pay with a ten."

"Did you take the money?"

"Nope. Told 'em to get out."

"Did they touch anything?"

George bent his head for a moment. "Nope. Didn't touch nothin'."

"Did you talk with them for long?"

"Not nearly as long as I've had to talk to you. You've got your warrant. Look at my books if you want, then get the hell out of here."

Sybil examined the credit card receipts and recorded the names and numbers.

"George, can you tell us where these people live?"

"I ain't their mailman."

Sybil was about to threaten George to get more information but changed her mind. It would only make him resist more. They could get the addresses and directions from Ed at the tavern. She glanced at the *Playboy* calendar—it was impossible to ignore it in the tiny office. She pointed at it as they were leaving. "Mom was Miss March that year." Turning to George, she asked, "1995, right?" She told Jones, "Mom was so proud, she hung the calendar in the kitchen. I had to look at that damned thing for years. The older Mom got, the more often she dragged it out when men stopped by."

Back in the JLTV, Jones asked, "You *were* just messing with that old guy, weren't you? Your mother wasn't really a *Playboy* model, was she?"

Sybil smiled to herself and looked up from examining the

names she'd recorded. "Stop at Ed's. If anybody in town knows where these people live, it will be him."

As Jones started the JLTV, she caught him casting sidelong glances at her. She smiled to herself. *Good. Let him gnaw on that for a while.*

As they headed toward the tavern, Jones asked, "Will we have to wear masks and protective gear?"

"The short answer is, we won't wear protective gear."

"Why not?"

"Most of the people we talk to won't be infected, and those who are infected are unlikely to be spreading the virus this soon. If I show up on somebody's doorstep wearing a mask and a moon suit, it creates a barrier between us. Many of them wouldn't pay any attention to what I said."

They stopped at the tavern, but it was locked and empty. Sybil elected to use her smartphone and the addresses she'd recorded to find the people. The first address was a house three miles south of Kirby. The driveway was empty, and no one answered the door when Sybil knocked. She waited, knocked again, and walked back to the JLTV. "Who's next on the list?" she asked.

Jones pulled out the list and handed it to her. "Nobody answered?"

"I assume they're at work. The way our luck is going, they're probably teaching or taking care of patients at the Tomah hospital. An infected person can expose hundreds of people in jobs like that. Then you, me, and the country will be screwed."

Jones looked at her. "You're exaggerating, I hope."

Sybil shook her head sadly. "Not really. If this virus gets out of Kirby, the whole country could have a huge problem."

"Man, so this job isn't important. It's critical, right?"

"Now you understand," Sybil said. She looked up directions

to the next address and gave Jones directions. The road was clear while they were on Highway 12. The last half mile was a side road. It was an easy drive too, as someone had plowed a single lane through the snow.

They came to a farm on the side road. The roof of a machine shed had collapsed, part of the roof of an ancient silo had blown away, the dairy barn hadn't been painted in decades, and a paddock between the highway and barn where the wind had swept the snow from the ground was overgrown with weeds. "Retired, probably a widow," Jones said.

Sybil dug through her supplies and picked up a package of paper masks. "How can you tell all that?"

"The pasture is overgrown, the fence is falling down, and the barn is surrounded by weeds. The door is half off the hinges. Nobody's done anything in the barn for years. The husband milked cows until his knees gave out when he was in his late fifties. He sold the cows and raised calves for a neighbor until his back gave out ten years later."

"Do you know this couple?"

"Never met them, but my dad milked cows on our farm, and I know the progression. Milking in barns like this was pure hell on the knees. Old dairy farmers worked until their bodies wore out. The condition of the buildings indicates they haven't been cared for in years. The lady here is likely a widow. Someone plows her driveway for her, probably a son or neighbor."

The 150-feet of driveway had been plowed, but only to the house. The other farm buildings were surrounded by deep snowdrifts. Several feet of snow covered whatever walk there might have been to the front door. Jones parked the JLTV at the back door. "Use the back door. Only someone from the city or government would use the front door."

Sybil looked at Jones to see if he was joking. Nothing in his face suggested that. She got out of the JLTV with a new appreciation for her driver and climbed three wooden steps to the back door.

A thin, white-haired woman answered the door. "I don't need insurance, magazines, Girl Scout cookies, or a new religion. Goodbye," she said, and moved to close the door.

Sybil blocked the door and showed her ID. "Mrs. Anderson, I'm from the Centers for Disease Control, the CDC. A visitor at the Kirby Motel brought a dangerous virus to Kirby, and you may have been exposed when you filled your car at the gas station."

The woman glared at Sybil. "Says who?"

"Me. I'm Dr. Sybil Erypet, a physician and epidemiologist working for the CDC. The problem is considered a national security issue, which is why the National Guard is assisting us." She pointed at the JLTV.

"Another way you bureaucrats have found to waste the taxpayers' money. So, what is it you think you're going to do to me?"

Sybil looked at Mrs. Anderson. The set of the jaw reminded her of someone. Was this old bat George Pecker's sister? "For the next two weeks, we'd like you to wear one of these paper masks if people visit you," Sybil said and handed her a small box. "We will deliver food and whatever else you need, so you won't have to travel to town. Should you feel sick, give us a call and a doctor will come to you. Nurses will visit you a couple of times a week to make sure you're well. Do you have any questions?"

"I have Bible study on Wednesday evenings. Are you going to try to stop me from going to that?"

"Yes, but only for two weeks."

"What if I tell you that you can stuff these masks up your ass, and I'll go where I damned well please?"

It was time to get out what Sybil considered her theatrical props. She reached in her back pocket for a set of handcuffs, hoping that the sight of them might convince this old girl that she meant business. "The governor has declared martial law. If you threaten to leave your home, I will place you under arrest now and take you to a military hospital. You will be kept under quarantine there until we can prove you haven't been infected."

"Does this hospital you're going to lock me in have cable TV and bars?"

"Huh? Bars? No. No alcoholic beverages are allowed in—"

"Not that kind of bar, stupid. Will I be able to use my cell phone?"

"Ah . . ." Sybil couldn't think of an answer. "Just a minute." She walked the few steps back to the JLTV. Quietly, she asked Jones, "Does the base hospital have cable TV and cell phone connection?"

"Sure. We have satellite TV available when we give blood or platelets. That carries cable channels."

She returned to the old lady with a feeling of foreboding. "Yes. Many rooms have cable TV, and cell phone reception is good."

"Sounds like fun. Let me get my coat. My husband died five years ago and my cat died last week. Lonely as hell out here, and the TV reception is awful. Can't wait to tell the girls I'm in the big house. Everybody in church will wonder what I've been up to."

The old lady turned, closed the door, and disappeared before Sybil could stop her. Sybil heard a snort from the JLTV. She turned and glared at Jones. The passenger window was open, and he'd apparently heard everything. He was collapsed across the steering wheel, laughing.

From the tightly pursed lips and bulging cheeks, she could tell he struggled for control. "Better get the cuffs ready," he said and burst out laughing again. "She may insist on them. It'll make a whale of a story to tell at her Bible study."

Mrs. Anderson was back on her stoop wearing a coat, gloves, boots, and a hat that hadn't been in fashion since the 1970s. She held out her hands. "Now, what about those cuffs?"

CHAPTER 15

MEETING THE PATIENTS

Wednesday, January 17, 2018
Anderson Farm
11:30 a.m. CST

Sybil put Mrs. Anderson in the back seat, took her own seat in front, and called the field hospital.

"Dr. Wickert, this is Dr. Erypet," she said. "I'm bringing a patient in for isolation. Are you set up for that yet?"

"How sick is the patient?"

"She is not sick. She may have been exposed to the virus and refuses to follow quarantine rules."

The radio was silent.

"Dr. Wickert, are you there?" Sybil asked.

"Yeah. I was thinking. If this lady doesn't have any symptoms and the exposure was only possible, not definite, you should take her to the base hospital. Once we have patients in the field hospital, she'll run the risk of actual exposure, perhaps to a large dose of virus. She'll be safer in isolation at the base hospital."

"That makes sense. We'll take her to the base," Sybil sighed. The base would be a longer drive, and she wasn't looking forward to an extended conversation with Mrs. Anderson. She put on a surgical mask and turned to Jones. "You heard the man. Back to the base and put a mask on."

She crossed her arms over her chest, sank into her seat, and sulked. Occasionally, she heard what sounded like a snigger from Jones. Each time she glared at him, and each time he acted innocent.

After the first few sniggers, it was a struggle to maintain her scowl. Those handcuffs and Anderson's reaction to them were ridiculous, and Sybil had no one to blame but herself. But two could play at this game. She decided to continue feigning outrage at Jones's humor and look for an opportunity to return the favor. He'd been incredibly perceptive about the Anderson farmstead, but could he laugh at his own mistakes?

Their "patient" was a chatterbox and full of questions all the way to the hospital.

"Will my meals be served to me, or will I have to order out?" Mrs. Anderson asked.

Sybil sighed and grudgingly answered. "Yes, all your meals will be served to you. You'll have a menu to choose from." After a moment she added, "I hope you like hospital food."

"Will I have roommates or a private room?"

"You will have a private room. That's what 'isolation' means."

"Good. I won't have to fight with anyone over which programs I watch." She tapped Jones on the shoulder. "Do they have male nurses?"

Jones shrugged. "The camp has several male nurses and medics, but I'm not sure if they'll be taking care of you."

She seemed dejected by that. A few miles down the road, Mrs. Anderson asked Jones, "These male nurses or medics, they'd be young guys in good shape like you, right?"

Jones glanced at Sybil. "I have no idea," he said. He covered his mouth with one hand, but his shoulders were shaking.

Sybil glowered at him. She was feeling more ridiculous every mile they drove. Mrs. Anderson was treating this like a holiday.

She tried to think of something to say that would make the old bat understand how serious this was, but she couldn't come up with anything appropriate. *This old lady doesn't realize it, but people with her attitude could put thousands of people at risk. In cases like this, the well-being of the population must take precedent over the rights of the individual.*

When they arrived at Fort McCoy, Mrs. Anderson lifted her hands from her lap. Sybil saw this out of the corner of her eye and winced. *She's making sure the entrance guards see the handcuffs. How the hell did I get maneuvered into this farce?*

They parked in front of the hospital. Sybil removed Mrs. Anderson's handcuffs, and she and Jones escorted Mrs. Anderson inside, one on each side of her.

Sybil sat with Mrs. Anderson during her admission to emphasize that she had to be put in isolation. Jones said he'd be in the hospital cafeteria. He struck Sybil as entirely too jolly as he headed off in search of food. She joined him later in the cafeteria and asked, "Do they serve anything edible?"

"The hot chocolate *is* good, and the breakfast rolls. Spend time in the cold and anything hot tastes good. By the way, they'd better beef up the staff on the roadblocks."

"Why more men on the roadblocks?"

"Mrs. Anderson has already said she's going to call her buddies. You've given her room service, cable TV, phone service, a warm and comfortable room, and attentive nurses to take care of her. That's like manna from heaven to bored, lonely old ladies living in the country by themselves. I'll bet Mrs. Anderson is calling her friends already and telling them to go to Kirby to gas up their cars."

Elbows on the table, Sybil put her head in her hands. Jones had been right too often to ignore his warning. She left him in the cafeteria and went to the nurses' station in the isolation ward. "First chance you get," she told the medic on duty, "you are to confiscate Mrs. Anderson's cell phone. We'll give it back to her when she leaves, but she is not to make phone calls from this hospital." When the nurse nodded but didn't take notes, Sybil demanded that she repeat her instructions back to her.

On her way back to the JLTV, Sybil passed a window that looked out on an open field piled with snow molded into drifts by the wind. It should have been sufficient to prevent people from moving around and spreading the virus, but bull-headed and ignorant jerks would always find ways even around a blizzard. If they kept it up, people would be dying in the streets. She shook her head. *How the hell has humanity managed to survive this long?*

Country roads near Kirby
1:30 p.m. CST

Sybil and Jones continued their search for people who had entered Kirby on Tuesday. They located and visited two couples, both retired. Both couples were happy to observe the quarantine rules for two weeks when promised free food delivered to their door, visits from a nurse twice a week, and house calls by military doctors if they felt ill.

On the road again, Sybil turned to Jones. "You sure were king of the smirks and sniggers when Mrs. Anderson showed her handcuffs off to the guards at the base this morning. You must remember that controlling people who've been exposed to the virus, like that old lady, is critical. If people like Mrs. Anderson are allowed to thumb their noses at our quarantine regulations, some of them will spread the virus and thousands will die."

Jones nodded sheepishly. "Sorry I was flippant about Anderson. I recognize the danger, but that old girl managed to make this epidemic work for her. It might help if you remember that civilians with no medical training won't understand the danger, and they'll resent being ordered around by officials from the distant headquarters of a federal bureaucracy."

Sybil conceded the point. Maybe she'd been a little heavy-handed with stubborn people. When their conversation ended, she turned and watched the scenery roll by. The day was bright and sunny, contrasting the dark pine trees and black skeletal bark of the barren hardwoods with the brilliant white snow drifts along the forest edge.

By half past five, they were back at the first home they'd visited. This time there was a car parked outside of the light gray, two-story farmhouse. Jones pulled up to the back door.

Sybil was met by a woman in slacks and a colorful sweater who looked to be in her late twenties. She introduced herself and asked if the lady, Mrs. Ann Jensen, had gone into Kirby the previous day.

"Sure. We had to gas up the car, and school was canceled because of the blizzard. My husband and I ate at Ed's." She paused, and slowly asked in a concerned voice, "Is there a problem with that?"

"There might be." Sybil explained the chance that they'd been exposed to a virus. "The odds that you were exposed are small, but the virus is deadly and any exposure is considered a national security issue. The entire village of Kirby is quarantined for at least two weeks, and we'll have to quarantine you and your husband for the same period. We'd like you to stay at home and wear these surgical masks when you answer the door." Sybil handed her a box of the masks. "We'll deliver food and medicine to you, provide visits from a nurse twice a week and house calls by a doctor if you feel sick."

Her hands clasped together, the woman took a step backward and frowned. She looked shocked. "Do we have a choice?"

"Sadly, no. We know the virus is easily transmitted, and it's deadly. We've had to admit one woman to isolation facilities in handcuffs because she said she wouldn't follow the quarantine rules. I'd rather not have to submit anyone else to that, but we can't risk exposed people wandering around and exposing others. People will die if that happens."

The woman nodded. "Yeah. My husband and I teach at Tomah High. We heard about that at school. But how do we square a two-week absence with the school administration?"

"Let me know who to contact and I'll take care of it. It's possible that local schools will be closed for two weeks or longer."

A car drove up and parked next to the JLTV. Ann introduced her husband, Rick, to Sybil.

Frowning, Rick asked, "Are you the one who dragged my aunt off in handcuffs this morning?"

Rick's aggressive statement came like a punch to the gut after the pleasant conversation Sybil had with Ann. Rick's face was serious, his brows were furrowed, and his stare bored into her. Sybil went into bureaucratic mode. "Mrs. Anderson refused to follow the quarantine rules or take the situation seriously. She gave me no choice. This is a matter of national security."

Hands on his hips, Rick laughed loudly and smiled. "God, I wish I could have been there to get a picture. My aunt can be the most cantankerous old biddy in the county, but it's all show. I'll bet she was laughing up her sleeve and being as difficult as she could. A friend called me from the base and said she was having a high old time at the hospital, ordering people around and being disagreeable."

Sybil's face warmed. *Your aunt isn't the only character in the family.* "Your aunt is, ah . . ."

"A pain in the ass?" Rick asked.

"She is unique. She insisted I put her in handcuffs and made a point of showing the cuffs to everyone."

Rick asked what the chance was that he or his wife might have infected any of their students. Sybil explained that their exposure, if it happened at all, would have been to a low dose of the virus. It would probably be two to five days before they could spread the virus to others—again, assuming they had been infected.

"Good," Rick and Ann said as one.

"I'd hate to think we've spread something that dangerous to our students," Ann said. Rick nodded.

Sybil gave them the phone numbers on base to call for food, fuel, and medical care. The Jensens waved goodbye as Jones backed the JLTV out of the driveway. Sybil returned the wave. It was a relief to find people who listened, recognized the risks, and behaved sensibly, even though Rick's faux anger had given her a bad start at first.

Fort McCoy
6:00 p.m. CST

Colonel Williams, along with his staff, Dr. Wickert, and Sybil had a working dinner in the conference room. The room was spacious but nearly filled with a large elliptical table and a bar holding beverages and covered serving dishes. Dinner was a choice of ribeye steak cooked to order or Southern fried chicken, mixed vegetables, and mashed potatoes and gravy. Wine or beer was available, but everyone stuck to decaf coffee.

Giving people enough information to understand how serious this was without creating a panic would require a delicate balance, a balance local politicians and medical professionals might be better at than CDC personnel. At Sybil's suggestion, they agreed to ask the governor to order closing the Tomah area schools, churches, movie theaters, and taverns for two weeks. Restaurants could stay open, but only half of their tables could be used, and people were encouraged to order meals as takeout. Meetings of local organizations would be postponed for the same period as a part of the declaration of martial law for the area around Kirby.

The colonel demanded of Sybil, "How did you arrive at a two-week quarantine period?"

"From what we saw with the original Swiss extraction team, those exposed to a moderate-to-high dose of the virus developed a headache and fever in less than a week and bleeding from the nose and eyes a few days after that. We don't know how long it will take people exposed to a low dose of the virus to become sick. Two weeks is our best guess."

Dr. Wickert asked, "Has anyone developed a test to identify infected people?"

"The Swiss have sequenced the virus and developed a PCR-based blood test to identify those who are infected. Unfortunately, it takes a while to run the test."

Colonel Williams looked confused.

"That's a test that uses DNA amplified with the Polymerase Chain Reaction to identify infected people," Dr. Wickert explained.

Sybil reluctantly put down her fork and agreed with Wickert. "I'd also like to develop an antibody-antigen test using blood from our two prisoners. There may be other ways we can use their antibodies in diagnostic tests—or even treatments."

"That sounds like months of work," Wickert said. "What will be available two weeks from today, and what are the sensitivity and specificity likely to be?"

"Sensitivity and specificity?" the colonel asked, his head tilted slightly to one side like an inquisitive crow.

Wickert glanced at Sybil and she nodded, indicating he should take the question. He finished chewing a piece of ribeye and dabbed his lips with a paper napkin before answering.

"Sensitivity is the likelihood that a test will find the virus if it is there," Wickert said. "And specificity is the probability that the test will only identify the virus—that is, it won't produce false positive results. Unfortunately, with some medical assays you can have high specificity or high sensitivity, but not both."

The colonel's eyes glazed over.

Sybil tried another tack. "We may have to use an inexpensive screening test to identify those who *might* be infected and a more expensive, secondary test to verify that positive reactions in people are real."

The colonel nodded at her over his coffee cup. He seemed to understand this time.

"So, how sensitive are the tests likely to be?" the doctor asked.

"No idea, but we've got a virologist on site. I haven't met him, but I like Grant Farnsworth's style. He came here, saw what needed to be done, and he did it without regard for regulations and without orders. That's a rare quality."

"Do we know if he has any experience developing assays?" Wickert asked.

Sybil chuckled as she took a small bite of a dinner roll. The butter had been flavored with garlic and another spice. She couldn't identify it, but the effect was marvelous. "Farnsworth is a virologist. Developing assays is more than half the work he does. If he's as good at that as he's been at other things, we'll be in great shape on developing assays." She hastily took a bit of ribeye before anyone else asked a question. The piquant flavor of the tarragon rich Béarnaise sauce melded beautifully with the rich, beefy, perfectly seared ribeye. Damn, why did this dinner meeting have such marvelous food?

"What about treating all people who have been exposed at the motel or the tavern?" asked Wickert.

Sybil held up her hand and finished chewing a bite of steak

before answering. "That's a tough one. I don't know. I'm going to ask for guidance from Sam Barker at the CDC. If we use treatment as a preventive, there's a chance the treatment may cause a false negative—"

"False negative?" the colonel asked.

"A false negative is someone who has the disease but tests as though they don't," Wickert explained.

"As I was saying," Sybil said, "a false negative test result for the virus could screw up everything we're trying to accomplish." Sybil worked at cutting the last bit of meat off the bone of her ribeye. God, it was good, and the mixed vegetables still had a little crunch to them. She should eat on base more often.

The meeting broke up after a few more questions. Sybil asked Dr. Wickert if Dr. Farnsworth would be at the Kirby Motel in the morning. She'd heard that Grant spent five years working as a veterinarian with dairy cattle. She looked forward to seeing if the old saw from medical school was correct. *Scratch a food-animal veterinarian, they said, and you'll find an epidemiologist. More likely, I'll just come away with cow manure under my fingernails.*

"I'll drop by the motel and hospital around nine tomorrow morning. Tell Dr. Farnsworth I'd like to meet with him and review the latest information from Switzerland. I need his opinion on our procedures from a virologist's viewpoint." *That ought to get his interest.*

Jones and the JLTV were waiting outside the office to take Sybil back to her room. "Where to, boss?" Jones asked.

She looked at her cell phone. It was 10:00 p.m. "Back to my room. God, I'm beat."

"You've worked the weekend and late every night. They don't give you much free time, do they?"

"I haven't had more than a couple of days off a month since . . ."

Sybil was about to say, *since the weekend my fiancé dumped me a year ago.* That wasn't something she cared to share. It sounded like whining and made her feel like a loser. "I haven't had much time off for over a year."

"Why do you let them drive you like that?"

"Sense of duty, concern for patients, fear about the spread of disease, plain old love of what I do. Maybe it boils down to an overdeveloped work ethic spurred on by insecurity." Sybil was tired, too tired to answer questions like this without saying more than she'd intended. "Whatever the reason, it's my problem, not yours."

She hadn't been watching where they were going. When Jones turned off the road, she saw it was into the driveway of a nightclub off base. "What's this? I told you to take me back to my room."

"You need to unwind for half an hour. Let's have a drink and bitch about our superiors for twenty minutes. It'll do you good. I'll drop you off at your room and pick you up half an hour later than usual tomorrow morning."

"But—"

"Working yourself into the youngest coronary on record won't help your patients. What are you drinking? It's on me."

Jones parked, came around to the passenger side, and gave her his hand to help her down from the JLTV. She grumbled but he ignored her complaints. Knowing that Jones worried about her and wanted to protect her gave her a warm feeling, and she took pleasure in letting him help her out of the JLTV. A lightly armored personnel carrier, she thought of it as an uncomfortable, underweight tank.

She had an Amaretto and felt guilty about letting Jones pick up the bill. That disappeared when he ordered a cognac, as the costs of the drinks were comparable. After a few sips of the Amaretto, she found herself talking about Sam and her many assignments. From there she moved on to the stupidity of the late Professor Antoine and her fears that Colonel Williams might be a problem in the future.

After her second drink, she told Jones what it felt like to be dumped by a text message. She cringed inwardly after the first sentence. It wasn't something she wanted to talk about, but once she'd started, there wasn't any natural place to stop, and the whole story came out. When she finished, she was close to tears, which made her feel even worse about blundering into that topic. *Two drinks and I'm worse than a jilted teenager.* As Jones helped her into the JLTV, she realized she'd done all the talking and more than her share of the drinking.

Back at the base, Jones helped her out of the JLTV again. She slipped and would have hit the ground if his shoulder hadn't broken her fall. It felt good to lean into him and let him put his arms around her. It felt even better when he kissed her.

She kissed him back and put her arms around his neck. Was she falling for Jones or for simple human contact? Did it matter?

"I don't even know your first name," she said.

"Tom. Tom Jones. But I'm warning you, I don't sing for shit."

"I think Fielding would forgive you. Thanks for the ride, Tom. Until tomorrow morning." She gave him another quick kiss.

As she climbed the stairs to her apartment, she realized Jones hadn't questioned her reference to Henry Fielding's wildly irreverent *The History of Tom Jones, A Foundling.* Was he familiar with eighteenth-century English literature? What kind of an education did Corporal Jones have, anyway?

CHAPTER 16

MEET DR. FARNSWORTH

Thursday, January 18, 2018
Fort McCoy
8:00 a.m. CST

Sybil paced back and forth across her room, her cell phone to her ear. "Sam, things are more complicated here than I'd anticipated. I'd like to run my plans by you if you don't mind."

"Okay. Shoot."

"We have four categories of patients here. The first are the two thugs and their girlfriends in Antoine's room. They are infected or heavily exposed. The second group is the people spending the night and the motel employees. I haven't had time to look at the air-handling diagrams for the building, but I'm willing to bet that anyone working or staying at the motel has been exposed to at least moderate doses of the virus. The third group is the people in town who frequented Ed's Tavern when the thugs were there. They could have been exposed to moderate to low doses of the virus."

"I'm following you so far," said Sam.

Sybil stopped pacing and leaned against the counter by the sink in the apartment's kitchenette. "Right. I'll get to the fourth group later. Group one, the thugs and those in close association with them, are being treated with the maximum doses of the three treatment drugs. That will continue for two to three weeks depending on their viral shedding, recovery from the symptoms, and how well they tolerate the drugs. Group two, the clinically healthy people staying in the motel, are being left in their rooms and treated as though they have the disease. After four days of treatment, they'll be moved from the motel and into clean housing on base to prevent infection by any virus loose in the motel. We'll keep them on a standard dose of medication for at least a week, and then on a reduced dose for a month. In the hospital they can be kept under quarantine where we can be sure they take their meds. They'll be monitored for symptoms and tested for infection for another month. Does that make sense to you?"

Sam answered with a note of caution in his voice. "Yes, but be ready to alter your plans if the Swiss come up with something new. We're still feeling our way on this."

Sybil nodded. "Point taken. The people in the last two groups are quarantined in their homes now, except for a Mrs. Anderson, who's on base. They'll be tested for the virus at two weeks, and monthly for two more months. If nothing shows up at fourteen days, they'll be presumed free of the virus and the quarantine will be lifted for them. Do you think we are taking too big of a chance by doing that?"

"You didn't describe the fourth group."

Sybil smacked herself in the forehead with her free hand and went back to pacing from one side of the kitchenette to the other. "Sorry. Those are people like Mrs. Anderson who bought gas in Kirby. They might have been exposed."

"I wouldn't bother treating them or the people in Kirby who didn't rub elbows with your thugs at Ed's," Sam said. "Test everyone ten days from now and monthly after that. We'll discuss it again when we hear more from the Swiss. They've got over a hundred active cases, about half of them patients they believe are recovering. Their PCR test for the virus is optimized, and they've identified a cell line the virus will grow on."

"Will do. I—"

"Sybil, you've never worked in a lab. Is there anyone at the base who can run a diagnostic lab and do these assays?"

"There might be. Ron Schmidt sent Grant Farnsworth, his postdoc here. He's a veterinarian with a PhD in virology. I'm going to meet him this morning."

"Will he be willing to help?" Sam asked, a note of concern in his voice.

"He's going to jump at it. He just doesn't know that yet."

"Can Farnsworth take the time from his job at the U?"

Sybil chuckled. "Sam, you have to use the right approach. It's called 'blackmail.' I've learned all about it. You find out who screwed up and caused your problem, and you twist their tail until they take corrective action. Everybody is happy if they behave. The moron who caused the problem might even get credit for solving it unless he's an idiot, digs in his heels, and chooses not to help. When that happens, I see to it that everything hits the fan. Blackmail should be a mandatory class for epidemiologists."

Sam snorted. "You don't let anything get in your way, do you? What dirt have you got on Farnsworth?"

Sybil shrugged. Sam had the wrong target. "The dirt is on his adviser. Schmidt had something to do with Antoine 'importing' those samples for him. If he didn't know Antoine was bringing them in illegally, he must have suspected it. Give him a call and ask about that. He'll know his career could vaporize. You might remind him that there could be jail time. Tell him we desperately need a well-trained virologist here at McCoy. Give him my phone number if he doesn't cave. Make sure Farnsworth's salary from the U covers his work here too."

"Wow. You're good at this."

"It'll save lives, Sam."

Concern crept back into Sam's voice. "What do you plan to do with the motel when everyone has been moved out?"

"We'll spray surfaces with bleach and let it dry. After that, the entire building will be sealed and gassed with formaldehyde a couple of times. Swabs will be collected from surfaces to test for the virus. The septic system will be treated twice with chloral hydrate—concentrated laundry bleach."

"Don't overdo it on the chlorine," Sam said. "I don't want to pay to treat the sewage as hazardous waste because of your treatments."

Sybil gestured broadly with the hand not holding the phone. Sometimes penny pinchers drove her nuts. "Sam, we're saving lives. This isn't a time to get picky with your budget. The news from the disaster in Zürich should keep the congressional coffers open for you."

True to his word, Tom didn't pick Sybil up until eight thirty. Neither spoke of the previous night. Halfway to Kirby, Tom said, "Thursday is a slow day for the restaurants around here. There won't be many people from the base out tonight, and the Frozen Fig will have half-priced specials. Like to have dinner tonight?"

"I'd love to," said Sybil. "How dressed do I have to get?"

Tom looked her over, his eyes traveling from her hair to her boots and back. He seemed to spend a little extra time looking over her chest. "What you're wearing will do fine. We can drop by the Fig on the way back to the base and take the evening from there. Not a lot to do after dinner, I'm afraid."

"We can play that by ear. See a movie in Sparta or even watch TV."

They arrived at the Kirby Motel shortly before 9:00. Half a dozen people were eating breakfast as they walked in. Sybil assumed the tall, thin young man eating at a small table in the corner was Grant. At least that was the corner the clerk had pointed to the previous day when she'd asked where Farnsworth was staying. Sybil put on a surgical mask.

"Dr. Farnsworth, I presume?"

Grant put his fork down and stood. Sybil shook his hand. "I'm sorry, but I've always wanted to paraphrase that," she said.

"Paraphrase?" Grant asked, his forehead creased.

"It's how Henry Stanley greeted Dr. Livingston on the shores of Lake Tanganyika in 1871."

"Were they at a conference?"

Sybil looked at Grant, but he didn't appear to be joking. "A century before those became problems. Livingston was an explorer searching for the headwaters of the Nile. No one had heard from him for years until Stanley found him in 1871."

"I can't imagine how I missed that in my education," Grant said dryly.

"Please, sit down and finish your breakfast before it gets cold," Sybil said, and she took a chair opposite Grant at the table. She realized she'd stepped into an educational gap and the muck was on her boots. Grant hadn't been posted to Africa like she had. Best to move on. "We were fortunate to have you in Kirby searching for Antoine shortly after he was murdered. You have saved the CDC and your country a great deal of trouble."

Grant finished chewing the last sausage link and wiped a drop of Maple syrup off his chin. "Thanks." He shrugged and shook his head. "I wish I could have saved Professor Antoine."

"Regrettable, true. We still have a lot of work to do, and you may be able to help us. You've been exposed to the virus, so you're stuck here under quarantine for a while." Sybil chose to leave the quarantine time vague in case she needed Grant for months instead of weeks. "How would you like to spend that time helping us set up a laboratory to run the Swiss PCR test for the Zürich

Virus? We also need to develop a rapid and sensitive assay for the virus and tests for antibodies to it. Are you game?"

Grant leaned back in his chair and thought a moment. "I'll give it a try if you'd like, but I think you'd be better off getting someone else. Most of my assays have been molecular. I've had limited experience developing the tests you want."

"Limited is more experience than anyone else here has."

"I'm working for Professor—"

"Given the importance of the work, I'm sure Professor Schmidt will agree to lend you to us for a couple of months. This will—"

"Months? My wife is due to have a baby in a few weeks."

Sybil assumed a serious expression and stared at Grant for a moment. He had to understand how important this was, but she recognized the bind he was in. "You can't risk exposing your family to this. As I was saying, this will be an enormous opportunity for you. You will head a laboratory critical for the safety and health of the citizens of the United States."

Grant's shoulders sagged and his face fell. He apparently knew when he was beaten. He looked up after a moment and asked, "Do you have a source of the Zürich Virus and antibodies to it?"

Sybil nodded. "Right. The Swiss sent us a sample of the virus, and I've ordered everything you'll need to grow it. Frank and Tony will pump out massive amounts of antibody if they survive." She smiled. "I believe you've met them."

Deep furrows formed in Grant's forehead. "Are Frank and Tony that civic-minded? Do they know you plan on collecting lots of blood from them?"

"They're facing life in prison for murder. They'll have to cooperate if they ever want to be paroled."

"I'm stuck here for at least a couple of weeks no matter what, right?"

Sybil glanced at the information she had on Grant. "At least. It *could* be up to two months or more. It will depend on how sensitive the Swiss PCR test is, and if we must develop a more sensitive test to verify people aren't infected. Your family's health will depend on it. You understand that better than anyone else here."

Grant muttered something Sybil couldn't make out and asked, "When do I start?"

"As soon as possible. I know this is rough on you, but if you can develop a sensitive and specific test, and do it quickly, you may be able to go home in two weeks."

Sybil arranged for Grant to have a room in the field hospital set up in the parking lot, started him on treatment for the virus, and gave him copies of the information sent by the Swiss. She promised him he'd be moved to the base hospital and lab after he'd tested negative for the virus three times over as many days.

"While you're stuck twiddling your thumbs in the field hospital," she told him, "you can plan your work and order reagents I missed. Be sure you get expedited delivery."

Grant sighed and glanced at the information Sybil had given him. "Good idea. The quicker I can start the work, the sooner I can get back to my wife and family."

He stood and shook Sybil's hand when she stood to leave. *Looks like he's on board.* She tried not to look smug as she walked to the JLTV.

St. Paul, Minnesota, College of Veterinary Medicine
11:00 a.m. CST

Ron Schmidt was relaxing in his office, leaned back in his chair with his feet on his desk. He was deep into the latest copy of *Virology* when the phone on his desk rang. He put his feet on the floor and sat up to reach his phone.

"Professor Schmidt, Sam Barker of the CDC here. How are you doing?"

Ron's heart sank. *Oh lord, the last person I want to talk to.* His next sabbatical would be in San Quentin if Sam thought he'd helped Antoine bring those samples in. He reminded himself to get caller ID. "Ah, hello, Sam. I'm doing fine, and you?"

"I'm calling about that little problem in Kirby, Wisconsin. Your buddy Professor Antoine created one hell of a mess for us to clean up. Were you aware that Antoine was smuggling the samples into the United States?"

Smuggling? Ron began to sweat. "It was a guess on my part. He, ah, that is Antoine, wanted to get the samples here quickly. He claimed he was following the regs, mostly. I followed the regs to a T on my end. I sent in the required requests to import the samples some time ago. You should have copies at the CDC."

"Oh, yes. I have them right here. The DOT and FBI have requested copies."

Ron thought he was going into cardiac arrest. He didn't trust himself to say anything.

"By the way," Sam continued, "it would be a considerable help if we could borrow your Dr. Farnsworth for a couple of months. Think you can manage that?"

Ron thought of the work he had lined up. He needed Grant, but man, he needed friends in high places more. Sam's goodwill might save his career. "No problem," he squeaked. "Glad to help. Keep him as long as you need to."

"Thanks. Can you believe those bone-headed thieves snorted and tasted Antoine's samples? They're sick as hell now. Your postdoc Farnsworth did a wonderful job finding Antoine's body, isolating it, and keeping the thugs in their room. He's agreed to set up a lab and work on the assays we'll need. We don't have anything in our budget to pay him. Can your department continue to cover his salary while he's here?"

Crap. He couldn't promise that, but if he didn't . . .

"Grant's salary comes out of a research grant," Ron said. "We can do it if I can connect Grant's work for the CDC to the grant somehow." Ron paused and sighed. "That won't be easy. Any chance you could suggest the Department of Defense make a grant available? I assume he'll be doing the work at Fort McCoy."

Sam said he'd look into it. As he put the phone down, Ron prayed Sam had enough pull with the DOD to push it through. If he didn't, Ron would have to scramble to find the money.

CHAPTER 17

LOVE AMONG THE ICICLES

Friday, January 19, 2018
Field Hospital, Kirby Motel parking lot
4:30 p.m. CST

As Sybil left the field hospital for the afternoon, she spotted Tom at his JLTV across the parking lot and headed for him. He had the engine going and the heater on by the time she got there. It was only four thirty, but Sybil was dog-tired. But it was a satisfying tired. Grant's agreement to spend up to two months working on Zürich Virus assays was a start, if not an enthusiastic start. Once he got involved, it shouldn't be difficult to keep him longer. She hoped Grant would become so invested in the work that he'd be reluctant to let it go. It was easy to see it in others now that she'd recognized it in herself.

Good scientists were like that. Once they committed to work on a problem, they'd immerse themselves in the problem so deeply it was difficult to pry them out of it. Minds committed to answering complex questions couldn't drop those questions easily.

Tom stood at the passenger door. He held it open and gave her a hand to get in. This was different, and a definite change for the better. She'd have resented the help a week ago. Now she appreciated it, even looked forward to it. He settled himself in the driver's seat. "Dinner at the Frozen Fig?"

"I'd like that," Sybil said. "How on earth did a steak house come up with a name like the 'Frozen Fig'?"

"No idea. The winters here probably had something to do with it. How's your work going? Do you have the virus under control yet?"

Sybil gave a derisive snort. "Too early to tell. Too much unknown. It's like feeling our way in the dark. We should be in good shape if the Swiss are telling us everything they know. That scares me, because bureaucrats tend to bury bad news until it bites them in the ass, and this time our ass is hanging out there with theirs."

"Then you'll be around for a while?"

"That's the only certain thing." She paused and, with arched eyebrows, looked at him with appraisal. "Will you like that?"

He smiled. "Having you around and getting off base all day are the two best things that have happened to me in the National Guard. I'm going to miss you when this is over."

"Because you'll have to go back to work on the base, or because you enjoy our scintillating conversation?"

Tom smiled at her, but they arrived at the Frozen Fig before he could reply. She enjoyed Tom's company. Bright and articulate, he had a wicked sense of humor, he respected her intelligence, and she looked forward to his hand in hers. It was a welcome surprise when he grasped her with both hands under her arms and lifted her down from the JLTV's running board. She put her hands around his neck, supposedly to stabilize herself, but she didn't want to let go of him when he put her down. Things were stirring within her that she hadn't paid attention to for over a year.

The Frozen Fig was a steakhouse, and anybody in their right mind limited their orders to steaks, chops, and ribs. She'd ordered walleye at a similar restaurant in rural Iowa once. The waiter hadn't even caught the sarcasm when she asked for a steak knife. She and Tom kept their orders simple—ribeye steaks and a California Pinot Noir.

For all the good qualities she'd seen, Tom was still a mystery to her. "You've never told me what you do, or what you've been trained to do," she said.

"Oh, that's easy. I've been trained to do absolutely nothing, and so far, I've done a splendid job of it."

She choked on her salad and shook her head. "Not being helpful tonight, are you?"

Tom put his fork and knife down and leaned back in his chair. "It's true. I'm in the National Guard, I work in a store that sells electronics and computers, and I have a bachelor's degree in philosophy with a minor in French. A couple of years ago I completed a master's and toyed with working on a doctorate in modern European history."

"Modern?"

"Yeah, 1645 to the present. I was so taken with Kissinger's *Diplomacy* and Barbara Tuchman's *The March of Folly* that I wrote my thesis on the political and military effects of wishful thinking. It's a common reason wars are started."

His expression remained bland, but Sybil thought she saw a twinkle in his eyes. He was hiding something, something he expected her to guess. She took another sip of wine and chewed on a piece of steak to give herself time to think. "Have you been published?"

"Not yet. It took me over a year to get a literary agent."

"Fiction or nonfiction?"

"I've tried my hand at both historical fiction and a history of the second Iraq War. I did the research for that when I wrote my thesis. The plans for that war were unadulterated wishful thinking. Last week my agent sent me a long list of revisions and additions she'd like me to make to the books."

I could fall for this guy if he writes as well as he talks. "I feel guilty," Sybil lied. "I'm keeping you from your work."

"You're not. My next book will be a history of the Zürich Virus. Chauffeuring you around puts me at the epicenter of the action. It's exciting. Nobody knows how things will turn out yet."

"Oh, I didn't hear that. You do understand that what we're doing might be classified."

"Only if things don't go well. Governments only bury their failures. If you prevent an epidemic, I expect your boss will pay me to write the book. I haven't detected any wishful thinking yet, so I'm depending on him for a job."

Sybil thought about Sam Barker. "You might get it. If you're still in the Guard, he may order you to write it—if everything goes well. And he'll want it done before we submit our budget for next year."

Tom had parked behind the restaurant to avoid drawing attention to an army vehicle, making for a long walk back to the JLTV after dinner. He held her hand as they walked and used the slippery sidewalk as an excuse; he didn't need the excuse. Having her hand in his felt good. It had been too long since someone had given her a hug, or kissed her. She hadn't known how much she needed human contact until the previous night when Tom had kissed her. She could become addicted to that.

Strange. Sybil was a highly trained physician and scientist. Though she'd seen papers on children's needs to be held and pampered, she'd never seen one on the need for physical contact in adults. She looked at Tom. Even in silhouette, his strong chin and smile stood out. Maybe she should read more romances. Or live one.

He drove her back to her room, and she invited him up to check the local paper for movies playing in Sparta. She wasn't sure why she asked him up. It just popped out when she realized she didn't want to let the evening end. *I don't even get the darn paper.*

She offered him Irish Cream, the only booze she had in the apartment. She got out her laptop and searched for movies in Sparta while they sat on the couch. It was easy and comfortable to lean into him. The making out started before her laptop connected to the internet.

Things progressed slowly, though. Perhaps Tom worried about the disparity in rank between them. *Well, somebody has to make the first move.* After a few minutes of necking, Sybil toyed with the top button on his shirt. That seemed to give him license, and he unbuttoned her blouse before she'd gotten to the second button of his shirt.

As frantic as their activity was, progress from the bedroom door to the bed was slow. Pants, shoes, shirts, and underwear came off as they moved across the room. Not a speedy procedure, but more fun than anything she'd done in a long time. What happened when they got to the bed was everything she'd hoped for. Even better the second time.

Tom woke up at 1:00 a.m. "Oh, crap. I have to get out of here."

Sybil snuggled close beside him, enjoying the feel of his warm skin against hers. She put a possessive arm around him. "Why? Aren't you comfortable?" She hugged him close. "I feel better than I have in ages."

"The JLTV. It's parked outside. Everybody on base knows I'm your driver. If anyone recognizes it, they'll know I've spent the night here. The military is fussy about stuff like that. I'd better get back to the barracks, or they'll assign someone else to be your chauffeur."

Sybil turned on a light, partly so he could find his clothes, mostly so she could watch him dress. "I hope you saved some energy for tomorrow. It could be a busy day." She wondered if they would have time to have a relaxed meal together tomorrow. It all depended on the virus.

He gathered her in his arms and kissed her. "I'll pick you up around eight," he said and left.

Sybil stretched and luxuriated in the warm, exhausted feeling. It was nice to have someone to care about again. She hoped he cared as much for her. He seemed to, but if he didn't, she'd take that chance. Better to enjoy a false romance than no romance at all. She didn't really worry about Tom. He didn't seem like the love-'em-and-dump-'em kind of guy. There was more brain behind those lovely brown eyes than most men had. Then again, Einstein had been a famous philanderer. More importantly, would Tom make the dinners or be satisfied with take-out?

She overslept and didn't wake until Tom knocked on her door. It took time to relinquish her sexy dream and face her cold room. She dragged herself to the door, opened it, and apologized. *Odd.* Now that they weren't in the throes of making love, she felt shy around him, dressed only in a patched robe, worn slippers, and tangled mousey hair. She collected the clothes she'd need and hauled them to the bathroom where she could dress in peace after she showered. It also allowed her to put on her makeup in private. That seemed important now.

She told him to make coffee while she got dressed. That would keep him busy. It normally wouldn't take that long, but he'd have to locate everything in the efficiency apartment.

When she came out, dressed and makeup applied, Tom looked at his watch. "I've had my coffee. Here's a thermos you can take with us. Grab a roll or something else to eat on the way. We're going to be late."

The ride to Kirby had more bounces in it today. Tom was hurrying.

"I don't have early meetings today, Tom," Sybil said. "You can slow down. It'll give my butt a rest." She adjusted herself in her seat.

"It's easier to plow through these drifts if we keep moving right along. After your meeting at the hospital, what's our itinerary today?"

She told him they'd stop in Kirby for half an hour to check with Dr. Wickert. Then they'd visit the county road entrances to Kirby and make sure they were still closed. They'd have to look at the snowmobile trails, too. All of those conveniently ended near Ed's Tavern.

They were finished checking the roadblocks and the blocks on the snowmobile trails by eleven-thirty. "I don't think I can face another one of Ed's frozen pizzas, and I sure don't want more commissary food," she said. "I saw a café on the way back to the base. Why don't we try that?"

When Tom stopped in front of the café, she suggested the JLTV would draw less attention parked behind the café. He gave her an odd look, smiled, and parked where she'd suggested.

Lunch didn't take long. Sibyl knew because she watched the clock. Her teleconference at the base wasn't until three o'clock, but she needed to have a talk with Tom. Things had gone too far, too fast. She chose a table away from the other diners and partially shielded by what looked like plastic plants. After the waitress brought their food, she started talking.

"Tom, I like you, and I think I could easily be serious about you, but our job here is critical. Lives depend on it. It's too important to have us sidetracked by a fling. I can't let a serious relationship interfere with it either. When I'm working, I must devote all of my energy to controlling this virus, and when I have time off, that time is too precious to waste on gratuitous sex. Last night was wonderful, but it ends there unless you're serious about a relationship."

Tom chewed on a bite of pizza, swallowed, and took a sip of water. "I am serious. You're the best thing that's come into my life in a long time." He reached across the table and held her hand.

Sybil relaxed. She hadn't realized how tense she'd been until then. "That's what I hoped you'd say."

"When do you have to be back on base?"

"I have a teleconference at three."

"Three o'clock. Do you have any reading or calls you have to make to prepare for it?"

Sybil shook her head. "Everyone I'd call to get ready will be in on the teleconference and I'm up to date on my reading."

With a wicked grin, Tom noted that it was only twelve-fifteen. He yawned—theatrically, Sybil thought—and suggested they have another cup of coffee. Sybil saw where this was heading. Damn, his hand felt good around her cold fingers. "As a physician, I'd recommend a nap instead of all that caffeine."

She let Tom pay for the meal while she strolled back to the JLTV. A mile down the road, Tom pointed to a sign for the motel. "Speaking of that nap, I've wondered how this place stays in business. I've never seen more than one car in the parking lot."

Tom pulled in and parked near the office. Sybil handed him a credit card and told him to use it for the room. She thought it would arouse less interest if he paid for the room. The office looked dusty, almost unused. When he asked for a room, the manager, a thin, middle-aged guy, chuckled and gave him a wink when Tom handed him the credit card. Greasy hair, stained and wrinkled clothes—the manager looked sleazy. He gave Sybil the creeps. *This guy would make anything feel dirty and cheap.*

Back in the JLTV, he said, "The room is in the back."

Outside their room, he opened the door, put his arms around Sybil, and kissed her.

They slept after making love. Tom woke up first, looked at a clock on the nightstand, and nudged Sybil awake. "We've got an hour before your teleconference. You realize if I'm going to write about a dangerous epidemic as fiction or fact, I'm going to have to spend at least a little time watching you work on saving the world. These practice runs on repopulating it won't fit in that kind of book."

Sybil leisurely traced a finger through the hair on his chest. "Maybe you should write the kind of book they would fit in. I hear those sell well," she said and snuggled against him. "I love the feel of you against me. I've never done anything like this before, especially on an assignment. You may have ruined me for work." She leaned forward and gave him a kiss. "Think your books will sell well enough to support us?"

He kissed her and nuzzled her neck. "I think this is where you're supposed to say we should take it slowly, but it's too late for that. And fast feels so damned good."

"You've got that right," Sybil said. "I promised myself this morning that if you stopped at a motel I'd say 'no,' but when the time came I couldn't. So much for best laid plans."

In the JLTV, she told him, "Back to the base for the teleconference with the CDC and Dr. Wickert from the hospital."

"Where to after that?"

"By four I have to talk to Grant in Kirby about his plans for the new assays."

"Did you plan it this way just so we could spend more time together going back and forth?"

"No, but I like it."

"Good. Keep it up."

Sybil smiled at him and relaxed into her seat as much as she could in the JLTV as Tom drove to the base. She got to the conference room as Colonel Williams made the internet connections and put a triangular speaker in the center of the conference table. He introduced the people on their end. Sam Barker joined them by Zoom from the CDC, and a clutch of congressmen joined them from Washington, DC. Barker asked Sybil to bring everyone up to date on the Zürich Virus.

She reviewed what had happened in Kirby and how McCoy had responded. "Dr. Grant Farnsworth is working on ways to make the Swiss PCR test for the virus more sensitive."

"What approach is Grant taking?" Sam asked.

"He's using antibodies from Frank to concentrate virus from samples, as well as other approaches I didn't understand."

"How critical will it be to have improved assays, and when do you anticipate they'll be completed?" Sam asked.

"If there are no surprises, we may not need them. I'm concerned about that because we've heard rumors of unusual problems the Swiss are having."

"What type of problems?"

"They've had isolated outbreaks they couldn't explain. The people who might have spread the infection were all negative for the virus by their PCR test. It suggests a carrier state that isn't being detected by the Swiss PCR test, or a virus that survives longer than expected in the environment. So far, we don't have a handle on what's causing it, and the Swiss have been tight-lipped about it."

A congressman harrumphed, and asked, "How much are the new tests likely to cost?"

"Much depends on how quickly Farnsworth comes up with something. Development and testing could be as high as two million."

The congressman's tone changed to that of a teacher instructing a slow student. "If we don't know that we'll need them, why spend the money? Money doesn't grow—"

Sybil would normally wait for Sam to answer this horse's ass, but she was losing patience with fools, especially those who talked down to her. "Congressman," she barked, "thousands of people will have to be treated for Zürich Fever if we suddenly need improved tests and don't have them. That would easily cost several billion and cost many people their lives."

"Well, can you describe a scenario that would cause this?"

"The Swiss test has only detected the virus in people who are sick. We don't know if it will detect the virus in early cases, before symptoms develop. We don't know if a carrier state exists or whether the Swiss test would detect it. We don't know how long the virus can survive in the environment, or if the Swiss test is sensitive enough to detect it in environmental samples. We don't know if animals carry—"

The congressman sighed and gave in. "Okay. I get your point."

Tired of congressmen making speeches instead of asking sensible questions, Sybil happily left early when Sam hinted that she had critical scientific work to look after. He probably did it to avoid another confrontation between the congressman and Sybil. It would be easier if Sam and the talking heads in Washington spoke to Grant instead of her, but bureaucracy had its chains of command.

The roads were another matter, Sybil discovered. They were still choked with snow. The sun had warmed the snow surface during the day, and as it gradually slipped behind the forested hills, the chill caused a hard crust to form on the snowdrifts. That made getting through them more difficult than it had been that afternoon.

As he worked to get through the drifts, Tom commented on it. "A couple of really warm days, and the roads will be passable to four-wheel-drive trucks or SUVs. You'll have to put roadblocks on County O and beef up the roadblocks on Highway 12 if that happens."

Sybil mumbled something in agreement, but she was still stewing over the congressman's opposition. The remainder of the ride to base was quiet. Tom gave her a questioning look as he stopped the JLTV in front of the field hospital in Kirby. As he helped her out of the vehicle, she told him, "Don't worry. I'm upset with a congressman, not you. Some jerk in Washington tried to pull my strings. I let him have it, and my boss got me out of the meeting before I said too much."

She put on Tyveks, an N95 respirator, gloves, and disposable plastic boots before entering the field hospital. The constant dressing and undressing was a pain in the butt, but the only way to visit Grant safely.

Grant met her at the entrance.

"Are you supposed to be out of your room before the three days of treatment are over?" Sybil asked.

Grant brushed off her concerns. "It's all right if I stay inside the hospital. I feel great. I'm negative for the virus by the PCR test. The Tyveks and the respirator I'm wearing will prevent virus shedding if I am infected."

They moved to a corner with a table used as a conference area. "How are Frank and Tony doing?" Sybil asked.

"Frank is feeling better—no headaches, no epistaxis—but Tony hasn't changed. Darn fool took a bunch of aspirin before treatment started. That's made it difficult to control his bleeding. His blood pressure is low, he still has a low-grade fever and a headache, and he hallucinates occasionally. They gave him several units of blood, he's on fluids with antibiotics, and he's getting platelets every day."

"Sounds like they have everything covered."

"Both Frank and Tony are still positive for the virus. Frank's viral load is barely detectable now. Tony's hasn't changed since we started. Frank will make it, but Tony won't unless his clinical picture improves markedly."

"What about the women who were with them?"

Grant chuckled. "They're furious with the guys. PCR tests proved they were infected, but the last test we did was negative for virus in their blood. I'm not sure I trust that yet."

"What do you mean?"

"Their viral load may have been reduced below the ability of the current test to pick it up, but they could still be infected. They'd have to have at least thirty thousand virions per ounce to detect an infection with the current test."

"Think you can improve the sensitivity?"

"We'll use antibodies to the virus to concentrate it. We purified antibodies from Frank's blood. Tony has too much virus in his blood, and he needs all the blood he's got."

"How do you purify the antibodies?"

"We collected serum from Frank and added enzymes that destroy RNA. Those destroyed the virus. Frank's blood has a phenomenal antibody titer. We diluted it fifty thousand times and still detected the antibodies. My guess is that we can increase the sensitivity of the test by a thousandfold using those antibodies."

Sybil smiled and nodded. She had a hard time imagining something diluted that much and still evident in the sample, or a test that could detect it. *That's why we have virologists*, she thought. "Push this work as hard as possible. It's going to be critical."

Grant leaned back in his chair and looked across the table at Sybil. "Suddenly there's pressure to move this really fast? What's up?"

"Don't repeat this. Through the grapevine, we've heard the Swiss are having problems. People with no known contact with infected patients are coming down with Zürich Fever."

"Zürich Fever?" Grant asked. "Is that the name they've settled on?"

"Yeah. PBS used it over the weekend, and it seems to have caught on. The damned virus is spreading somehow. Maybe through water or air. They don't know. The standard test for the virus hasn't identified where people are getting it."

"That's bad news. The Swiss test can be automated to run hundreds of samples at a time. Modifications to improve sensitivity won't be easy to automate. We'll be stuck running a few samples at a time for a while. That'll cripple attempts to control the disease if it gets out of Kirby."

Sybil leaned back in her chair. "In a little while, important people are going to put pressure on you to get answers fast. Some will insist you take shortcuts based on assumptions about the virus they think are obvious. Don't do it. Take things in a logical, step-by-step program. Tell the loudmouths and bigwigs to back off, but do it so they think you're sucking up to them."

"How the hell do I do that?"

"I wish I knew. I've never gotten it right. Sam Barker has always run interference for me. Give that problem to him. Protecting us from self-important jerks and politicians is his job."

"Thanks, I think. I'll keep you posted." Grant went back to his room, shaking his head.

She went to Dr. Wickert's office next. Wickert agreed with her that Betty and Cindy shouldn't be left in Room 221, exposed to Tony's viral shedding. They'd be moved to rooms in the field hospital that afternoon.

"What about Frank?" Wickert asked.

"What about him?" Sybil asked.

"Do we move him to the field hospital?"

Sybil shook her head. "Not until he's negative for virus by the Swiss test."

As they left Kirby, Tom asked, "How goes the battle?"

"Grant is a good scientist with a lot of promise, but he's a postdoc. He hasn't had much experience. I hope he has the confidence to ignore most of the advice he'll be getting from opinionated big shots, and the wisdom to separate good advice from bad. In science, there's a fine line between a determined, farsighted genius and an arrogant, pig-headed fool."

"That doesn't sound good. What's going on?"

She told him about the problems the Swiss were rumored to have. "Maybe it's problems in tracking contacts. That would be the simplest answer, but I've never been lucky enough to get 'simple.'"

"So, what are you afraid the problem is?" Jones asked.

"Take your pick. A carrier state in people or—God help us— an animal reservoir. Either could be disastrous. An insect that spreads the virus is possible but unlikely in winter. It would be just as bad if the virus survives in water or air for several hours. If any of those are true, there's going to be enormous pressure for Grant to get his new tests up and running. I hope he's up to the challenge."

Monday, January 22, 2018
Fort McCoy
2:30 p.m. CST

Sybil put down the printout of people known to be exposed to the Zürich Virus and picked up her phone. It was Dr. Wickert.

"Dr. Erypet, I believe we have our first death from Zürich Fever," Wickert announced.

"What? I hadn't heard of anyone but Tony and Frank who were sick."

"It's George, the old guy at the gas station. He hadn't opened the station for the last three days. Everyone thought it was because nobody had any reason to buy gas, since the town's quarantined."

"How'd they find him?"

"The sergeant in charge of delivering food to people has been calling him for several days. They didn't get an answer. Didn't think anything of it, knowing what a grouch the guy was, but today they sent somebody over with a food delivery and asked them to check on the old coot. The door wasn't latched properly and swung open when they knocked. They called his name. Nobody answered, so they did a search. Found him dead in bed and bleeding from his nose, eyes, and ears."

"How long had he been dead?"

"Hard to say. The place was cold. George heated his house with an old wood-burning stove. The fire was out, but the pipes hadn't frozen yet. Although he had symptoms of Zürich Fever, he might have died of carbon monoxide poisoning. Do you want us to do a postmortem?"

Sybil thought about it. The symptoms of Zürich Fever were obvious and present, and doing a postmortem would increase the chances of spreading the virus. "No. Double bag the body and rinse everything in bleach. Lock the house up. We'll deal with fumigating it later."

Sybil put her phone down. *Shit.* That meant everyone who had stopped at the gas station since this nonsense started may have been exposed to the *Zürich Virus*. At least a few would be infected. She called Dr. Wickert back and told him she'd send him a list of people his nurses would have to visit to collect blood samples.

Her next call was to Grant. "George Pecker at the gas station died of Zürich Fever," she said. "We'll have to test samples from anyone who was at the station. You could be asked to test samples from up to a dozen people in the next two days."

"Oh damn," Grant said with feeling. "I stopped at the station and talked to George the day I arrived in Kirby."

"So did Tom and I, although it's more important for you and your family," Sybil said. "It's even more important now to get a sensitive test developed."

There wasn't an answer.

"Are you there, Grant?" she asked.

"Yeah, I'm here," he said. He sounded dejected. "I guess I'd better get my butt in gear if I'm going to get back to Sarah before the baby is born."

"Don't be afraid to ask for help if you need it," Sybil said. "We'll provide as much assistance as we can."

"Thanks," he said and hung up.

CHAPTER 18

IT'S IN McCOY

Monday, January 22, 2018
SleepyTime Motel
8:00 p.m. CST

Sybil and Tom returned to the motel they'd stayed at previously. The manager was a creep, but the room and bed were clean. The place was old, bordering on decrepit, but it was cheap and no one else was there. It didn't have a café and didn't offer a complimentary breakfast, reducing the chance they'd run into someone visiting the base.

Sybil hung her coat in the motel room as Tom closed the door. They embraced and he undressed her. She yawned, he noticed, and caught himself yawning too. "You're exhausted and so am I. How about just cuddling tonight?" he asked.

She rested her head on his chest and hugged him. "You're tired too, huh? Snuggling sounds good. Maybe tomorrow morning if we wake up early enough . . ."

The bed squeaked just lying down on it. Sybil couldn't imagine how much noise it must have made the afternoon they'd made love. *Maybe we should look for a better motel,* she thought as she slipped off to sleep.

She slept late, too late for fun and games. They shared a shower, dressed in a hurry, and ate at the base cafeteria. An hour later, she walked into Grant's office at the Fort McCoy hospital lab. "How does it feel to be out of isolation and in a lab again?" she asked.

Grant wore scrubs and a lab coat. The only biosafety equipment he still used was a surgical mask. "Great. Wearing Tyveks all day was a pain." He paused and changed the subject. "The lab techs here are superb. I could sit at home and run the lab by phone if I had to."

"You'd like to get home to your wife, huh? When is she due?"

"Three weeks. Think I could leave for a home visit in two weeks?"

Sybil wished she didn't have to break the news. "Better test this first." She handed him a blood sample sealed in a plastic bag. "We may have a problem. This is from Lieutenant Jeager, one of our nurses."

"And?"

"Nurse Jeager has a headache and fever. She developed a nosebleed a few minutes ago."

Grant took the blood sample and looked at the identification on it. "Did she work at the field hospital in Kirby?"

"No. As far as we can tell, she hasn't had contact with anyone who is positive for the Zürich Virus." Sybil felt rotten. Grant had done great work. Anything that prevented him from visiting his wife seemed unfair. "*If* this sample is positive, no one who's been exposed to the virus will be allowed to leave Kirby or Fort McCoy. You won't want to visit your family until we sort this out."

Grant's face fell and he turned pale. "You've got that right. Is this the kind of problem the Swiss are encountering?"

"Yes, according to the rumors. They still haven't commented officially. But let's not get ahead of ourselves. Do the test and find out if Jeager has the virus. Maybe we'll get lucky and it's just a sinus infection and dry air from our ancient heating system. I'll have her complete a questionnaire on possible contacts just in case."

Tuesday, January 23, 2018
Fort McCoy Hospital Lab
12:45 p.m. CST

Abby, the civilian lab tech, received the sample from Grant. She added water to burst the red blood cells and put the sample in a small centrifuge in a biosafety cabinet. The cabinet was stainless steel and glass. Metal panels enclosed a narrow table on three sides. Above, the panels merged with a hood four feet above the work surface. A glass panel covered the front of the compartment except for the bottom six inches. The opening was large enough for Abby to insert her hands and forearms into the cabinet to work. Filter-sterilized air circulated within the hood in a way that ensured that neither the work nor the worker were contaminated.

Doing the PCR test had become routine. Abby's thoughts dwelled more on Ryan, her new hunk, than they did on the lab's strict biosafety procedures.

Abby waited until Grant returned to his office before she took off her lab coat and gloves and walked to the break room. Ryan, a blond guy in his mid-twenties, also in scrubs, sat reading the funnies with a cup of coffee. His chiseled chin and dimpled smile always got to her.

"Have a minute?" Abby asked and took a seat across from him. "Last night you said you hadn't worked with RNA viruses. If you don't blab about it, I can show you what I'm doing with the Zürich Virus."

Ryan put the newspaper and coffee down, flashed the smile and dimples. "I'd love to learn more about that," he said and followed her back to the lab.

In the hallway, Sybil whispered, "Farnsworth doesn't want anyone visiting or hanging around the lab, so if he comes back, tell him you brought me a shipment of enzymes and leave, okay?"

Ryan nodded. She dressed in protective gear and took a seat on the lab stool in front of the biosafety cabinet. Flipping up the lid of a small centrifuge, she retrieved Lieutenant Jeager's sample, put ten microliters of white cells—a drop little larger than a fly speck—into a mixture of enzymes and fluids, and let it incubate for a few minutes.

"First the viral RNA is transcribed to DNA by the reverse transcriptase enzyme I added," said Abby. She described the enzyme mix used. On the Thermocycler, the machine used to run a PCR test, she showed him the time and temperature settings.to produce DNA from RNA. Then she added the reagents for the PCR and put the test tube into the Thermocycler. The Thermocycler, a smooth, gray rectangle a bit over a foot tall and almost a foot wide—small enough to sit within the biosafety cabinet—would put the sample through the temperature changes necessary for PCR.

Abby had little to do for an hour after she'd loaded the samples in the top of the Thermocycler and started the sequence of temperature changes. Ryan was familiar with PCR amplification, so there was nothing to demonstrate or explain to him. He stood behind her, massaging her shoulders.

She relaxed and enjoyed the massage. It wasn't long before she felt his erection pushing against her back. He leaned forward and put more effort into the massage, which pressed his erection firmly against her.

"Feel good?" she asked.

"Hmm. Yeah, but I bet you could make it feel better."

"We can't do anything here. Wait until tonight," she told him.

"But you're so desirable," he said. "It's cruel to ask me to wait. I'll never make it."

"Bullshit!" she said. Ryan continued the massage and pressing against her. After a moment, she sat up straight and glanced at the lab door. "All right. Maybe we'll be safe in the stock room." She stood and looked out the small window on the lab's door, making sure no one was out in the hallway. Then she grabbed Ryan's dick with a gloved hand and led him to a windowless supply room a few steps away. He tried to kiss her, but she leaned away. "Don't do anything until we're behind closed doors."

The PCR amplification lasted an hour. Ryan didn't take that long, but longer than he had last night.

Ryan lacked several qualities as a lab tech, but he made up for them as a lover. Abby could get used to that. She glowed with the memory of their workout as she loaded samples of the amplified DNA and a dye in special depressions made in a gel slab bathed in a buffer in the depression of a small black box. She twisted dials to adjust the voltage and set the timer for the electrophoresis. A slight current would drive the dyed DNA through the gel and separate DNA fragments by size.

Later that afternoon, Abby turned off the current, put the gel on a glass plate, and turned on an ultraviolet light. The amplified DNA segments and associated dye showed up as a short, fluorescent yellow line at the right place. Nurse Jeager was positive for the Zürich Virus.

Abby's mind was elsewhere. Her divorce had just gone through. It still hurt. She'd been a heavy girl all through high school—over two hundred pounds on a five-foot-five frame when she graduated. College and beer packed on more pounds. It was only by extraordinary good luck that she'd found her husband, thin as a stick and a chubby chaser who liked her for her personality and her pounds.

She'd been so sick after her daughter's birth that she'd gone weeks eating only a cup of soup and a glass of fruit juice per day. It was a long recovery. The prolonged illness and change in the normal flora of her gut produced a significant weight loss. It was the first time she'd been able to lose weight in a lifetime of trying. It spurred her on to make a concerted effort to lose even more. She'd stopped drinking beer, dieted, and worked like mad in the gym until she weighed only 130 pounds.

She felt great, and for the first time in her life, men on the street paid attention to her. Every stroll on a beach, every summer walk downtown served up temptations she found it hard to resist. Ryan was only the latest temptation she'd succumbed to.

Grant slumped in his chair at his desk, picked up the lab phone, and dialed. "Sybil, we have a problem. Nurse Jeager is positive for the virus. She'll have to be quarantined and treated. Any idea where she might have picked it up?"

"The only person we know she was exposed to was Mrs. Anderson," Sybil said. "We know Anderson was exposed to the virus at George's gas station. Anderson has been healthy and negative for the virus for as long as she's been here. She was to be released from enforced quarantine in a few days. A blood sample from her is on its way to your lab."

Ten minutes later, a nurse delivered the sample from Mrs. Anderson and Grant gave it to his best lab tech. "You may have to stay late to get the PCR and electrophoresis done," he told them. "I wouldn't ask you to do this if it weren't important. If the amplification is negative for the virus by electrophoresis, set up a Southern blot and save the rest of the sample for antibody concentration."

The tech nodded. "I've wanted to try the antibody concentration on a real sample. With the martial law rules, there wasn't anything my wife and I were going to do tonight anyway."

Grant thanked the tech and headed back to his office. He thought how personnel working in science accepted night and weekend work as a matter of course. It was almost like veterinary medicine or farming in that way.

First thing the next morning, he received a call from Sybil. "What'd you find?" she asked.

"Mrs. Anderson's blood was negative for the virus by the standard Swiss methods. We've set up a Southern blot, but we won't have answers until tomorrow."

"Remind me what a Southern blot is."

"We transfer the DNA from the electrophoretic gel to a nylon filter and probe it with matching DNA that has a chemical tag. If the tag lights up a line at the right place on the filter, we'll have a positive. It's ten to a hundred times more sensitive than the initial Swiss test."

"Glad I've got you here," Sybil said. "The only part I understood was that the Southern is more sensitive than the standard test. Does the test require special equipment?"

Grant smiled as he remembered the hundreds of Southern tests he'd run. "You could say that. We use a glass baking dish, a stack of paper towels, and a weight on top of the stack."

Sybil was silent for a moment. "Are you pulling my leg?"

Grant laughed. "Nope. That's what we use. You'd be surprised how much cooking and molecular biology have in common."

"What do we do if that test is negative?"

"My lab tech is setting up the next improvement, the antibody capture test I told you about. We've only tried it a few times."

"How can you be sure you won't be contaminating Anderson's sample with virus from Frank?"

"A PCR test on a sample of the antibodies is run as a negative control. We're in trouble if Anderson is positive by either the Southern blot or the antibody capture test."

"Why?"

"Those tests take time and individual attention. They aren't suitable for screening large numbers of people. We need a test that will identify carriers, be suitable for automation, and, preferably, provide an answer within an hour or less. With the tests available, you'll have your answer no sooner than Monday morning."

Grant broke the connection and called Sarah. "Hi," he said. "How, ah, how have you been doing?" He worked to keep his voice even, but he missed Sarah so much he was afraid he'd start to cry. "How is Jimmy behaving?"

"I'm tired of being pregnant. My back hurts, my feet hurt, and I can't find a comfortable position to sleep. Delivery can't come soon enough, Jimmy is driving me nuts, and I'm worried about you, honey. You're surrounded by people and samples containing the Zürich Virus. All it would take is one little slip."

"God, I've missed you, Sarah, and I wish I had some good news for you." He'd racked his brain to find an easy way to break the bad news to her, but he hadn't been able to think of any way to cushion it.

"What? You're not sick, are you?" she gasped.

"I'm not sick, but . . ." He tried, but there was no way to make it sound less threatening. "It looks like I might have been exposed to the virus. It won't be safe for me to come home until I've developed a test sensitive enough to identify healthy people carrying the virus."

"Oh my God, Grant. Are you safe? How long will it take to develop a new test?"

"We have medication that prevents the virus from replicating, and we're working over the weekend on a new test. I can't promise when we'll have an adequate test."

The call ended with Sarah crying. Grant's tears were flowing when he hung up, but he avoided weeping until the phone connection was broken. Hearing him cry would have made it worse for Sarah.

Tuesday, January 23, 2018
Office, SleepyTime Motel
1:00 p.m. CST

Bob, the manager at the of the SleepyTime Motel, rummaged through his desk. The colonel's phone number was written down somewhere. He paged through an old notebook. Nothing there. He found it in the third notebook he searched. It had been years since he'd had a chance to use it. Colonel Williams had stiffed him the last time he'd called with information. He wouldn't consider calling that cheap bastard if there hadn't been so much excitement about the virus in Kirby. If the strange woman and her driver had anything to do with that, he could squeeze some real money out of Williams. He dialed the number.

He got the runaround when he asked for the colonel. Typical military. "Tell him Bob at the SleepyTime Motel called. I have information for him." The secretary promised to transmit the message. *Crap.* He'd be lucky if they remembered to tell the colonel about it before they went home tonight.

The colonel called back an hour later. "Bob, you said you had something for me. I hope it's better than your last tip. That got me nowhere."

Bob was torn over how much information to give him without getting cash up front. "Colonel," he said, "one of your men and a female officer have been stopping here, sometimes at night, sometimes at noon. I thought you should know about it."

Bob thought the colonel's voice was hesitant and suspicious when he replied. "Other than the nurses, we don't have any female officers on base now. Who is this woman? What does she look like?"

"What's it worth to you? I'm a businessman. I get paid for information."

"What you have may not be worth anything."

"She's kind of tall, brunette. She's in charge. It looks like the guy is her driver. They're always in one of those oversized jeeps. What do you call it? A Humvee."

"Like I said, I don't have . . . Wait, was she dressed in a uniform?"

"Hard to tell. Didn't look like it. She had on an army parka, but her pants and boots didn't look regulation."

"I'll give you a couple hundred if you can give me a list of times and dates they've gotten a room. You will have to provide ID on the vehicle. I'll give you an extra hundred if they pay by credit card and you can give me the lady's name."

Bob demanded money up front. The colonel didn't agree. "I pay on delivery."

"Yeah. That's the shit you gave me last time. I never saw a dime. Make a five-day reservation right now and give me your credit card information, or I'll tell the lady and her boyfriend that you're watching them."

The colonel remembered the "last time." It had been a sharp, up-and-coming lieutenant colonel who'd been banging one of the nurses and angling for the colonel's job. The colonel caved. Bob had already found the payment record for Dr. Sybil Erypet. She and her boyfriend had been the only guests the previous week.

Wednesday, January 24, 2018
Guest Quarters, Fort McCoy
7:00 a.m. CST

Sybil was in her bathroom, toweling off after her morning shower when her phone rang.

"Sybil, it's Grant. We got a positive on our antibody concentration test. The standard Swiss test, even with a Southern blot, was negative."

Sybil rubbed the sleep from her eyes. "Can you back up and give that to me again?"

Grant explained that Mrs. Anderson's blood was negative for the virus by the standard tests, but his new test—the one that used Frank's antibodies to concentrate the virus—was positive. The control samples of Frank's antibodies were negative. "It means Mrs. Anderson is a carrier, a regular Typhoid Mary."

Sybil dropped her towel. "Oh my God," she said as the implications sunk in. "There could be others like her spreading Zürich Fever across the state, despite our quarantine and testing. Will it be difficult to use your new test to screen people who've been exposed?"

There was a pause before Grant answered. "The concentration step adds another eight hours to the test, and a lab tech can only set up about thirty tests a day. I've only got two lab techs. How many tests will you need to run?"

"The extra time will delay the test results a day. That's not good. Sixty tests a day will handle what we have now, but if this gets out of Kirby, we might need hundreds of samples run per day."

"We could cut the manpower requirements if we prepare test tubes coated with antibody ahead of time. There might be other ways around this, but I'll have to spend some time thinking about it," Grant said. "Call me again tomorrow and maybe I'll have something."

Sybil thought about the consequences. They had asymptomatic carriers for a potentially fatal virus, carriers who may not have been quarantined. They could spread the virus all over the state. *Fuck, all over the country. God help us if that's true.* She picked up her phone and called Sam.

CHAPTER 19

FRANK IS OUT

Wednesday, January 24, 2018
Kirby Motel
6:00 p.m. CST

Frank lifted himself off the bed on one elbow and glanced out the window of Room 221. It was six o'clock and already dark out. The motel room had been transformed into a hospital room. With his gun still hidden in the cubbyhole above the closet ceiling, he thanked God they hadn't moved him to the field hospital yet.

He looked at Tony and shook his head. The guy had tubes in both arms and his port, an oxygen tube in his nose, a feeding tube in his mouth, and a drain tube in his bladder. *Poor bastard.* No way could you call that living. Blood-stained fluid drained from Tony's eyes, nose, and ears. Frank could handle Tony's nosebleeds, but the thin trickle of blood from the corner of his eyes and the bloody urine draining through the tube to a bag on the side of the bed got to him.

He couldn't carry the guy with him when he made his break. What was the point? Tony looked like he'd be dead in a couple of days anyway. Then why did he feel guilty? Two weeks ago, the worst things he'd ever done—even for work—were threatening people, beating up guys who hadn't paid up, and maybe breaking a leg on somebody. Since then, he'd ordered Louis to be killed, he'd tried to hold two women hostages, and now he was going to abandon his best friend.

Wickert and Grant said they'd move him to the field hospital tomorrow. His viral counts were low enough that he wouldn't be a threat to others. If the counts kept decreasing, they'd move him to the base hospital in another week. For what? To try him, convict him, and sentence him to life in prison without parole? Grant would keep him in prison and suck blood out of him for years. His life wouldn't be much better than Tony's. They could shove that up their collective asses.

He'd been on his best behavior for two weeks, and some of the nurses and guards seemed to buy his story that the murder was Tony's doing. His escape had to be tonight, before they transferred him to the field hospital. Once there, he wouldn't have access to his street clothes or the gun. No way in hell could he escape in this weather wearing a fucking hospital gown. It made his ass feel cold just thinking about it.

He'd make a break when Smythe, the nurse with the softest heart and weakest mind, took over duty tonight. A middle-aged woman, Smythe had the worst case of the uglies he'd ever seen. A chubby face, a poorly healed scar across her left cheek, and acne covering the rest of her face—God, what an awful combo. Her face reminded him of a potholed road that had cost him a tire and realignment. That's probably why she'd fallen for it when he'd flirted with her. She'd even started to wear a little makeup.

They still had him handcuffed to the bed by one hand. No way could he get a good night's sleep like that. It did make it easy to give people a line of poor-me complaints, and other nurses had swallowed it. He'd polished his whining technique such that even Grant might cut him some slack. He should get an Oscar for the performances he'd given the past couple of nights. With luck, Nurse Smythe would fall for it tonight.

Midnight medications would be the perfect time. That's when they gave him his last daily pills for the virus. While he was planning, he heard the door open and pretended to be asleep. Nurse Smythe walked in and gently shook his shoulder. "Are you awake, Frank?"

Why the hell do they ask stupid questions like that? "Huh? What? Sure. Nobody can sleep chained to this godforsaken bed like I am." He faked a big yawn. "Can't you take the cuff off just for tonight? Or at least loosen it? I can't sleep worth shit tied up like this."

She looked like she might do it, but her supervisor stuck her head in the door and asked if there was a problem. Frank waited until the door shut again before he told Smythe, "I swear, you've got the touch. You're gentler than the other nurses. You understand what it's like to be this sick." He pretended to try to sit up, moaned a couple times, and held a hand over where he thought a kidney might be.

One of the docs had asked him yesterday if he had any pain there. He didn't know if this Zürich shit caused kidney pain, but Tony had often bitched about it hurting to the left of his backbone. It was worth a try.

Smythe ate it up. Even passed a soothing hand over his forehead.

"You know, you've got a deeper beauty than any of those bimbos and Hollywood models," he told her.

That might have been a mistake. He didn't think anybody could believe shit that deep. She stared at him. "What are you after?"

Yup. It was a mistake. She was suspicious. Frank assumed the most doleful expression he could manage and looked up at her. "What do you mean? In case I don't make it, I just wanted to let you know how much I appreciate you." He followed that by grabbing his side again and groaning.

Smythe seemed to relax a little. "I'm sorry, but they warned me that prisoners would try to manipulate us." She passed her hand gently over his forehead. "Nobody has ever said anything that nice to me before."

Dodged that bullet. Frank knew he'd have to tone the flattery down a bit in the future.

He asked if she could take the handcuff off so he could make a bathroom run. She was supposed to have a male nurse present to do that, and man, they had some big bruisers here. Those guys didn't take any guff at all. One of them looked like he'd break Frank in two at the first excuse.

Good old Smythe gave in when he told her he had diarrhea and didn't think he could hold it any longer. He could see her thinking of the mess she'd have to clean up. She rushed out of the room and came back with a key fast—must have rustled it up from somebody. Frank saw the pocket she put it in. He made his trip, relieved himself, groaned a few times for sound effects, and returned to bed. Smythe cuffed him, but she didn't do it as tightly.

She gave him his pill and water and got all concerned when he pretended to have a coughing fit.

"Sorry about that," he said. "Water went down the wrong tube. It happens a lot because of the way I'm tied up." He coughed a couple more times and said weakly, "Makes coughing hard, too."

He lifted the key while Smythe patted his back and held a spit tray under his mouth. It wasn't difficult, but he got a mild smack on his hand when his hand roamed over her dress. He figured he'd tried to feel her up so often she looked forward to it. Apparently, she didn't think about the key.

She'd slapped his hand and walloped him on the head the first time he'd felt her up. She'd gradually reduced that to a desultory pat on the hands, and a few times she pretended she didn't notice. He suspected she appreciated any attention she could get. As she left, she turned and waved at him before she closed the door. The flattery had worked after all.

He unlocked the handcuffs a couple of minutes later.

Some idiot had washed and sterilized Frank's street clothes and put them in the cheap dresser the TV sat on. That was stupid. He would have been stuck in the motel and field hospital if they'd tossed them.

Betty and Cindy had already been moved to the field hospital. Tony wouldn't snitch on him—he was out of it. Frank stole out of bed, dressed in his civvies and coat, and retrieved his gun from the closet. He went through the air lock next to the door inside the room, peeked out the room door, and scoped the hall.

Shit. An MP on his rounds was doing bed checks. Frank closed the door and tiptoed back to bed. He made sure the sheets covered his clothes, and at the last minute hooked one cuff over his hand so it looked like he was still cuffed to the bed. The MP's route would make Frank's room one of the last he checked. He pretended to sleep when he heard the door open. The MP, that lazy coward, didn't even bother coming through the air lock inside the room. Probably afraid Tony would infect him. He peered through the plastic sheeting of the air lock, checked something off in a notebook, and left.

Frank started to count when he heard the door close. When he got to six hundred about ten minutes later, he slipped out of bed, went through the air locks, and peeked down the hall. The hallway was clear. It took only seconds for him to get to the stairwell at the end of the hall, take the stairs to the first floor, and ease out the side door.

He stayed in the shadows of the motel until he could sneak across the parking lot past the field hospital. His street clothes didn't cut it in central Wisconsin. He'd learned that the first day in Kirby, but he had other things on his mind tonight, hadn't even thought about the cold. That didn't last long. TV News said it would be twenty below zero. His toes were frozen, his ears burned, and so did his nose and fingers as he hid in the shadows. Even his ass was cold, and that was well padded. He stamped his feet and waved his arms—all in the shadows—when he started to shiver.

He bolted for the highway when he couldn't stand it anymore. Somebody might see him, but that wouldn't be as bad as losing his toes. And to hell with worrying about the tracks he left through the snow. By the time anybody spotted those, he'd be long gone. Tracks weren't a problem once he got to the highway—the snow had been cleared, and salt and sunshine had melted what Ed's plow had missed.

The highway was still closed to traffic, so at least he didn't have to dodge headlights and cars. Once across the highway, he made his way to a house he'd watched since the day he and Tony were locked in the motel room. The only people around the house were an elderly couple. An old Arctic Cat was parked in front of their detached garage.

The sidewalk was still covered in snow, but the couple's driveway had been cleared of all but hard-packed snow. The house was a white clapboard, two-story building with a large porch that covered the front of the house, with four wooden steps leading up to it. The snow covering the steps was undisturbed. Not a footprint. If he went to the front door, his footsteps in the snow would be like a red light telling the cops to look here first. He followed the driveway and moved rapidly to the back of the house before he became a block of ice.

With every step, he heard the irritating squeak of stepping on packed snow in subzero weather. It was like crushing a nest full of baby mice with his shoes. The squeak traveled right up his spine. Or maybe he imagined the mice running up his pants. The noise made him feel like a freaking popsicle.

Navigation was easy. The moonlight and snow made the night so bright he could have driven a car without headlights. The back steps were clear and the door to the small porch unlocked. So was the door to the house. Man, people in small towns were sloppy about safety. *It probably keeps them from freezing to death searching for their keys.*

He let his eyes adjust to the dim light in the kitchen, but it wasn't enough. He turned on the lights and found keys hanging on the wall near the back door. Next to the sink, he found a drawer with knives. Damned sharp ones, too.

Take this one step at a time. Let my fingers, ears, and toes thaw. Make sure I've got the keys I need. When he had feeling back in his fingers, he collected the keys, turned out the lights, and slipped outside. It took a few tries to find the key for the snowmobile. His fingers and ears were turning to ice. He turned the key farther than he'd meant to. The engine sputtered and coughed.

Frank almost had a stroke. He scrambled off the machine, slid around the corner of the detached garage, and plastered himself against the wall. The fingers of his right hand felt something, but they were so damned cold he didn't trust them. He slid sideways and found the edge of a door.

Moving a little farther, he found the doorknob. It turned and the door opened. In the silence of the snowy night, the slight creak of the door opening sounded like a claxon to Frank's ears. He ducked into the garage, closed the door, and leaned against the side of a car until his heart stopped pounding. Then he felt his way to a set of three windows in the garage door and watched nearby houses for activity. No lights went on. No doors opened. No dogs barked. He started to breathe again. He'd been so scared he hadn't realized he was holding his breath.

As he scanned the houses for signs of life, he thought of what he'd need besides the snowmobile. At the top of the list was warm clothing. Money was essential, and food. The old guy who lived here probably had all of that. Money and ID would be on his dresser or in his pants.

As Frank's hand moved to open the side door, his frozen fingers brushed against the light switch. The lights blazed on. He made a few frantic swats to turn them off and missed. By the time he found the light switch again, he'd noticed tools and junk sitting on a bench attached to the back of the garage. *What the hell?* The lights were on. He might as well look through the tools. Maybe there'd be something he could use. Hammers, screw drivers, a couple of saws—those wouldn't be of much use. A couple rolls of duct tape? Those might come in handy. He grabbed them and headed to the door.

Outside the garage, he peered around the corner and checked the neighboring houses for lights again. Still nothing. He walked back to the house as though he owned the place, in case somebody was watching.

The money, ID, and the warm clothing he needed were most likely in the bedroom, on or in the couple's dresser. If he did this right he wouldn't have to kill them. As things stood with the law, he could get away with blaming Tony for killing Louie. They'd send him up for ten years maybe, but he'd be out in less than half of that on good behavior and parole. Kill this couple, and he'd be in prison for life if he got caught.

He found warm clothes—boots, gloves, a coat—in a closet near the back door. In the bedroom, he'd be quiet and see if he could get the old guy's wallet without waking them up. If he woke up, Frank would tie them up with duct tape.

He took the stairs slowly, testing each step for creaks and squeaks before taking the next one. The door to the bedroom opened and Frank ducked back down a couple of steps. The old man shuffled across the hall into the bathroom. Didn't look like he'd even opened his eyes.

Frank got to the bathroom door, put his back to the wall, and listened as the old guy peed. It sounded like a dribble. He must have had prostate problems. *Damn.* He hoped he wouldn't have that when he was that age.

As granddad toddled past him headed for bed, Frank tapped him on the shoulder and shoved the pistol's barrel into his back. "Keep quiet and nobody gets hurt. Put your hands behind you."

His victim gasped and woke up fully. Frank had to repeat his order before the geezer put his arms behind his back. "What, what," he babbled. Duct-taping the hands together took only a couple of seconds.

The old guy kept up with the "what" until Frank explained what was going to happen. "Now we're going into the bedroom," he said. "You're going to get in bed with your wife, and I'm going to duct tape your feet together. Got that?"

The old guy nodded. Frank flipped on the lights as they entered the bedroom. A pile of quilts and blankets nearly obscured the woman. The old guy needed help getting into bed, but his wife slept through it. Frank wouldn't have found her except for her snoring. She slept so soundly he'd had her hands duct-taped together in front of her before she woke up and looked around. She seemed too confused to ask questions and settled down when her husband told her to relax.

Frank got their attention. "Stay in bed, be quiet, and I won't hurt anybody. I'm going to get something to eat and leave. Wait for daylight before you try to get loose and call for help. Got that?"

The old man nodded.

A phone sat on a night table sitting next to the bed. With a quick jerk, Frank ripped the connection from the wall. To be safe, he tore out the wire and pocketed it.

The wallet was on the dresser. One credit card, driver's license, and thirty bucks. Not much, but enough if the snowmobile had a full tank of gas. The dresser reminded him of how cold he'd been. He opened the drawers from the top down. His first major find was an unopened package labeled "thermal underwear." It was long underwear, both top and bottom, with a thick checkerboard pattern woven into it. *Insulated.* Frank cocked his head to the side and shrugged. *That sounds good.* He undressed and put the thermal underwear on. It was long in the sleeves and legs, and tight around the waist, but he felt warm before he even got his pants back on.

His next find was a pair of woolen socks. Once he got those on, he couldn't get his feet back in his shoes. He remembered the boots by the back door and prodded the husband with the pistol. "What size shoes you wear?"

"Huh? Size twelve."

Frank wore ten and a half. The boots would do.

"Stay warm in bed until dawn. I've torn out the phones. Sit here and wait until the sheriff's deputies come by. You can tell them all about me then."

Frank clambered down the stairs. He was famished. Reluctant to turn on the kitchen lights for too long, lest someone see them and get curious, he cooked by the reflected light from outside and a small light over the stove. A couple of fried eggs, a slab of bacon, and toast didn't take long.

He went through the closet near the back door. He collected a hoodie, a scarf, and a bunch of insulated clothes: coveralls, gloves, lace-up boots—it felt good to get his feet out of his tight shoes—and a cap with ear flaps.

Everything was too big for him, but the coveralls slid easily over the rest of his new clothing. He was sweating by the time he'd put everything on. For the first time, stepping outside into bitter cold felt good. After he adjusted the scarf to cover the lower part of his face, he felt downright comfy.

The snowmobile started on the first try. It didn't take long to figure out that the throttle was on the right-hand handle and the brake on the left. Frank drove to the end of the driveway and looked up and down the highway. The only lights were a couple of streetlights, the motel's advertising sign, and a light over the field hospital entrance. He veered left and headed toward Ed's. That's where all the snowmobile trails were said to start, but that's what the army and cops would be expecting. He reversed course and headed north toward the junction of Highway 12 and County O.

Once past the last section of plowed road, he let the snowmobile rip through the ditch of County O. That didn't last long. His nose was numb. Moisture from his breath collected in the scarf and froze. The frozen scarf itself felt like a piece of medieval armor. Ice built up in his eyelashes and eyebrows, and blurred his vision. He soon couldn't open his left eye because of the ice. *Jesus.* It must have been thirty below.

Frank cut back on the throttle and putted into the countryside. He gradually increased speed as his eyelashes thawed, and he could open both eyes. He didn't push the throttle past halfway. There was no point in escaping if he just turned himself into a block of ice or had a stupid accident.

MRS. ANDERSON'S SAMPLES

Monday, January 22, 2018
Guest Quarters, Fort McCoy
8:00 a.m. CST

Sybil dressed and, before she left her apartment, called Grant to ask if he had more ideas for testing possible carriers of the Zürich Virus. He said he hadn't been able to think of a different approach to testing the samples, but perhaps concentrations of the virus would be higher in samples other than blood. Since it was mainly a respiratory disease, maybe nasal samples would be better. It was also related distantly to both Ebola and coronaviruses. Ebola was primarily spread by contact with infected skin, and the coronaviruses that caused common colds could be spread by touch. Skin samples might work too.

"Do you think Mrs. Anderson will let you collect samples from other body sites?" he asked Sybil.

"That could be a problem. Mrs. Anderson likes Nurse Jeager, but she's not fond of me. If Anderson believes you or I ordered the collection, she might demand a warrant. If what you want collected isn't invasive, I think Tom—ah, Corporal Jones—can talk her into it. She enjoys giving him a hard time so much she might allow him to collect simple swabs where she'd throw a nurse out of her room.

If you're thinking of collecting rectal or vaginal swabs, I think you can forget it. Jones would refuse to collect those."

"I'd like to collect them from her nose, mouth, and hands. Why Jones? Isn't he your driver?"

"Don't ask. She likes him and he understands her." At least she might agree to those samples, and Tom wouldn't freak about collecting them.

She gave Tom his new job a few minutes later. The poor guy went rigid in front of Sybil's desk when she suggested he collect the samples.

"No deal. I don't even know how to collect samples, and that old lady might get frisky with her hands. Why don't *you* take the damned samples if they're that important?"

The phone rang and Sybil ignored it. She put the virology text she had been reading on her desk and looked Tom in the eyes. "I would collect the samples if I thought she'd let me. Mrs. Anderson likes you and she hates me. She won't let me near her, might even demand we get a warrant. We don't have time for that."

"This is horse shit."

Sybil had never tried wheedling, but then she'd never ordered a lover to collect samples. "C'mon, Tom. It may be horse crap, but the problem is serious. You understand the old bat, and we really need these samples. It's a matter of national security."

"I've heard that so often it's wearing a little thin."

He sounded whiny. So much for wheedling. "I know it sounds like an excuse, but thousands, maybe millions of people will be put at risk if we don't find a simple way to identify carriers."

Jones gave her a calculating look. "Have the Swiss mentioned carriers?"

"No, they haven't." Sybil leaned back in her chair. "But they're having problems that could be caused by carriers, and they have so many infected people to track, they might not realize carriers are their problem. We've already proven Mrs. Anderson is a carrier, but the tests Grant had to use take too long. If any of these samples are positive by the PCR test, it will completely change how we test people for the virus."

Jones paced back and forth and ran a hand through his hair. "But damn it, she pinches!"

Sybil thought of the countless women who put up with unwanted sexual advances from men. Tom got no sympathy. "Tell her to behave," Sibyl said. "Tell her if she pinches or grabs you, the doctor will get a warrant to collect samples from her large intestine by colonoscopy. She'll have to drink a gallon of vile liquid that will give her the trots for days, and then they'll run a tube three feet up her butt."

"They'd do that?"

"No, but I thought you were looking for ways to make her behave. One of the nurses taking care of Anderson will show you how to take the oral and nasal samples."

The phone rang again and Sybil ignored it. "It's easy. You just put a swab in the nose, mouth, and on the skin, and roll it around. The nurse will show you how."

Fort McCoy Hospital
9:00 p.m. CST

Because she'd been exposed to the Zürich Virus, Mrs. Anderson had a private room, but in other respects it was standard for the base hospital. It was painted a cheerful pale yellow and smelled strongly of disinfectant. She was sitting in a recliner watching *Jeopardy* on television when Jones arrived.

He coughed to get her attention as he entered. Dressed in Tyveks, surgical mask, and gloves, he felt like a Pillsbury Doughboy.

He stood just out of her reach. "Mrs. Anderson, I've been ordered to collect samples for virus testing."

Mrs. Anderson turned off the TV with the remote. "Call me Lydia. What's your first name?"

Jones looked at the floor and back at Lydia. This was already going in the wrong direction. "Tom. I'd rather we keep this on a professional level. Please call me Corporal Jones."

"Why Jonesy, you look worried. Why are you dressed in that weird getup?"

"Nurse Jeager has come down with Zürich Fever. The only person she could have caught it from is you. They used a new, extra-sensitive test on your blood. It proved you carry the virus."

Lydia's face fell at mention of Nurse Jeager. "That poor girl." Lydia held a tissue to her nose and sniffed. "She was always so nice. And you're sure she caught the virus from me? I haven't had a sick day in years."

"That's what they think. You were positive for the virus on a new, super-sensitive test."

"But I'm not sick. I haven't been sick since I had the flu last fall."

"You remember Typhoid Mary? She spread typhoid to fifty-one people, but she was never sick herself. Now, I only need to get swabs from your nose, mouth, and the skin of your hand. I won't use a needle—and you won't pinch."

"Party pooper." A disheartened-looking Lydia agreed to the terms, and Jones collected the skin and oral samples. When he inserted a swab in her nose, she laid a hand on his thigh. He glared at her.

"Just steadying you. You're bouncing all over with that swab. Your hand is shaking."

He disagreed, but he didn't want her to volunteer to steady his hand either. He continued and completed the sample collection.

A nurse watched from the doorway and closed the door behind him as he left the room. In the hallway, she sprayed disinfectant on the tubes the sample swabs were in and placed them in a plastic bag. She sprayed disinfectant on Jones's Tyveks and handed him a form after he'd removed the protective gear. "Sign this on the bottom. It states you collected the samples from Mrs. Lydia Anderson." She giggled. "Was she a little frisky with the hands again?"

Tom glared at the nurse and ignored her question. "I'm out of the sample-collecting business. Be sure these get to Grant Farnsworth in the lab and let Dr. Erypet know the samples were delivered."

He walked quickly out of the ward, but not before he heard another nurse snicker.

Thursday, January 25, 2018
Sybil's office, Fort McCoy Hospital
9:30 a.m CST

Sybil picked up the phone. It had been ringing wildly as she walked into her office.

"Dr. Erypet, this is Colonel Williams. Don't you ever answer your phone?"

"What's the problem, Colonel?"

"One of the killers escaped. He terrorized an elderly couple, stole an old snowmobile, and beat it out of Kirby. We're trying to determine which way he went."

Sybil was speechless.

"Are you there, Erypet?"

"I'm here, Colonel. This is a disaster. Do you think you can catch his ass before he makes it to a town?"

"What do you mean, *I* catch him? You're supposed to oversee everything pertaining to the Zürich Virus, Erypet. I'm holding you responsible."

"The MPs, doctors, and nurses caring for and guarding Frank are your people, Colonel. Catching him will be the State Patrol and Sheriff Department's job. The Sheriff's Department is guarding the snowmobile trails. I'm a physician and scientist, not a guard dog or a bloodhound." She hung up on the colonel and called Grant.

"Grant," she said. "I have some bad news. Frank has escaped and beat it out of town."

She heard something drop and quiet swearing when she mentioned Frank. "Sorry," Grant said. "I dropped the phone. Did I hear you correctly? Frank is on the loose?"

"Yes. The State Patrol and Sheriff's Department will be hunting for him. Stay near a phone. I may need to have you take Tyveks and other biosecurity equipment to the cops and show them how to use it."

Thursday, January 25, 2018
Fort McCoy
10:00 a.m. CST

Colonel Williams invited Dr. Wickert to have a seat in his office. "Doc, what is this I hear about a civilian carrier of the Zürich Virus being admitted to our hospital?"

The doctor's face suggested he didn't agree with that description of events. "Yes, Mrs. Anderson. She appears to be a carrier. It came as quite a surprise. Her blood samples had been negative for the virus by the standard Swiss test."

"You know, Doctor, one of our nurses has succumbed to the

virus. She was infected by Mrs. Anderson because of the sloppy way this project is being run."

Wickert sat up straight and his face turned red. "Nothing has been sloppy, Colonel. You can't blame—"

"If Dr. Erypet had taken reasonable precautions, we wouldn't have a sick nurse, and we wouldn't have the problems encountered because of a carrier on base. There was no sensible reason to bring Mrs. Anderson on base. I'm going to file a complaint, and I'd like you to sign it, Doctor."

"It wasn't her fault—"

"Nice to see you understand, Doctor. Nobody would want you to put your advancement in question or have that night with the stripper at the SleepyTime Motel put on your record."

The doctor's face fell. He said nothing.

"And did you know that Dr. Erypet has been fraternizing with Jones? A corporal! They've been shacked up at the SleepyTime. It's a cheap, run-down excuse for a motel, as you probably remember. I'll feel safer, and I'm sure this project will be run more efficiently and safely, if we have military personnel in charge of all phases. I don't trust academics like Erypet."

Colonel Williams sat back in his chair, his eyes daring Dr. Wickert to disagree with him. That slimy little sneak who managed the motel was coming in handy, even if he was greedy as hell.

Thursday, January 25, 2018
CDC, Atlanta, Georgia
11:30 a.m. EST

Sam Barker was at his desk, reading a report from Sybil when his phone rang. He answered.

"Doctor Barker, Colonel Sean Williams of Fort McCoy here. How are you today, sir?"

"How can I help you, Colonel?" Sam answered warily.

"We've had a few problems with your Dr. Erypet. A carrier of the Zürich Virus was moved to the base when there was no good reason for her to be here. The carrier infected one of our best nurses, and now Erypet has let that murderous thug Frank escape. She's also been shacking up with an enlisted man. These are things the military takes very seriously, and I'd feel safer if the project to control the Zürich Virus were put under control of military personnel. We have several army doctors here, and if they can't handle it, we can bring in army scientists."

Sam took a deep breath. Sybil was blunt, short on patience, and didn't take crap from anyone—not a good combination for someone working in a huge bureaucracy—but she was rarely wrong about infectious medicine, and she had little to do with housing prisoners. The colonel's phone call sounded like a brewing turf battle. Sam had been through these before, and with the Zürich Virus wreaking havoc in Europe and already in the United States, the CDC had Congress's ear in a way they'd never had before.

Sam adopted a belligerent tone to his voice. "I'll be happy to talk to Dr. Erypet about your concerns, but your suggestion is way out of line. The CDC is the department properly charged by Congress with handling infectious problems. The army doesn't have the scientific expertise or experience to control epidemics. Dr. Erypet is one of the best people we have, and if a criminal has escaped, that's got nothing to do with her. I'll get back to you later, Colonel."

"Then I'll have to take this up the chain of command."

"Do that, Colonel. I'm fielding panicked calls from congressmen daily, and I'm scheduled to discuss the virus with two congressional committees and the Joint Chiefs this week. I'll be happy to mention your concerns to the army secretary."

Sam hung up. Williams would have to be an unusually dense officer to take this further.

Sam asked his secretary to get Sybil on the line. She was busy but promised to call back within the hour. When she finally called, Sam asked, "What's the skinny on Colonel Williams at McCoy?"

"Oh, him," Sybil said. "He tried to take over the project once, but I straightened him out, or I thought I did. I know he'd feel better if the army was in control here. He tried to shift the blame for a murderer's escape onto me, but I thought I made it clear to him that security personnel were the army's responsibility. Why do you ask?"

"He's a problem now. He's saying that you improperly put Mrs. Anderson on base where she infected one of the army nurses."

"If you're reading your reports, Sam, you know I had no choice about Mrs. Anderson. The old bat said she wouldn't follow quarantine procedures unless we forced her to. The Swiss hadn't reported a carrier state, and we had no reason to suspect one at the time. Mrs. Anderson was free of virus according to the standard test. It was only because of Grant's new version of the test that we proved Anderson is a carrier. The colonel has his head up his ass."

Sam smiled to himself. "That's what I thought. Watch your back around him and try a little flattery. He's the sort who might respond to ego-stroking." Sam told her how he'd handled the call from Williams. He then asked, "Have you been fraternizing with Corporal Jones?"

Sam thought he heard a gasp. The line was silent for a moment until Sybil said, "None of your goddamned business, Sam. I'm not in the military. For that matter, Tom is probably smarter than the colonel. He speaks fluent French, has a bachelor's in philosophy, and a master's in European history. His literary agent is shopping two of his books around to publishers."

"I should have guessed he'd be quite a guy if he has your interest. Watch—"

"Christ. This means they're going to raise hell with Tom too. Williams is a damned snake in the grass."

"Like I was going to say, be more careful. And for God's sake, get a different motel. The colonel has somebody watching the one you're using. Jones is in the National Guard. He may be in the reserves or close to shifting to them. That will limit how unpleasant Williams can make life for him."

Sybil agreed and Sam hung up. God, he hated these turf battles. Maybe a walk would settle his nerves. He grabbed his coat and left his office, telling his secretary he'd be gone for half an hour.

CHAPTER 21

THE GETAWAY

Thursday, January 25, 2018
Fort McCoy Hospital
11:00 a.m. CST

Grant watched his lab tech leave his office and looked at the results he'd been handed. It looked like they'd found a way to identify carriers, but a lot more work needed to be done to prove it. He called Sybil.

"I've got good news and bad news. Mrs. Anderson's nasal swabs were positive using antibody concentration of the virus and the Swiss PCR test. From there, the virus can be spread by sneezing and coughing, but it simplifies detection of carriers."

"We'll have to test a hundred or more other patients to make sure you can consistently replicate these results. You've made a critical breakthrough if this stands up."

"That's the hitch," Grant said. "We'll have to contract out to have antibody-coated tubes produced, and it could take us months to test enough infected people. I'll bet the Swiss have sufficient patients, antibodies, and suspects to do a study in a couple of days."

Sybil promised him she'd call Sam Barker with the news. "We'll let Sam negotiate with the Swiss. Assuming they back up your results, you'd better gear up to test large numbers of nasal swabs. At least the samples will be easier to collect than blood. Do you have the equipment to automate the Swiss PCR test?"

"No," Grant said. "At best, what we have here is a small research lab. But there are commercial labs that can make the tubes and do the PCR."

"I'd rather keep it in-house, if we can," Sybil said. "We'll have to test all of the people on that bus the stupid state patrol let through. If any of them are positive for the virus, we'll have to start wholesale testing in Tomah and all of the little towns around here. That could easily be over twenty thousand samples."

Jesus Christ. Grant looked around his office and, through a window, glanced into his lab. He didn't know what planet Sybil was on, but he was still firmly planted on planet Earth. No way in hell could his lab run one hundred samples a day, let alone a thousand. It would take the technological equivalent of a moon shot for him to gear up to run twenty thousand samples in a month, let alone in a week. "Sybil, we couldn't run that many samples in a year. I'll get back to you with a list of commercial labs."

He was so stunned he forgot to ask how the hunt for Frank was going. Grant had barely put the phone down when it rang again. It was Deputy Krueger.

"Grant, what gear do we need to chase and arrest Frank?"

"Gear?" Thinking of commercial labs and their automated equipment, Grant had a hard time switching topics. He drew a blank.

"Safety equipment," Krueger said.

"You'll need two layers of Tyveks, surgical masks, face shields. Do you have a lead on him?"

"Not yet. We expect to hear something soon. A plane is up looking for tracks."

"This could be complicated. I'll come to Kirby with the equipment and we can talk it over. Give me half an hour. Have other deputies start looking for him, but tell them to stay ten feet away from him if they corner him."

Grant stopped at Sybil's office and asked if he could borrow her JLTV and driver. She was on the phone but nodded in agreement. Returning to his office, he grabbed his coat and boots and went to the cafeteria in search of Tom. He found him toying with a cheese Danish and reading the paper.

"Hi, Tom. Got time to talk?"

"Sure. I'm hiding out from my sergeant. Scuttlebutt has it the colonel wants to reassign me to cleaning waste oil tanks in the motor pool. I've done that before. It's the dirtiest job on base." He turned a page of his newspaper. "But it won't happen until Sarge finds me."

"Frank has escaped. He stole a snowmobile from an elderly couple and beat it out of Kirby. Deputy Krueger is frothing at the bit to chase him, but he needs biosafety gear to get near him. I need wheels and a driver to deliver the gear to him. Are you up for it?"

Tom shrugged. "Sure, as long as Krueger and his pistol stay between us and Frank. I'm no good at dodging knives or bullets."

"We shouldn't be within a mile of Frank. I'll give the gear to Krueger with instructions on how to wear it, and we're done."

As they cleared the Fort McCoy entrance, Tom said, "I had to wear the Tyveks and the rest of that gear once. I can't imagine trying to drive a snowmobile wearing that stuff. The faceplate or goggles are guaranteed to fog up, and the Tyveks will be torn. The boots and boot covers will get in the way and be torn up too."

Grant was quiet for a moment. "I was worried about that, but standard protocols require they wear the gear. It doesn't make sense on a snowmobile. I'll suggest the deputies wear the biosafety equipment only after they've got Frank cornered."

"So, we'll have to trail behind Krueger with the biosafety stuff until they catch him?"

"Yeah," Grant said. "Cops aren't biologists. I should be there to supervise their use of the protective gear. This job just got more complicated."

In Kirby, they found Krueger pacing back and forth outside the entrance to the field hospital. Grant explained the problems with the biosafety gear. Krueger pointed at the JLTV. "Can that machine take a snowmobile trail?"

"No sweat," Tom said, "unless Frank has a fifty-caliber. With the chains on, this beast can go through almost any terrain you've got here, except cranberry bogs. Has anyone figured out which way he went?"

"It looked like there were fresh tracks in the ditch beside County O headed east out of town. Fort McCoy put an observation plane up. They'll find him fast if he stayed next to the road."

Krueger's radio crackled. A moment later he ran for a snowmobile near the JLTV, waved to Tom and Grant, and yelled, "Follow me." Grant noticed that Krueger rode like a pro, a pro who expected bumps on the trail. He kept his arms bent and was almost standing on his machine instead of sitting, allowing his arms and knees to act as shock absorbers.

Grant and Tom jumped into the JLTV and followed Krueger east on County O. The tire chains clanking on the road provided a background beat to their conversation. "Okay," Grant said as he buckled himself in. "Fill me in on what this machine can do."

"Most of the trails around here are old railroad beds," Tom said. "Those are wide, the snow is packed, and the trails are groomed. This buggy can handle those and any snow drifts around here. The trails between taverns could give us a problem if they go through swamps or woods with close-set trees. Otherwise, this thing can take anything nature can throw at it. We're even armored against IEDs."

Grant snorted. "Kind of overkill, isn't it?"

"Yeah. I think either the Humvees were all in the shop, or

Colonel Williams wanted to impress Sybil—er, Dr. Erypet. JLTVs have great heaters, and she complained once about the cold when she first got here."

Krueger pulled off the road and roared into the ditch, following Frank's tracks. The steering skis on either side of his snowmobile lofted waves of snow into the air. Tom slowed and steered the JLTV through a large snowbank that marked the end of the plowed section of the county road. The JLTV paused, lurched forward, tipped from side to side, and waddled through the packed, crusted snow. Tom followed Krueger but stayed on the road.

With a rooster tail high in the air behind him, Krueger sailed along the ditch, throwing plumes of snowy on either side. Grant grabbed the safety handle to steady himself as Tom did his best to keep up. Grant was thrown around the cabin as far as the safety belts allowed. He told himself he wasn't scared, even though he held his breath at every drift. His heart pounded, and his legs and arms were tense. He was able to relax by watching Tom drive. The guy was like a teenager on an amusement ride, grinning and whooping as they cleared each drift until they fishtailed out the other side.

Finally, about five miles down the road, Krueger turned into a pine forest. Tom pointed the JLTV toward the trees and stopped. The trees, planted in rows, all had trunks about six inches in diameter. There was little underbrush between them. "Pine plantation?" Grant asked.

"Yup." Tom paused. They'd be entering the plantation at a right angle to the rows. "These trees are too big to roll over. They'll make it a tight fit, but I think there's room for us. When we cross the ditch, we might get hung up coming out of it. Should I chance it?"

"Go for it," Grant said. "We don't have a choice."

The JLTV didn't even pause as they climbed from the ditch to the woods. They made it through a gap where a tree had been removed and followed Krueger's tracks. Krueger still appeared to be sailing along through the woods. The JLTV couldn't match that as it squeezed between trees and crashed through low-hanging branches. It rapidly fell behind. A compass on the dashboard indicated they were headed northeast.

"Do you think Frank knows where he's going?" asked Grant.

Tom chuckled. "Hell, I don't know if Krueger knows where he's going. He's either a darn fool or a semi-pro snowmobile racer. He must be bouncing all over. Bounce high enough and a tree branch will knock him out."

"What about Frank? Do you think he's headed somewhere specific, or is he simply running away from us?"

"The only things in this direction are small villages, cranberry bogs, and a national forest. We're likely to get in trouble if he goes through the bogs. Ice in the bogs will be strong enough for a snowmobile, but I doubt it can hold our buggy. He'll go like a bat out of hell if he finds the logging roads, if he knows how to ride a snowmobile."

"How far can he go?"

"Depends how much gas he has. There are no gas stations in the area. A full tank and an old machine, he might make it 150 to 200 miles. He'll be hungry—his last meal at the motel was yesterday, and cold weather really fuels an appetite. If he gets on a logging road, he could head out of the forest looking for food, or go deeper into the forest and hope to find a home or a stocked cabin."

They came to a gravel road, its surface covered with hard-packed snow, the surface shimmering with light where it was melting. Krueger's snowmobile tracks indicated he was riding in the ditch again.

Tom hesitated and turned east onto the road. "Looks like they're headed toward the bogs. See that shine on the road?"

Grant nodded.

"It's a sunny day," Tom said, "and it's melting the snow. It's going to be slippery as all hell. If I'm not careful, we could be upside down in a ditch." He took his foot off the accelerator.

Frank hadn't ridden a snowmobile before. Fear drove him and he learned. But not fast enough. It didn't help that he rode an antique. Frank sat on the machine like he would a chair. He didn't get in a crouch or spread his weight between his legs, butt, and arms. Every bump he hit tossed him into the air. Luckily, he was riding in the ditch again and no longer had to worry about tree branches. The bumps had knocked him off the machine twice. The snow cushioned his fall.

Even with the long lead he had, when he stopped to rest he heard a snowmobile catching up to him. Frank ducked into the woods, crossed two rows of trees, and doubled back. The pines hid him from that damned observation plane, but he had to take it slow. He didn't have a snowmobile helmet. If he went too fast, the bumps tossed him up and tree branches scraped his face, threatening to blind him.

He cursed himself. A helmet had been sitting next to the door in the old couple's house where he stole the snowmobile. He should have grabbed it, but he'd been in a hurry and he hadn't understood its importance.

The trees on the interior rows were trimmed by the first four feet, but the ones at the edge of the forest hadn't been trimmed and their branches reached the ground. Frank found a dense tree overlooking the ditch he'd ridden in earlier. Frank turned off his snowmobile, dismounted—God, it was nice to stretch his legs—crawled under the tree, and pulled out his Glock. No way could he miss at this distance.

Though muffled by the snow, the roar of the approaching snowmobile grew loader. It was that fucking Krueger, and he was coming on fast. He flew past Frank in a blur. Frank pulled the trigger once, but the Glock's sensitive trigger got off four rapid shots. One shot hit Krueger, tore his helmet off, and knocked him off his seat. He lay on his belly in the snow, unmoving, his head turned to one side. Frank did a celebratory fist pump under the tree, crawled to the ditch, and scrambled to his target.

His luck was still with him. Krueger's forehead was barely grazed. Blood oozed from a wound above his right eye and trailed along his nose. He moaned, blinking.

Frank grabbed the deputy's service pistol and shoved it under his belt. "What size shoes you wear?"

It took a few repeats of the question before Krueger came around enough to answer. "Eleven."

Almost his size. He duct-taped the deputy's hands and knees together and stole his boots. Putting on his new pair of boots required taking his gloves off. The weather had warmed up, but temperatures were still subzero and his fingers were freezing by the time he had the boots on. They were a little big, but it no longer felt as though he were wearing snowshoes.

Frank looked at Krueger's helmet. The bullet had smashed the right side. He tossed the helmet away in disgust and ran to where the deputy's snowmobile was idling. It was a newer, faster machine than the piece of shit he'd been riding. It would get better gas mileage and possibly have more gas in the tank.

"You gonna leave me here in this snowbank?" Kreuger yelled. "I'll freeze my balls off."

"Stick your head in the snow. They say cold is good for head wounds." Engine noise drew Frank's attention down the road. "Besides, you've got help coming."

In the distance, a vehicle on the road rumbled into view headed toward him. It looked like one of those Humvees, only taller. It was probably following Krueger. Army.

Shit. They'll have me outgunned by a long sight.

Frank jumped on Krueger's snowmobile and headed away from the oncoming vehicle. He followed his track where he'd left the ditch and turned into the forest.

A few yards farther, his previous track turned right where he'd backtracked to set up his ambush. Now he turned left, parallel to the road. He aimed his machine down the long alley of trees. There weren't as many bumps as before, and he gave the engine more gas. He raced under the interlocking branches above him. They covered him from aerial surveillance. If the guys in the Humvee followed his old trail, it might give him a few minutes of extra time. Whoever followed him would at least be delayed as they helped Krueger and dithered over which track to take—his old one to the right or the new one to the left.

The speed scared him. His heart thundered—he knew he was a rank amateur on a snowmobile. A few hundred yards later, he slowed down and looked behind him. Nothing visible. He slowed to a stop, turned off the snowmobile, and listened. He didn't hear an engine.

He got off the machine and peed on a tree. That wasn't a simple task in the layers of clothes he wore. Taking off his gloves, he dug through the flies of the insulated coveralls, his pants, the thermal underwear, and his regular underwear. *Damn!* His dick almost didn't make it out to fresh air before he let fly. Thank God it was warmer than it had been early in the morning, or he'd have frozen both his hands and his dick. When most of the pressure on his bladder was relieved, he found he'd dribbled down the front of the coveralls. Tony would have never let him forget it. He got back on his machine and moved forward sedately. *Saving gas,* he told himself.

Thursday, January 25, 2018
County Road O
Noon CST

Tom slowed to twenty miles per hour. Something was in the ditch fifty yards ahead. He pointed the JLTV down the road and took his foot off the gas. From the uniform, Grant identified the body as Krueger as they drew closer. Tom tapped the brakes. Even with chains on, the heavy JLTV slipped sideways and continued forward at nearly the same speed. It ran out of momentum and slowed to a halt a few yards past the body.

Krueger sat up as they approached. His phone had fallen out of his pocket, and his helmet had been thrown three yards away. Grant ran to Krueger and helped him up.

"Thanks. Got a knife to cut through this damned duct tape?"

Grant had a pocketknife and cut through the tape.

"That son of a bitch stole my fricking boots," Krueger complained. "My socks are solid ice. I can't feel my toes."

Grant helped him limp to the JLTV and got him inside.

From the woods he heard the roar of a snowmobile. He closed the JLTV door and told Tom to get them out of there, but the sound lowered in decibel and tone, indicating the machine was headed away from them. Tom didn't move the JLTV, and Grant returned to where he'd found Krueger. There, he picked up Krueger's phone and radio.

On the radio, he fingered the "transmit" button. "Officer down.

Officer down. Deputy Krueger has been shot. We're on County O southeast of Warrens."

The radio crackled. "Who is this?"

"Grant Farnsworth. Deputy Krueger was chasing a fugitive. Corporal Jones and I were following in a . . ." JLTV wouldn't mean anything to most people.

"What's Krueger's condition?"

"He might have a concussion. A shot tore off his helmet and grazed his head. We were following in a . . . Humvee." Grant figured everyone knew what those were. "The fugitive fled on a snowmobile. I believe he has two guns, his own and one he took off Krueger. The fugitive is infected with the Zürich Virus. It's important to keep him away from people. Do you have anyone in Warrens?"

"One cruiser is there now. We'll send backup and alert the recon plane. Are you armed?"

"No."

Grant heard a muffled, "Jesus Christ," and other conversation he couldn't make out. "Stay in your Humvee. Keep the motor running and bug out of there if the fugitive returns. A deputy on a snowmobile will be with you shortly. Do not, I repeat, do not follow the fugitive."

For once, Grant heard an order he was happy to obey.

CHAPTER 22

ON THE LAM

Thursday, January 25, 2018
Pine Plantation
2:30 p.m. CST

Frank came to a dirt road cutting across the rows of trees about the time his butt and fingers became sore and tired. His arms and legs were cramping too. With practice, riding the snowmobile had become easier, but he still bounced around plenty. He guessed he'd covered at least five miles since he'd shot Krueger and stolen the better machine. *Time to slow down, take fewer chances, and give my ass a rest.*

He climbed stiffly off his machine. His muscles protested every move. After he stretched a few times, his legs limbered up enough for him to walk to a small clearing where he scanned the sky. The dead silence of the forest seemed creepy after the continuous roar of the snowmobile.

He couldn't see or hear the observation plane, but he knew his respite would be short. Unless he found another snowmobile trail or a road covered with packed snow, sheriff's deputies on the ground would have no trouble tracking him. Even crossing this road would leave tracks in the ditch that could be spotted by air.

It couldn't be helped. He stretched one last time, got on Krueger's snowmobile, and goosed the throttle to climb the side of the ditch and scoot across the road. He looked at the tracks he'd left. He needed to steal a car the first chance he got. It might take them a while to figure out he'd left the woods and taken to the roads. With a little extra time, he'd make it to a city and disappear among the locals. But finding a car in this godforsaken wilderness wouldn't be easy.

The forest on this side of the road was a mix of burr oak, pine, birch, and what he thought were poplar. These trees hadn't been planted or pruned. The lower branches were black and twisted, almost skeletal against the white snow. They seemed to reach out to ensnare him like something from a horror film. It gave him the creeps.

He continued straight ahead, or what he thought was straight ahead. At least the rows of planted trees had made it easy for him to navigate. Dodging trees, as he was now, made it impossible to determine whether he was going in a straight line.

Riding slower took less out of him, but he was hungry. He was sure there wasn't anything like a city out here, and he didn't know where the towns were. A town was the last place he wanted to stumble into. Small population centers would be crawling with cops looking for a short, chubby bald guy on a sheriff's department snowmobile, and locals would recognize him immediately as a stranger.

He crested a hill and smelled woodsmoke. An old farmstead stood in a clearing in the trees below his hill, the roofs of the buildings bent under the weight of snow and probably rot, their gray wooden walls weathered. But the house and detached garage looked solid, their rooflines straight and the siding freshly painted. A plume of gray smoke rose lazily from the chimney and an old SUV sat in the driveway.

No matter how old the SUV, the driver's seat had to be easier on his ass than the snowmobile.

Frank inched ahead until the garage and barn blocked his view of the house. If he couldn't see them, he figured they couldn't see him. He cut across what looked like abandoned fields and headed for the farmstead at half speed. Good thing, too. He didn't see the old barbed wire fence. The top wire snapped when it hit his windshield. If the wire had been new or had he been going faster, it would have sliced through his throat and taken his head off.

He left the snowmobile in a tangle of brush along a fence line fifty yards from the house. It was dusk, and the smell of baked ham filled the air as he crept around rusty farm machinery to a corner of the garage where he could watch the house. Nothing moved. His empty stomach rumbled, aching with hunger. That improved his sense of smell, but it twisted his gut in knots. He had to eat.

The SUV was still parked in front of the garage, so whoever lived here might be planning to drive somewhere yet this evening. The SUV was so old it had axles with knobs that had to be turned in to put it in four-wheel drive. Anybody who drove something that old was either too poor to get good wheels or didn't put many miles on in a year.

An elderly hermit—perfect.

This guy might be old enough Frank could take him without firing a shot, and the farm was so secluded nobody would find him soon.

Frank tried a door on the side of the two-car garage. It wasn't locked. He found the light switch and flipped it on. The bay next to the door he'd come through was empty, and the other bay was being used as a shop. Duct tape, a hammer, saws, wood chisels, and woodworking clamps hung on one wall. The adjoining wall held a variety of equipment, some for plumbing, a few things for electrical work, an axe, a hatchet, and several shovels. *Everything he needs to live in the boondocks.*

Frank picked up the hatchet. It had a nice heft. Even the handle was steel. *Hey, I got me a regular tomahawk. I can knock him out with the blunt end.*

As he walked across the bay toward the side door, the garage door began to rise. Frank dove for the switch and hit the lights.

A white-haired guy with a heavily lined face lifted the door and turned to walk through the snow to the SUV. He was over six feet tall, and even with his winter coat, his broad shoulders and thick neck were visible, suggesting a once powerful build.

He was putting his car away, and he hadn't seen Frank.

Frank didn't hesitate. He sprinted for the man and brought the flat side of the hatchet down on the back of his head. The old guy collapsed onto the hood of the SUV, and Frank held him there. It was easier to search his pockets that way.

He pocketed the guy's wallet, his cell phone, and key ring, and let the body slide off the hood onto the packed snow. It didn't take him long to find the keys to the SUV. The car started easily. He checked the gas—half a tank. That should get him out of the woods and onto a highway with gas stations. And the SUV was white. On snow-packed roads, they might not even spot him from the air until he had to turn on the headlights.

The old man slowly rolled up to a kneeling position as Frank backed the SUV away from the garage. He stopped the SUV, turned off the engine, and ran back to the garage. He briefly considered loading the old guy in the car, but Betty and Cindy had turned him off on taking hostages.

The smell of the ham got to him again. *Shit.* The old guy was barely conscious. He would drag him into the house and get something to eat. And then when the guy came to, he could tell Frank how to get out of these damn woods.

Thursday, January 25, 2018
County O, Pine Plantation
1:30 p.m. CST

Grant couldn't relax until a sheriff's deputy arrived on a snow-mobile. It didn't take long, but knowing that Frank had a gun and had no compunction about using it made the minutes drag. Tom spotted the deputy approaching from their rear.

"We've got company." Tom put the JLTV in gear.

Grant poked his head out the JLTV's passenger window and looked. Even from a moderate distance, he could tell it wasn't Frank. "You can relax. Looks like a deputy."

They both got out of the JLTV and waited in the road for the cop.

The deputy rode up, cut the engine, and took off his helmet. "Deputy Eustace Mankey. You the guys who found Krueger?"

Mankey wasn't as tall as Krueger, he didn't have Krueger's muscular build, and his comb-over failed him when he took off his helmet. Running a hand through his hair didn't fix it. His waistline matched his chubby face, which quickly turned pink when exposed to the cold. On his approach, he'd ridden flat-footed and heavy-butted on the snowmobile. He definitely lacked Krueger's athletic style and verve.

Grant went to the door of the JLTV and motioned Mankey over. "Here he is. It looks like he was following Frank's trail and got caught in an ambush. I think he has a concussion."

Mankey confirmed Grant's story with Krueger, and asked Grant and Tom how much they'd disturbed the crime scene. "Only enough to help Krueger to the vehicle," Grant said. "After that, we stayed in the JLTV, ready to beat it out of here if Frank came back."

"Smart move. The ambulance will be here soon. They tell me it's critical to corral this Frank guy. I'll see which way he went and get in touch with headquarters." Mankey got on his snowmobile and took off.

"Wait, wait," Grant yelled as Mankey rode into the ditch and onto the trail left by Frank. He turned to Tom and threw his hands in the air. "What the hell are we supposed to do now?"

Krueger was no help. He just leaned back in his seat and complained about his cold feet and frozen toes.

"Let's wait for the ambulance," Tom said. "We can transfer Krueger, and then follow Mankey." He paused a moment. "Would have been nice if he'd told us what band his radio is on." Avoiding the crime scene, Tom walked into the trees and returned, zipping up his fly. "These trees look far enough apart to squeeze the JLTV through them."

Grant smiled to himself. *That's a novel way of measuring.*

A siren wailed in the distance. A moment later, the ambulance and its emergency lights came into sight. He and Tom stood in the middle of the road to meet them. Tom suddenly stood straight, turned, and tackled Grant. The two rolled into the ditch as the ambulance skidded past them on the frozen snow.

Grant came up, spitting snow. "What the hell?"

Tom pointed at the ambulance, a hundred yards down the road. "Those jerks were going way too fast for this road. They slid right through where we were standing."

Grant looked at the road. There weren't even any tread marks on the frozen snow. "Jesus. Thanks."

The ambulance backed up to the JLTV while Tom dug his driver-side mirror from the snow on the other side of the road. He waved it at the ambulance driver. "Kinda close, weren't ya?"

"Sorry about that. I didn't realize how slippery this road is." The driver turned and pointed at Grant, who was helping Krueger out of the JLTV. "That our patient?"

"Yeah. He's all yours," Tom said. "Head shot. Grant thinks he has a concussion, and his feet may be frostbitten."

The ambulance crew helped Krueger in and laid him on a cot. A sheriff's department cruiser pulled up. Even with chains, it skidded a few feet. It barely kissed the bumper of the ambulance. The deputy got out and checked the front of his SUV. "Good. No damage, no report. Damn, but this road is slick."

"Four-wheel drive doesn't help stopping, does it?" Tom noted.

"Good thing I put chains on." The deputy searched through equipment on the back seat of his car and came out with two pistols and a radio. He handed them to Grant. "You guys need communications with Deputy Mankey, and you're supposed to follow him. Handing out guns to people not in the department isn't protocol, but it's insane to let you follow an armed murderer without something."

Grant put the guns and radio in the JLTV.

"Those guns are for your self-defense only," the deputy said. "You are to let Deputy Mankey take the lead if you get close to Frank. Got that?"

Tom and Grant nodded.

The deputy went into lecture mode. "I'd like to *hear* that. You will let Deputy Mankey handle it if it comes to a showdown."

"Yes," Tom and Grant said eagerly, but Grant feared it might be wishful thinking, and he assumed Tom had the same concern.

The deputy backed his vehicle out of the way, and Tom drove past the ambulance to the place where Frank had ducked into the forest. Tom's eyebrows peaked, and he looked at Grant.

Grant shrugged. "All we can do is give it a try."

Tom jockeyed the JLTV around to hit the ditch at a ninety-degree angle, told Grant to buckle up, and gently accelerated into the ditch. Even buckled in, Grant's head hit the roof hard.

"Sorry about that," Tom said. "I forgot how deep and steep some of the ditches are." He threaded their way ahead through the trees. Following the snowmobile tracks, they moved at right angles to the planted rows of trees until they came to where the tracks diverged to the left and the right. Tom looked at Grant.

Grant pointed to the right. "That's probably the one laid down when Frank set up his ambush."

Tom nodded and turned left. Grant felt easier, certain they were on the right trail, and Mankey was between them and Frank. Driving between the rows of trees was faster than on the road. It wasn't slippery and they hit fewer bumps and dips.

The radio crackled to life a few minutes later. It was Mankey. "I've just come out of the trees. Looks like Frank crossed a logging road. How far back are you?"

Grant picked up the radio. "No idea. We're still following your tracks. I'll call back when we hit the logging road."

"We might get stuck trying to climb out of the ditch there," Tom said toward the radio. "Ditches on the logging roads can be steep and unstable."

There was nothing to do but keep moving forward. They reached the logging road as the sun turned the sky yellow and pink. The radio made sizzling noises and Mankey came on. "I'm in a clearing about a mile and a half past the logging road. The tracks have turned toward a farmstead. Looks . . . yeah, it looks like Frank abandoned the snowmobile and walked the last hundred feet to the barn and garage. Lights are on in the house. Over."

Before Grant could answer, another radio cut in. "This is the observation plane. We've been tracking your signal, Mankey. I think you're looking at a home on a side road about three miles from County O. Real long driveway. There's an SUV parked in front of the garage. Your target may be in the house."

"This is Deputy Fischer at the Kirby Motel. The last meal Frank had here was last night. It's about five o'clock, that's suppertime in the woods. He might have stopped to eat."

Tom took the radio from Grant's hand. "We've just reached the logging road. Do you want us to follow Deputy Mankey or approach the house by the road?"

"Go south on the road you're on for about a mile. Turn left at the first crossroads. You'll be looking for a long driveway to your left. It'll probably be the only one that's had the snow cleared. Turn your lights off when you hit the side road or the perp might see you."

Tom headed the JLTV down the road. Half a mile in, a white SUV blazed past them, headed the other way. It almost forced them off the road.

"Jesus Christ," Tom said. "What the hell is wrong with that asshole?" He concentrated on keeping the skidding JLTV on the slippery road.

Grant could hardly believe his eyes. He turned in his seat and watched the car drive away. Excitedly, he thumped Tom on the shoulder. "Holy shit! Turn around, turn around. I think that's Frank."

"I'll look for a place to turn around. Radio Mankey and headquarters. Tell 'em what Frank's doing."

Thursday, January 25, 2018
Logging road
5:00 p.m. CST

Frank tested his brakes. Even though the sun was down, the melting ice on the road remained slippery as hell. He'd reduced speed to only twenty miles per hour when he came to a sign warning of a T intersection ahead. Pumping the brakes accomplished nothing.

He clutched the steering wheel and watched in horror as his SUV slid sideways, the intersection and ditch looming ahead. The SUV finally stopped in the middle of the intersection.

Damn. Four feet farther and I'd be in the goddamned ditch, twiddling my thumbs until the cops picked me up.

He looked both ways and then in his rearview mirror. No headlights were coming from any direction. The cops thought he was headed east. He didn't know where he was, and he didn't have a reason to head east. It had simply been the easiest direction to head away from Kirby. If they thought he was headed east, this intersection was a chance to reverse course and go west. Maybe it would throw them off his trail.

He headed into the last glimmer of the setting sun. Two miles later, the snow-covered gravel road turned to salted and sanded blacktop. The road was straight for as far as he could see, and it wasn't covered by that film of wet ice. He eased down on the accelerator. The speedometer inched up to fifty miles per hour. Funny how a few minutes on a slippery road made that seem like flying.

Mashed potatoes, ham, green beans, and beer filled his belly. The hermit had been a decent cook. He'd left Grandpa tied up in his kitchen, still unconscious from the whack on his noggin. Frank congratulated himself for not killing him. Damned unlikely anybody would find the old duffer until tomorrow. The geezer would be waking up by then, and Frank would be in another county, maybe even another state.

He considered making a run for Canada. That wouldn't make sense unless he could find a car with a cushy seat and enough cash to buy the gas—and it would take a lot of gas. He'd have to drive into Minnesota and skirt Lake Superior.

Even if it were close, driving to the Twin Cities and then heading for some place colder didn't tempt Frank. He remembered listening to an interview with one of Gorbochev's Russian bodyguards when the Soviet leader was in Minneapolis. When asked what he thought of the Twin Cities, the guy said, "Nice. Much like Moscow, only colder."

Nope. He wasn't going home to Minneapolis or any place north of there. Besides, it would be crawling with police watching for him. They probably had his wife's phone tapped, waiting for him to call home again. That wasn't going to happen.

He fought a yawn. A full belly, a bottle of beer, and no sleep for twenty-four hours were catching up to him. He should have left the beer alone. Staying in his lane was a challenge. *Sleep*. If he didn't get some soon, he'd end up in the ditch or a head-on collision. Better slow down.

Over the next hill he came to the driveway of another farmstead. The driveway had been plowed, but the plowed section went to the barn, not the house. Though it was early in the evening, it was already dark. There were no lights on in the house, and the mailbox hung at a precarious angle on its post. Turning into the drive, he saw broken windows as his headlights swept over the house. The barn looked to be in better shape.

Frank followed the driveway behind the barn and parked. The barn doors were locked. That seemed odd, but if he couldn't get into the barn, he could sleep in the car. He hadn't taken time to check out the SUV before. Nothing under the seats, a flashlight, old receipts for oil changes, the vehicle registration in the glove box, and an old blanket in the back seat. *Not bad.* The blanket might save his life.

The flashlight worked, and he returned to the barn to peek through the windows. He brushed off the frost from one, put the flashlight up to it, and looked. He did a double take. The place was packed with boats, some new, some old. *Storage!* That's what the owner did. He was renting out the barn to store boats and camping equipment. That meant safety for him. It was unlikely anyone would visit their boat, and by this time of year, all boats were already stored.

Frank peed on the fieldstone barn wall. The temperature had plummeted when the sun set. His fingers felt stiff and frozen. Getting his dick past the many layers of clothing was harder than ever, and the pee froze as soon as it hit the stone face of the barn. What splashed off the barn wall landed as yellow snowflakes on the surrounding drift. He zipped up, climbed into the SUV, and wrapped himself in the blanket. That night was the best sleep he'd had in weeks.

Thursday, January 25, 2018
Tomah, Wisconsin
8:30 p.m. CST

Abby was tired. It had been a long day in the lab, and when she picked up her five-year-old daughter, the kid was already screaming about something. She'd fed her and gotten her to sleep when her cell phone buzzed. She was lucky to get out of the kid's room without waking her before answering.

"Hey, Abby. Is there, ah, anything I should know?" Ryan asked.

"Why? Did you want to come over?" Even though she was tired, Ryan's attention had a way of revivifying her. She changed her tone to what she hoped would be seductive. "The kid is asleep, so don't make any noise when you come in."

"We didn't use protection when we did it in the lab stock room, remember?"

"Yeah, but I'm on the pill, and we're both clean," Abby said. But she had an itch that she'd thought was another yeast infection. Maybe. "Are you screwing around with somebody else?"

A pause convinced Abby she'd nailed it.

"Ah, no, no. I'd never mess around on you, but you didn't take your gloves off right away. You handled my dick with those gloves on, remember? Well, now I've got a rash on my dick, and I've had a headache all day."

Shit. He *was* screwing around. "Go into the free clinic in town so it won't show up on your military record, and have yourself checked for an STD. I'll do the same."

"What if it's something from the samples you were working on? Your gloves had contact with the sample and my dick, and my dick had plenty of contact with you."

Is he trying to make this my fault? "Damned unlikely to be anything from the sample. We can be tested for that if everything else is negative."

Abby hung up. Man, she'd be in trouble if it came from a lab sample. They'd probably fire her ass. The sample she'd been working with came from a nurse, a nurse working with that old lady who was giving everybody trouble at the hospital. The virus she was testing for was the Zürich Virus. It was supposed to be something like Ebola, and that was transmitted—

Oh, shit.

It was transmitted by contact.

CHAPTER 23

DISAPPOINTMENT

Thursday, January 25, 2018
Logging Road
5:10 p.m. CST

It took a lot of jockeying back and forth to turn the JLTV around on the narrow logging road.

"It's like trying to turn an elephant on a dime," Tom muttered.

The moon was out by the time they were pointed in the right direction. Enough light reflected off the snow that the headlights seemed superfluous. He knew Frank had an almost insurmountable lead, but they had to try. They came to a T intersection with too many tracks to tell which ones were Frank's.

"Okay. Which way do we go?" Tom asked.

"Not sure. There's been no information from the spotter plane. He'd headed due east before. Take a right and see if he stuck to that."

Tom turned east and eased the JLTV up to thirty-five. Ten minutes later, they hadn't seen a farm, a house, or a set of taillights.

"What now?" Tom asked.

The radio crackled. Mankey had arrived at the T intersection and wanted to know where they were. Grant told him they'd gone east five miles and hadn't seen anything. "I'll let the sheriff know what's going on and alert the other deputies, especially those to the west," Mankey said. "You might as well pack it in for the night. We'd stumble all over ourselves in the dark."

It wasn't the answer Grant would have expected from Krueger, but he was ready to call it a day. "Want to drop by Ed's for a pizza?" Grant asked.

"I don't think he's open. Sybil said that all of the people who could go to Ed's are quarantined at the motel or in their homes. It saved her from officially shutting him down."

"Back to McCoy, then."

It took an hour to drive back to McCoy. "Where are you staying?" Tom asked as they passed through Fort McCoy's main entrance gate.

"I've been staying at the base hospital in case I'm still shedding virus. Might as well drop me off there."

Tom frowned. "Should I be checked for the virus after spending the whole day with you?"

"We should all be checked for it, but not tonight. Just drop me off at the front entrance to the hospital."

"If Frank makes it to a town, what are the odds he'll spread the virus?"

"Depends when we catch up with him. His last antiviral treatment was late last night. If treatments suppress shedding, and we haven't proven that yet, he might not be shedding today, maybe not tomorrow. I suspect he'll develop symptoms of Zürich Fever and be shedding gangbusters a day or so after that."

Tom pulled up to the hospital, and Grant got out and returned to his room. He collapsed in a chair and called Sarah.

She answered on the first ring. "I've been worried about you all day. The news said one of the murderers escaped and headed into the national forest. When I couldn't reach you in your room, I figured they'd asked you to join in the hunt."

"They did," said Grant. "I was supposed to be backup—just supply the biosafety gear when needed—but Frank disabled a deputy. Grazed his head." *Aw, shit.* Grant realized he'd screwed up as soon as he described Krueger's shooting. He would have kicked himself if he'd had the energy. He wouldn't call when he was exhausted and mention danger ever again.

"My God, Grant, don't put yourself at risk. Don't get in the line of fire. I don't know what I'd do if something happened to you." She paused. "I . . . I guess this means you won't be able to come home soon."

"I'm afraid you're right. We haven't proven our new techniques will dependably identify carriers of the virus. Besides, I can't see how I can get away with Frank on the loose." He sighed and tried to think of something optimistic to say. He couldn't. "I'm so sorry, honey."

Exhausted and on the edge of tears, he put down the phone.

Friday, January 26, 2018
Abandoned Farm
6:00 a.m. CST

Frank woke up, peed against the barn wall, and ate a ham sandwich he'd made the night before at the hermit's. He didn't wash his hands. His old man had told him, "Don't pee on your fingers and don't bang whores, and your hands will be clean. Hand me another beer."

Maybe they hadn't found the old geezer he'd left taped up in the house, but he couldn't count on that. He needed to find a motel, something out of the way and cheap. Once they found the old guy, it wouldn't take them long to figure out Frank had his car.

He revved up the SUV, modestly surprised it started, and

headed west. When he came upon the entrance to I-94, he pulled over to think about it. If they'd found the old geezer, every cruiser in the state would be watching the main roads for his SUV. With luck, they'd be looking farther and farther east with every passing day. It still wouldn't be safe to take the interstate during the day. At night might be safer, but if the state patrol stayed awake, it would be even easier to spot him on the empty roads at night. Best leave the interstate for driving between 2:00 and 4:00 a.m.

The Twin Cities and home were only a little over two hours away, but the cops would have his house under surveillance, his wife would be furious, and his boss would have a hit out on him. The cops had found and confiscated the drugs he was carrying. Nobody could lose a shipment that valuable and expect to live.

Chicago was only six hours away, but he expected it would be watched. Cold and windy too. He had to target a smaller city—a town with less money to train their police force, and fewer contacts with his boss. It had to be someplace where nobody knew him. Sioux Falls, Moorhead, Fargo—all on or near I-29. He'd take I-90 across southern Minnesota, turn south a couple of miles on I-29 in South Dakota, and he'd be in Sioux Falls. That should be safe if the old jalopy held together. If worse came to worst, he'd steal another car. Maybe he should anyway. If he left this area at midnight tonight or tomorrow night, he could be most of the way across Minnesota by the morning.

Even though it made him nervous to be this close to Kirby, he drove straight ahead and took Highway 12 south. With Fort McCoy nearby, there should be some cheap motels around, cheap enough for soldiers to use for one-night stands or a two-hour shack-up.

A few miles south of the intersection between Highway 12 and I-94, he came to the SleepyTime Motel. It was a single-story row of dilapidated rooms. Paint peeled from the wooden doors, door frames, and window frames. Weeds sprouted in the parking lot. The place looked like a dump even in the morning's early light. He wouldn't have known it was still in business had it not been for the flickering VACANCY sign.

It was only 7:30 a.m. He'd need a story on why he wanted a room this early. Tell the clerk he'd been driving all night and he needed to get some sleep. That might explain why he'd settled for the SleepyTime.

First, he had to fill the tank. This old SUV probably only got fourteen miles to the gallon, or less, and something about the steering felt wrong. It had been all right on the gravel road, but on salted blacktop or concrete it felt funny. Five miles past the SleepyTime, he pulled into a gas station on the northern edge of Tomah.

He was in luck. The gas station was old enough to have a service bay. Unwilling to use one of the credit cards, he paid cash at the register before filling up. The clerk was older than Frank and wore overalls, just the kind of guy he was looking for.

Frank sauntered casually up to the clerk. "Say, I've got a problem with my car. The steering has felt funny ever since I got off the gravel road and onto blacktop. Any idea what it could be?"

"Yours that old white SUV?" the guy asked.

Hell, it was the only car still at the pump. Frank wondered if the guy was senile. "Yeah. Ain't she a beaut? She'll be an antique in a couple of years."

The only other customer had just paid and driven off. The clerk walked out and looked at the car. He gave Frank a hard look. "How long you owned this car?"

The tone made Frank put a hand on the pistol in his coat pocket. He thought fast. "I, ah, I bought it from an old geezer last week."

"You've got the transmission in four-wheel drive, and you've got the hubs locked in. You can't leave old jalopies in four-wheel when you're on dry pavement like this. You're lucky you haven't seized the front transmission." The guy bent down and locked the nearest hub out. "Do that with the one on the other side, take it out of four-wheel, and you shouldn't have any problem. Don't ever leave it in four-wheel on dry pavement again, or this thing will be a pile of junk."

Frank thanked the guy, let go of his pistol, and filled the tank. That had been a close call, way too close for comfort. He picked up a small mountain of junk food and a couple of newspapers and drove back to the motel.

It was still early when he checked in at the SleepyTime. He stashed a roll of duct tape in his pocket, just in case, and entered the motel lobby. He had to slam the button on the bell sitting on the counter a couple of times before the manager came to the desk.

"Normally, we don't allow check-ins until three in the afternoon," the manager said. He had "Bob" embroidered on his rumpled white shirt with coffee stains down the front.

Bob's hair looked greasy, his teeth were yellow, and his fingernails dirty. A sleazeball if Frank had ever seen one. He sure as hell wouldn't eat breakfast here.

Bob grabbed a Kleenex from a box on the counter and blew his nose, but not quite getting it clean. Frank found something else to look at. "Checkout is noon and check-in is three, so you'll have to pay for two days," Bob said with a gleam in his eye.

Frank pretended to yawn. "I'm in no shape to argue. I drove all night. Headed to Chicago, but I can't keep my eyes open."

"We haven't had time to clean all the rooms yet. I'll see if I've got a room ready." Bob flipped through a Rolodex and shuffled some papers. "Number—"

Frank tuned the jerk out as he looked around. The newspapers in the office's small lobby were a week old. The soda vending machine was empty, and the windowsills were loaded with dust. Faded postcards and advertising materials sat in a wire rack. The place probably hadn't had a customer in a month.

"I'd like a room as far from the road as you can put me," Frank said. "I don't even want to see it out my window." When the manager gave him a suspicious stare, Frank added, "I'm a real light sleeper. Almost any noise wakes me up."

That seemed to satisfy Bob. The dust suggested there wasn't a woman around, married to Bob or hired. Frank had planned on paying with cash, but if Bob was alone, he had options. He could save his cash *and* avoid using a credit card.

"Can I ask your wife to recommend a nearby restaurant?" Frank asked as he handed Bob a stolen credit card. "I've found that women's recommendations are usually better than men's when it comes to eating."

"You're shit out of luck there." Bob put the card in the machine to run it through. "My wife walked out on me twelve years ago. Ran off with a soldier from Fort McCoy."

As Bob concentrated on the card, Frank pulled out his gun. "I changed my mind. I'll put this on a different card. Can you hand that one back to me, please?"

Bob mumbled under his breath and gave the card back to Frank. His eyes became wide ovals as he focused on the gun.

Frank nodded. "I see you understand. Now, if you'll put your hands up and step to this side of the counter, I won't have to put a plug in your ugly face."

Shaking, Bob complied, and Frank quickly duct-taped his hands behind his back and prodded him in the back with the Glock. "Let's go back to your office. You first."

Bob marched at gunpoint down a hallway behind the check-in counter. He entered an open door on the right and turned to face Frank. "This . . . this is it."

Frank waved the pistol toward a swivel chair behind a cluttered desk. "Sit."

Bob complied. Frank duct-taped him to the chair and taped his feet together. "Be nice and quiet, and I won't tape your mouth shut. Make noise and I'll have to tape you up. You might not be able to breathe if you have a cold. That would be a shame, 'cause then some prosecutor will nail my ass for murder. I don't want that." Frank shrugged. "But I'll do what I have to. Understand?"

Bob nodded, his eyes still wide and focused on Frank's gun.

Frank checked the desk for money. There wasn't any. He left the office and locked the door behind him. *Should have shot him.* It would have improved the gene pool and the quality of motel management around here.

At the front desk he cleaned out the till, only $53, and found a switch that changed the sign outside from VACANCY to NO VACANCY. It didn't look like it had been used in years. He found a bunch of keys—real keys, not those damned key cards—and pocketed them. Then he put a Closed sign in the office window. He locked the office and parked the SUV out of sight behind the motel. It didn't take him long to find the key to a room near the office.

Frank didn't worry about leaving a trail the cops would follow. The motel had little traffic. Hell, it could be a week before someone found Bob or asked questions. He'd have to give the sleazy bastard water before he left and maybe phone in a tip to the cops about Bob when he was out of the state. Nobody deserved to die of thirst.

There was so much dust on the bed that Frank took the bedspread outside and shook it. It must not have been made in months. Relaxing on top of the sheets, Frank pulled out the stash of junk food he'd bought at the gas station. He munched chips, downed a bag of M&Ms, and swilled a Diet Coke.

As he did, he paged through the newspapers. His exploits and picture were on the front page. He laughed as he read that his old SUV had been reported in several towns to the east and north, one report from as far away as Wausau. That would focus the search for him ninety miles northeast of where he was. The news on TV said the same thing, but with better pictures of him. *Not bad.* He was home free unless somebody local recognized him. He'd nap this afternoon and decide later whether to leave tonight or tomorrow night. With any kind of luck, he'd be in rush-hour traffic in Sioux Falls before the yokels knew they were chasing phantoms—that is, if Sioux Falls had a rush hour.

CHAPTER 24

A NEW CAR

Friday, January 26, 2018
Fort McCoy Hospital
10:30 a.m. CST

Grant bounced a tennis ball off the wall of his office as he waited for a call from Deputy Mankey or somebody—anybody—from the sheriff's department. He misjudged on a throw, and his ball went sailing out his office door and down the hall. An orderly tossed it back.

He put the ball away and got down to work. He made several calls and found two commercial labs in Madison that could handle large numbers of samples for the Zürich Virus testing and were willing to do the work. It wouldn't be cheap, but it was less expensive and faster than trying to remodel the lab at McCoy, purchase the required equipment, and train techs. It would have taken months to do that, given the government rules on letting contracts. He called Sybil mid-morning to give her the contact information for the labs.

At the end of the call, he asked, "What are my responsibilities vis-à-vis Frank?" He pushed a map of Wisconsin to the side. He'd drawn an arc from the north to the east of Kirby, supposedly the places Frank was headed.

"We need a virologist for biosecurity," said Sybil. "I wouldn't trust a physician with this unless they've had special training, and I sure as hell don't trust law enforcement to get it right. We need you there to maintain biosecurity when they catch Frank."

Grant had feared that. He couldn't go home until they caught Frank.

Sybil continued. "I've set up a teleconference with the head of the State Patrol, the sheriffs of Jackson, Clark, Wood, and Marathon counties, people from the governor's office, and Sam Barker. I'll suggest they call us after they've located Frank. The Wisconsin Air National Guard will fly you and your equipment in as soon as he's located. There's nothing you can do until we know where the hell he is."

Grant drummed the fingers of his left hand on the desk. "You want me to sit and wait?"

"I want you to assemble the equipment you'll need. Make sure it's a small enough package to fit in a helicopter or single-engine plane."

"I'm not good at waiting," Grant whined. "Do they have any ideas where he is?"

"None. They're watching for the credit cards he stole from the two old guys. The ancient SUV he took has terrible gas mileage, and he didn't get much cash from his victims. He'll have to use one of the cards sooner or later. I just hope he doesn't infect anyone."

"Is Tom still your driver?"

Grant heard a sigh. "Tom's been relieved of that duty," Sybil said. "Williams said I don't need a driver. The roads are clear enough now for a car to get through. He's assigned Tom to the worst detail in the motor pool. Tom gave me the keys to his car, so at least I have wheels."

"Have you lined up people to track down everybody Frank exposes to the virus?"

"That's going to be a job. Sam has a crew at work in the Tomah area, ready to go wherever Frank has been. I rented an office, computers, and office equipment for a central staff to coordinate things. They are limited to testing locals for now. It's frustrating. We don't know whether Frank's holed up in a cave or out spreading the virus in a city."

The call ended and Grant hung up. Frustrated, he grabbed his tennis ball and fired it at the wall again. It barely missed him as it bounced back, but it came too hard and fast for him to catch. He let it go, stood, and paced back and forth across his small office until he was able to settle down and study the maps spread on his desk.

Grant's office phone rang again an hour later. It was Deputy Mankey. "Any idea where Frank is?" Grant asked.

"Like a ghost, he's disappeared. The leads in Black River Falls, Neillsville, and Marshfield didn't pan out. We got a call from a bar in Pittsville. I doubt he had enough gas to get to Marshfield or Pittsville, but to be safe we sent a cruiser up to check it out. Turned out the calls were made by locals with a snootful."

"Anything you want me to do?" Grant asked.

"Not at the moment. Just be ready to go when we locate him."

Mankey took Grant's cell phone number and hung up. Grant tried to read a virology journal but couldn't concentrate, spent several hours catching up on the latest news on the outbreak in Zürich, and gradually went stir-crazy.

An email from Sybil advised him that she and Sam had contracted for all PCR testing for the virus to be done by the commercial labs he'd told her about. That was good, but it didn't give Grant anything to do.

His medical degree was in veterinary medicine, so he couldn't legally treat sick patients or Mrs. Anderson. Worse, he couldn't go home to Sarah and Jimmy until his nasal swabs tested negative twice and Frank was safely tucked in a prison hospital. The baby was due next week, and he desperately wanted to be home for the birth.

He called Sarah but had nothing concrete to tell her and no estimate of when he could be home. It made for a deeply unsatisfying conversation.

Saturday, January 27, 2018
SleepyTime Motel
8:30 a.m. CST

Frank had a headache. It was getting worse, and he feared he might have a fever. *Probably because I'm thinking too damned much about Grant and his virus.* Maybe ibuprofen would help. His last dose of the antiviral pills they were giving him was a couple of days ago now, but that shouldn't make a difference. They'd said his antibody level to the Zürich Virus was sky high. If that couldn't protect him, what could? Smythe had said that all antibodies weren't protective, but he thought that was just another excuse to keep him cuffed and under control.

Hell. Maybe the junk food he'd been living on was causing it. One day at the SleepyTime had turned into two because he hadn't slept well during the day, and he'd been too exhausted to start a long trip that night. It might help if he could find a restaurant and get a decent meal. Until then, all he could do was sit in the office, feed and water Bob, and twiddle his thumbs. He needed cash. The easiest way to get it would be to let out rooms and give a discount for paying cash.

He'd missed a golden opportunity yesterday. A Lexus had pulled into the motel lot—an army officer, alone. The guy banged on the office door, swore a lot, and left. Frank wanted to be ready if he came back. A guy that desperate for a room might pay cash, full rate.

Nobody stopped at the motel in the morning. Big surprise. He took Bob to the can and listened to his whining. He told him to shut up and just be happy he took the duct tape off his hands so he could pee. Bob asked for more water a couple of times. He gave him that, but when he bitched about being hungry, he told him to get used to it. It would have required cutting his hands free again, and that was just too much trouble. Later, Frank leaned back in Bob's chair behind the check-in counter and fell asleep. The chair was too darn comfortable.

His own snoring woke him. He went to the back office and made sure Bob was warm and gave him more water. If he got cold, Frank would have to give him more trips to the can, and he didn't want to be bothered with that. But now Frank was hungry, and he'd had his fill of junk food. He locked the door to the office as he left. What the hell, the officer hadn't heard Bob yesterday, or maybe Bob hadn't heard the officer. He put a CLOSED sign on the lobby door. Bob should be safe for an hour.

He headed away from Kirby to avoid being identified at lunch. The road was almost empty, so he took a chance and drove the eight miles to Tomah. The cafés and diners in town were too small, too easy for somebody to remember him if a cop came around with pictures. Besides, the ancient SUV would stand out. He drove east to a busy truck stop at the junction of I-94 and I-90 and splurged on a ribeye steak, baked potato, and green beans. He ate it too fast to enjoy it. Then he spotted a couple looking over the SUV. With luck, they were looking because it was almost an antique and not because it matched a description they'd heard on the news. They didn't seem to pay attention to the license plates. *Yup. Car buffs.*

He took the same route back to the SleepyTime, but once out

of Tomah he pushed his luck with the speed limit. The road was empty, and he figured all the County Mounties were looking for his ass to the north and east. No one was on his tail when he drove into the SleepyTime's parking lot. Maybe it was the full belly, but he was too tired to park behind the motel and walk all the way back to the office. He parked a couple of units from the rear door to Bob's apartment.

Ibuprofen helped his headache and fever for a while. He swallowed another dose, unlocked the front door, and settled into Bob's comfy chair. A jerk yelling and banging on the bell at the front desk woke him up an hour later. It took him a couple of seconds to wipe the sleep from his eyes and focus. Damned if it wasn't the army officer he'd seen yesterday, and one with some rank. The emblem of an eagle on his cap indicated he was a colonel.

"Jesus H. Christ, what do I have to do to get service here?" the officer thundered.

"Okay, okay," Frank said in his most conciliatory-sounding voice. "I'm sorry, but I haven't been feeling well. How may I help you?"

"Where the hell is Bob? I have something for him." The colonel pulled an envelope out of his coat pocket.

Frank had handled envelopes stuffed with tens of thousands of dollars in cash. The fools always skimped on the envelope. Always a size too small. This envelope had the same look. "Bob isn't in right now. I'll give it to him when he comes back," Frank said sweetly and held out his hand for the envelope.

The colonel jerked the envelope away and pocketed it. "Bullshit. I'm not giving this to anybody but Bob."

Frank reached for his gun. It wasn't there. *Shit.* He'd left it in the car. "Wait here a moment. I'll see if Bob is back. He might be working on, ah, on repairs in a unit."

Frank hustled down the hallway to Bob's apartment, checking to make sure the office door was locked as he passed it. He picked up speed when he reached Bob's dingy quarters and sailed through the back door to his SUV. Frank was out of breath and puffing from the exertion as he rushed back inside with his Glock.

Something warned him that the colonel might have found Bob. He tiptoed from the apartment to Bob's office. The door and lock were cheap and could easily be forced. The sound of splintering wood greeted him as he crept down the hallway to the office, followed quickly by the crash of the door being thrown open. *Rats.* The colonel must have heard Bob call for help.

Frank heard, "Oh, my God! Bob, what on earth . . ." as he rounded the corner into the office. The colonel bent over Bob and ripped the tape off his hands as Bob explained what had happened.

Frank brought the gun up. "Good. You can hand him your envelope now."

The officer turned to face him, saw the gun, and raised his hands. Even the eagle on his hat seemed to stare bug-eyed at Frank's gun.

Frank liked that. "Put the envelope, your wallet, cell phone, and car keys on the desk."

The colonel complied and continued to stare at Frank's gun.

Frank had an idea. He thought of it as inspiration. "Thank you. Now, off with your coat, shoes, pants, shirt, and underwear."

"What? You mean get naked?"

"Brilliant deduction. I see why you're an officer." Frank waved his pistol. "Off with all of it."

"Why? What are you going—"

"Naked guys don't run away in this weather. Happy now?"

The colonel complied and Frank duct-taped his hands behind him before forcing him at gunpoint back to Bob's apartment and bedroom. "Onto the bed."

The colonel stalled and started to argue. Frank fired a warning shot over his head and the colonel dove into the pillows.

"See," said Frank. "That wasn't so hard, was it?" He duct-taped a foot to each side of the bed.

"What are you going to do with us?" the colonel asked.

Frank smiled. "I'm going to get Bob and have him strip. You guys can snuggle and keep each other warm until the cops find you."

Frank returned to the front office, took Bob's clothes off for him, and forced the naked and shivering manager back to his bedroom. "Into the bed, on top of the colonel," Frank ordered.

Bob's expression became desperate. "That's sick!"

"It'll keep you both warm in case the cops take a couple of days, and I can be sure you won't go roaming around outside."

Bob did as he'd been ordered, and his feet were quickly duct-taped like the colonel's. Frank threw a quilt and a couple of blankets over the two and returned to the front office.

He carried their clothes to the far end of the motel and stomped them into a snowbank. The rest of Bob's warm clothes from a dresser and closet were given the same treatment. Frank found the main telephone connection for the entire motel in the office and cut the wires with a knife from Bob's kitchen.

It didn't take long to find and smash Bob's cell phone and to collect the colonel's wallet, cell phone, and keys. Frank found only $300 in the envelope. A disappointment, as the swollen envelope had seemed to promise more. In Frank's line of work, envelopes were usually stuffed with hundreds. This envelope held tens and twenties. Frank shrugged. Life was hard and full of disappointments, but the person who found those lovebirds would have a surprise.

Frank dumped the white SUV behind the motel and returned

to Bob's bedroom. "How are you guys doing? Getting comfy? Now, don't do anything I wouldn't do."

"You perverted bastard," the colonel hissed. "I'll see that they send you up for life."

"You can try," Frank admitted. He used the kitchen knife to cut the tape on one of Bob's hands. "There. It'll take you a while to get free, but when the sun goes down, it's going to be colder than a witch's tit out there and I cut the phone lines. I'd suggest you stay in here where it's warm." He clicked his heals together and gave the colonel a snappy salute before he hustled out to the Lexus.

Saturday, January 27, 2018
SleepyTime Motel parking lot
1:00 p.m. CST

Frank luxuriated in the Lexus. The soft leather of the seats was unbelievably comfortable, but his foot barely reached the brake pedal—damned colonel was over six feet tall. Frank had always been touchy about how short he was. He played with the little levers and slides on the side of the seat, moving it forward and back, tilting it back and forth, and moving it up and down. He'd never been in the driver's seat of a luxury car and was unlikely to be again, so he took his time getting everything about the seat right.

He tucked Krueger's service pistol safely away in the leather-lined door pocket of the Lexus. Even that leather was soft and supple. Yup, he was going to enjoy riding in a luxury car. It took his mind off his headache for a while.

He gave into temptation to use the GPS navigation system, trying to put in Sioux Falls, but nothing happened. The GPS system had been inactivated, he assumed by the colonel. Now, why would the owner do that? Frank thought it over. It didn't take long. That SOB didn't want anyone to know he was at the SleepyTime. Hell, he didn't want anyone to know where he was either. Frank left the GPS system inactivated as he'd found it.

He took Highway 12 from the SleepyTime to I-94, and I-94 to I-90 east. He set the cruise control at sixty-nine to drive through Wisconsin—no sense exciting the State Patrol—and tried to look as though he hadn't a care. Adrenaline kept him going for the first hour, then his headache intruded. He needed a rest and wanted to top off the gas tank. He stopped for a late lunch at a fast-food joint outside La Crosse. That was a mistake.

Normally, you could count on these joints being too busy for anyone to notice a guy. Even their patrons were in a hurry. But it was two o'clock. The staff was relaxing as the noon rush wore off, and in the back of the place a group of old guys were reading the paper, bullshitting each other, and gossiping like a gaggle of hens. Frank grabbed the funnies section of the paper and hid behind it when he saw his picture was on the front page. He ate fast and got the hell out of there. The gas could wait.

The ibuprofen helped his headache but only a little. It kept his temperature normal, or at least it felt that way. He briefly wondered if Grant's virus had something to do with his headache, but to admit that would be to admit that Grant had been telling the truth and he might die. It was easier to blow it off as stress, a sinus headache, or a cold.

He pulled into a rest area in Minnesota and used the restroom facilities. There weren't any paper towels, only hand driers. He shrugged and ignored the sink. He examined a map on the wall. I-90 would soon cross I-35, which headed north to Owatonna, a city at the juncture of US Highway 14 and I-35. Owatonna looked like a small city with several major exits.

Back in the car, he closed his eyes and napped an hour. His headache was back and he had little energy. He remembered that he hadn't had headaches while he was on the antiviral medication for AIDS. Every pharmacy should have those. Maybe that could be worth a try.

He took I-35 north to Owatonna. The town would be perfect— far enough off the interstate that people might not associate a theft with him, and small enough not to have much of a police department. Hell, if they did figure out it was his work, they might think he was making a run up I-35 for the Twin Cities.

In Owatonna, he filled the car's gas tank and got a tankard of coffee at a truck stop. Gas to fill up the Lexus cost close to fifty bucks, a small dent in the colonel's envelope. The coffee was a bladder-buster. He really needed the restroom after that.

He parked at the nearest Walmart and checked to see when their pharmacy closed. 9:00 p.m. The only thing he knew about his meds was that they were given to AIDS patients and blocked viral enzymes. That's what the doc had said. He had to get there before the pharmacy closed. Frank didn't know what an enzyme was, or the names of the drugs, so the pharmacist would have to tell him what he needed. He'd claim to be an AIDS patient.

There was plenty of time before he had to act. When he got hungry again, he didn't make the same mistake he'd made for lunch. He waited until five-thirty when every fast-food joint he passed was loaded with customers. Nobody paid any attention to him, and he felt safe taking his time eating, even going back to the counter to order dessert.

He took a chance and slept for a couple of hours in the Walmart parking lot. Nobody bothered him. At a quarter to nine, it had cleared out a bit. He moved his car to the door closest to the pharmacy and strolled into the store. He walked past the men's sweaters, grabbed one that looked like it might be his size, and headed to the pharmacy. There, he got in line behind a middle-aged lady. He waited patiently as she picked up her script. The closer to nine o'clock when he talked to the pharmacist, the better for him.

At the counter, he asked to talk to a pharmacist. A tall sandy-haired guy in a white jacket approached him. A badge on his jacket identified him as Steve.

"Hi. How can I help you?" Steve asked.

"I'm on vacation and I've, ah, I've misplaced my medication for AIDS. I can't even pronounce its name. It's the one that blocks three critical enzymes the virus uses to make my life hell. Know which one that is?"

"There are several with two or three active ingredients. Think you could remember a name?"

Frank had heard a few drug names bandied about by the nurses, but he wasn't sure he could remember them. *What the hell.* Let the guy rattle off a few and pick one at random. Anything was better than nothing. "Try me. I think I might be able to remember."

The pharmacist named a few and Frank chose one at random. "Genvoya, that's it," he said.

"Do you have your pharmacy's number? I can try calling them to verify your script."

"No. And they don't stay open this long either. Can you just give me a week's worth of meds? Something to hold me over until I get home?"

Steve shook his head sternly. "Sorry. I can't hand these medications out without proof you have a prescription for the drugs."

Frank shrugged, pretended to search his pocket for the script, and pulled out his pistol. "Oh, here it is. How's this for a prescription? Call your assistant over and ask them to bring you ninety days' worth of, what did you call it? Genvoya?" He dropped the sweater over the gun so the assistant wouldn't see it. Neither he nor Steve could verify that the barrel was still pointed at Steve, but they both had to know that Frank couldn't miss at this range.

Wide-eyed, Steve did as he was told, and the assistant brought a large plastic bottle of medication. Frank checked the name, sounded it out, and decided it was close to the pharmacist's pronunciation of "Genvoya." He nodded to the pharmacist. "Thank you. Would it be too much trouble to ask for one of your pharmacy sacks? I'd rather not have anyone ask questions as I leave."

The pharmacist's shaking hand made the sack dance. Frank snatched it quickly before it drew too much attention. As it was, the pharmacist's assistant had a strange expression and was looking from the sack to the pharmacist and back.

"Thanks again. It was a pleasure doing business with you." Frank motioned the pharmacist closer. In conspiratorial tones, he said, "I'm going to turn and leave now, and you're not going to call for help until I've had time to get out of your parking lot. That's because you're a compassionate man, and you'd hate to see your fellow workers taken hostage or gut-shot in a shootout. I'd advise you not to say a word until I'm out of town and well on my way back to Minnea—ah, Austin."

Frank didn't know if his hint that he was headed to Minneapolis would work, but it was worth a try. He left the pharmacy quickly, located a clerk in another aisle, and asked her to show him where the sauces were in the grocery section. He looked back toward the pharmacy to make sure the pharmacist watched as he and the clerk headed toward the sauce aisle, which Frank had confirmed was close to the exit door.

Near the door, Frank walked rapidly to the exit, but not so rapidly that he'd draw attention to himself. He hopped in the

Lexus and drove at a sedate pace to the freeway. He was heading south on I-35 well before he expected any response from the local sheriff or city police, and turned west onto I-90. The law enforcement response would be divided six ways: north and south on I-35, and east and west on both I-90 and US 14.

Sioux Falls, South Dakota was only over two hundred miles away. Frank increased his cruise control until he was almost reaching eighty. That was nearly ten miles over the speed limit. He'd heard of the Iowa and Wisconsin State Patrol stopping people going over five miles, but that wouldn't happen in Minnesota. On the freeway he hadn't seen anyone going under seventy-five, and most were going over that.

Sunday, January 28, 2018
Sioux Falls, South Dakota
Midnight CST

It was past midnight, and he was exhausted by the time he got to Sioux Falls. What the hell, he'd driven 350 miles since leaving Tomah *and* robbed a pharmacy at gunpoint. It was time to call it a day.

He didn't dare use any of the credit cards he'd stolen, and most motels wouldn't take cash. He found the Sunset Motel, on a road that had once been a major highway prior to the interstate. The manager might have been an upstanding citizen once, but that was before the interstate diverted traffic from his motel.

The sign was faded, and the neon tube looked like it hadn't been lit in a decade. As he turned in the drive past some tall shrubbery, he saw units that looked like something out of the sixties that needed a fresh paint job. It wasn't as decrepit as the SleepyTime, but was otherwise exactly the sort of place he wanted. He drove up to the office and walked in.

The manager came out after Frank had pounded the bell repeatedly. Frank recognized him as a calculating weasel. He acted unhappy about taking cash, but he took it—for three nights lodging. Frank hadn't wanted three nights, but the manager—the greedy bastard—insisted on it if it was to be a cash deal. Frank was sure neither the payment nor the "taxes" collected would ever make it to the motel's account books.

That emptied what was left in the colonel's envelope. He didn't have the energy to argue. Besides, the way he felt, resting all day tomorrow sounded good. Traffic on this highway was light, and the shrubbery around the motel was so overgrown he needn't worry about the Lexus being spotted. The room was bare but clean and the towels fluffy. The TV was so old it probably had vacuum tubes instead of transistors. He was too tired to turn it on.

The motel's idea of a complimentary breakfast the next morning was cold coffee and a stale roll. Screw that noise. He was tempted to get out Krueger's pistol, blow the manager's head off, and get his money back, but that would draw attention and the cops would know where to concentrate their search. Better to lay low and catch up on his sleep. The coffee washed down more ibuprofen and one of his AIDS pills, and he went back to bed. He'd walk to the diner down the road later for breakfast.

CHAPTER 25

ABBY

Monday, January 29, 2018
Fort McCoy
10:30 a.m. CST

Abby swallowed hard and gathered her courage outside Grant's office door. He might fire her. She might even face disciplinary action affecting her license to work in a lab. It would all depend on how she worded her story. She'd been positive for chlamydia at the free clinic, but nothing about that STD should cause the headaches and fever she had. She'd checked on Google.

She tapped lightly on the door frame of Grant's office. "Dr. Farnsworth, could I talk to you for a minute?"

Grant looked up from the papers on his desk. "Sure. What's the problem?"

"I . . . I've been having headaches for a couple of days and I ran a fever this morning. When I . . ." This was the part she had to get right. "When I ran Nurse Jeager's samples, I discovered I had a tear in my gloves."

She cringed inwardly. Farnsworth had ordered her to double glove whenever she handled Zürich samples. The chance of having a tear in both gloves on a hand was infinitesimal. The chance that the tears would line up so something could penetrate both gloves approached zero.

"I think I should be tested for Zürich Fever."

Dr. Farnsworth's eyes burrowed into hers, his forehead furrowed and eyebrows arched. His expression suggested he didn't believe a word of it. She cowered before his glare, crossed her fingers, and said a quick prayer as he put down his paper, gave her another searching look, and reached for his phone.

"We'll run the samples here. Collect swab samples from each nostril and give them to Al in the lab. I'll give him a call and tell him you're coming down. Then go home and quarantine yourself."

Relief washed over Abby. *He didn't buy it but he's not arguing.* "Ah, my boyfriend is having the same symptoms. Can I collect samples from him and have them tested too?"

Dr. Farnsworth was talking on the phone to Al in the lab. At this, his head whipped around, and his eyes bored into hers again.

Oh shit. I said too much.

Monday, January 29, 2018
Fort McCoy
11:30 a.m. CST

Grant was surprised by how quickly Abby got the nasal swabs to Al. He had Al process his nasal swab and those from Tom, Sybil, and Ryan along with Abby's. They were tested with the Swiss PCR test. Swabs from Abby and Ryan were positive. The other swabs were negative.

At least he didn't carry the virus, but he wouldn't be able to go home until he had a second negative test and Frank, or his corpse, was safely in custody. There was nothing to do but wait.

He told Abby and Ryan to report to the hospital. Abby's story of the torn gloves might have convinced him had he not seen Abby's behavior when Ryan was around. She could hardly keep her hands off him. Ryan wasn't supposed to be anywhere near the Zürich Virus samples or patients. What the hell had they done to get infected so quickly? Screwed in the biosafety hood? How hormones routinely overrode common sense for some people never ceased to amaze him. He called Sybil at the end of the day.

"How are the treatments going for Mrs. Anderson?" he asked.

"It's too early to tell," Sybil said. "She's been on high doses of medication for three days now. We submitted her latest swabs to your lab this morning. You should have the results any time now."

Grant looked through papers on his desk to see if he had missed copies of the submissions or testing results. They weren't in yet. "Have you considered local treatments?"

There was a pause. "Hadn't thought of it," Sybil said. "We can run a semi-quantitative PCR on her first nasal samples and a recent one. If there's been no drop in the amount of virus, we might give it a try. Any suggestions?"

"Use a solution of the drugs and spray them in her nose. Even better might be to incubate the drugs with Frank's antibodies to the virus. If the antibodies and drug bond, the antibodies would direct the meds right to the virus. Check with a biochemist on the best way to get an antibody-drug complex formed."

"Do you have enough serum from Frank to make treatment with it a viable option?" Sybil asked.

Grant laughed. "We have enough for up to four thousand treatments, more if we catch Frank alive."

"Lord, I hope that's more than we'll ever use. It's not going to be much of a study though, unless we have a negative control."

Inspiration hit Grant. He'd been in a study in which different treatments were used in the left and right side of each cow's udder and the results within each cow compared. Two nostrils to treat— same principle. He recommended treating one nostril and using the other as a negative control. They didn't have enough patients to make it much of an experiment yet, but there might be more patients soon. He took a pass on telling her where he got the idea.

"Damn," Sybil said. "I like the way you think. We can do it, but getting permission to use an experimental treatment on a patient will take time. Hmm. I might get approval faster if I stress that it's a national emergency and all treatments for this virus are, at best, experimental. It would be nice to have treatments worked out for carriers before we're swamped with them."

While Sybil was in a good mood, he gave her the bad news. "Two lab techs tested positive for the Zürich Virus. One gave me a bullshit story on how she picked it up. I don't believe it, but there's no point in arguing with her about it. Thing is, they both have reputations for active sex lives."

"No! Lab techs weren't stupid enough to . . . ?" Sybil was briefly at a loss for words. "Assuming they would be having affairs with people like themselves, they could spread the virus over the entire county. Do you think this means it's an STD?"

"No. I think it means they swapped spit and breathed hard on each other during sex."

Grant was kicking himself for not providing more supervision, or for having such stupid lab techs that they needed watching. "I can't prove it, but after seeing those two running their hands over each other, I think they were having sex in the lab when they got it. Abby and Ryan have been excellent workers in the lab, but right now I could wring their bloody necks. They're being checked in to the hospital. Someone can interrogate them there about their contacts."

CHAPTER 26

FALSE LEAD

Grant tried to catch up on reading his scientific journals, but he couldn't summon the level of concentration it required. It drove him crazy thinking about the number of screwups and the incomparable stupidity shown by people who should have known better. It also kept him in McCoy, away from Sarah and Jimmy. He gave up trying to read and paced around his office.

There was little for him to do now that contract labs were handling the bulk of the PCR testing and Sam's professionals were tracking down contacts the busload of elderly people from Kirby had made. Jesus, what a cockup that had been. It's what happened when you didn't share relevant information with people. They were lucky it happened before anyone was likely to have started shedding the virus in large amounts. They could have had a dozen Mrs. Andersons.

He called Sarah. When she picked up he could hear Jimmy wailing in the background.

"Grant, just a second. Jimmy's having breakfast and throwing a fit. Can I call you back in five?"

Grant hung up, his throat choking with frustration and longing. It was easy to concentrate on the problems in Kirby and the surrounding area—until he talked to Sarah. Then everything hit him. He should be there helping. Jimmy could be a handful for her, especially now, only a week from delivery. He responded to Grant better, at least when it came to discipline.

The phone rang ten minutes later. When Grant picked up, he could still hear Jimmy's muffled wail from another room. Must be having a time-out. "Got him under control?" he asked. God, he wanted to be home.

Sarah's voice was flustered. "I told him he couldn't talk to Daddy unless he behaved, ate his breakfast, and was quiet while we talked. He was okay with breakfast, and he worked on being quiet while I cleaned him up. I'll let him talk to you when he quiets down. When are you coming home?"

"Everything except Frank is ready on this end. They want me to supervise handling him once they have him cornered. I have no idea when that will be." He explained that Frank's last medication was four days ago. They expected him to be shedding large amounts of virus by now, possibly infecting dozens of people near him. "What we fear most is that Frank might die unseen on a back road. If we don't know where he is or where he's been, we won't know where to concentrate our people. Infections could get out of control before we know where to look."

"I'm due soon. The doctor said the stress of worrying about you and not having help at home could bring it on early. The neighbors are helping when they can, but most of them are going to school and taking care of their own families. Every time I get to sleep, the baby starts to kick and wakes me up. My belly is huge—I'm not even sure I can fit behind the steering wheel anymore, and my feet are so swollen I can hardly get into most of my shoes. Jimmy has been impossible this week. Oh, Grant, it would really help to have you here."

Grant started to sniffle again. He didn't want Sarah to hear it.

She had enough on her plate. When he had himself under control, he asked, "Have you called your mother? Can she come up from Milwaukee?"

"No, and I'm not going to call her. If she comes here, it'll just be a vacation from fighting with my dad and she won't be any help at all."

"But couldn't she—"

"Maybe she could, but she won't. Remember when she was here for Jimmy? We spent more time taking care of her than we did caring for him."

"The babysitter for Jimmy is arranged though, isn't she?"

"Martha next door said she'd take him. I still want you here."

"And I want to be there with you, but I'm sitting on a potential national disaster." Grant's landline phone rang. "Wait a second. I have a call on the other phone. Nobody calls me on it except for emergencies."

It was Tom. "Grant, you won't believe what I heard walking past the communications office. Air reconnaissance was on a landing pattern coming into Volk field and they spotted a white SUV behind the SleepyTime Motel. They're sending a team of MPs from McCoy and deputies from the sheriff's department to investigate."

"Just a second." Grant picked up his cell phone. "Sarah, I have to get ready. They may have found Frank. Love you." He disconnected and picked up the handset for his landline again. "Can you drive for me if they have Frank?"

Tom grinned. "Yeah. Nobody is paying attention to me."

"Oh? Is that why you were eavesdropping at the communications center?"

"That's such a harsh way to put it. I happened to wander by and be at the door at an opportune time. Get this—Colonel

Williams has been missing for a couple of days. The brass is trying to keep it quiet, but the officers and secretarial staff are edgy. When I figured out weird shit was going on, I walked in and asked if I could speak to the colonel. The staff in the front office looked like they were about to have a collective fit."

"They should have you in Intelligence. Bring the JLTV around. I'll make sure everything is loaded and ready to go. Let me know if Frank's at the motel."

"Will do. Your stuff is still in the JLTV from our last goose chase. We can head straight to the SleepyTime. No reason to wait for those bozos to call us."

They arrived at the motel behind a truckload of MPs and three sheriff's department cruisers. Grant introduced himself to the MP in charge and the deputies and filled them in on the biosafety equipment they'd need *if* Frank was found at the motel.

"Okay. Just stay out of our way until we know if he's here," the MP said.

Grant was happy to do that. He noticed Tom stuck to his job as driver, not leaving his seat in the JLTV. *That's out of character for him,* Grant thought until he remembered that the JLTV was bulletproof where light arms fire was concerned.

Grant returned to the JLTV. No point in getting hit by stray bullets. He and Tom watched the MPs surround the motel as the deputies checked out the SUV. A team of four deputies in flak jackets broke down the office door and piled in. Two of them came out laughing ten minutes later and told the MPs they could pack it in. "Only two pissed-off naked men wrapped in blankets," they said, "and neither of them is the guy everybody's looking for." The deputies walked off, snickering. Grant's hopes sank.

"I wonder what's so funny," Tom said to Grant. "Let's go see."

"Are you sure? Do we—"

"If Frank was here, then so was the virus. You've got an excuse to be in there. Grab your sample kit, look official, and let's check this out."

Grant did as he was told and they headed to the office. Tom looked like he was fighting to stifle a grin. At the office, holding a package of swabs in front of him, Grant explained to the deputy why he thought he should see what they'd found. Tom worked at looking innocent as he glanced around the lobby.

"They're in the bedroom," the deputy said. "Try not to laugh. That really set them off when the deputies did."

"Can I collect nasal swabs?" Grant asked.

"Go ahead. It's up to them," the deputy said, nodding toward the bedroom. "I'll be in my cruiser calling headquarters for clothes to give them."

Grant and Jones walked in as the colonel and Bob were sitting on the bed, glaring at each other. Tom broke into a grin, snickered, and saluted. "Colonel! Are you all right, sir?"

The colonel looked startled. He stood, returned the salute, and the blanket wrapped around him dropped. He fixed Tom with a glare that challenged him to repeat his snicker. "What are you doing here, Jones?"

"I'm escorting Dr. Farnsworth. He's here to take samples to make sure Frank didn't infect you."

The colonel wrapped himself back up in his blanket, and he and Bob sat for Grant to collect the nasal swabs. Grant bit his cheek to keep a straight face. It was hard to forget about the image of the colonel standing naked to salute. "I'll arrange to have the samples repeated in a week," he told them. "If you're negative on both, you can relax." He turned to Bob. "A technician will come to collect your samples next week. I'm sorry, but because Frank stayed here, your motel will be closed until we can disinfect it. Corporal Jones will take these samples to the lab. We'll have the results in three or four days."

On the way back through the motel office, Grant told the deputies that they'd be sampled in five to seven days. Tom asked how they'd disinfect the motel. "This whole building," Grant said, "will be fumigated with formaldehyde to make sure all surfaces Frank touched are exposed to a strong disinfectant. The bedding from the room or rooms he stayed in will be autoclaved."

Tom glanced around the office. "That'll cost more than this place is worth. Couldn't they just burn it?"

"Oh my God, no! With a fire there'd be thousands of tiny particles in the smoke. They'd be spread all over hell and many would still have active virus."

In the front office they overheard the deputy in charge call in an All Points Bulletin for Wisconsin and surrounding states for a late-model black Lexus. He made it clear the governor and Homeland Security said that finding the Lexus or Frank took priority over all other investigations for every cop in the region.

Back at the base hospital, Grant handed the swabs he'd collected to a lab tech and made a phone call. "Sybil, Frank has moved up in the world. He's driving the colonel's Lexus now. He's been driving it for a day and a half, so he must be at least hundreds of miles away. Probably a lot farther."

"The colonel's Lexus. Is the colonel one of the men they found in the SleepyTime?"

"Yeah. He and the manager. Tom will tell you all about it. Don't believe a word of it if he gives you his favorite version of the story."

"Huh?"

"You'll recognize it if he does. Say, you know the hierarchy here better than I do. Can you arrange to have a pilot and an airplane set aside for me when they find Frank? Speed will be important. I'd like to load all the gear in it now so we can lift off as soon as we hear about him."

"I'll take care of it. Mind if I come along when they find him?

He's liable to be sick as a dog and need medical attention. If I catch Colonel Williams in a good mood, I might get approval to bring Tom along to drive for us when we get there."

Grant spent the rest of the day checking to see whether an aircraft had been set aside for him and glaring at his phone, hoping Sybil would call to tell him Frank had been found.

She finally called again late that evening. "Grant, Sam Barker at the CDC just called me. He said Homeland Security notified him and the Minnesota State Patrol that Frank was recently in eastern Minnesota on I-90, headed west. They wouldn't say how they knew, but Sam suspects Homeland has surveillance cameras on parts of the interstate system. He thinks it's a pilot project. We're lucky that some of the cameras are on I-90."

"I'll bet that's a sensitive subject."

"This may not have anything to do with Frank, but I heard there was also an armed robbery at a pharmacy on I-35 in Owatonna. It's only sixteen miles from I-90. A guy fitting Frank's description stole drugs used to treat AIDS patients. They think he fled north to the Twin Cities."

Grant's heart sank. The Twin Cities was the third largest metropolitan area in the Midwest. Frank could hide there for years without being reported.

CHAPTER 27

IN ISOLATION

Tuesday, January 30, 2018
Fort McCoy Hospital
10:00 a.m. CST

Abby checked in to the hospital with her five-year-old daughter, Amanda. Ryan met them just outside the hospital. The bozo acted as though nothing was wrong, even after stumbling over his words when he said he hadn't slept with any other women. And Abby had hoped their relationship would turn into something permanent. She could hardly stand to look at him now.

They were asked to take a seat in the waiting area, but Abby's and Amanda's names were called before they could walk the fifteen feet to a pair of chairs. That was fine with Abby. She didn't want to be near Ryan. He still acted as though he hadn't done anything wrong.

A nurse dressed in ill-fitting protective gear introduced herself to Abby. Abby had never seen anything like the nurse's getup in any of the hospitals she'd worked in. It reminded Abby of something an astronaut might wear.

A different nurse, dressed in the same spacesuit, talked to Ryan and led him out of the room.

Amanda had an iron grip on her mother's hand.

"Here," said the nurse, handing each a surgical mask. "Put these on and follow me."

Abby put it on Amanda. The bands that went around her ears got tangled in her daughter's hair, and she threw a fit. Abby would have been fighting with the kid yet if the nurse hadn't brought a doll-sized mask for Amanda to put on her doll. That made all the difference. Abby wrapped the doll in Amanda's favorite blanket, which was soon trailing on the floor.

The nurse took them through empty hallways to an area with a newly painted sign identifying it as an isolation ward.

NO ADMITTANCE EXCEPT BY AUTHORIZED PERSONNEL, and WARNING: BIOLOGICAL HAZARD signs were posted on the wall next to the new entrance doors.

The entrance to the ward was decidedly different from any others Abby had seen in the hospital. There were two sets of doors only ten feet apart that formed an air lock at the entrance to the ward. Electronic controls prevented one set of doors from opening until the other had closed. She noted the recently installed air pressure gauges on the wall outside the first set of doors, and on the walls in the air lock. *They're controlling air pressure, keeping the ward negative to the hallway so no air will leak from here to the rest of the hospital. My God, how sick am I going to be?* She looked at her daughter standing beside her, still holding her hand. Tears formed in Abby's eyes. *What chance does Amanda have to survive?* There was a low buzzing noise and the second set of doors opened.

Ryan and his nurse came through the air lock after them. She glanced at Ryan. There'd been little conversation between them, and nothing in his expression indicated fear or even curiosity about this special ward. The memory of his hesitation when she'd asked if he'd slept with other women still rankled. *Prick. I hope he gets damned sick. I'd like to tear his eyes out.*

The ward was nearly empty, but the few nurses and doctors they saw were dressed in the same weird getup their guide wore. They were put in a private room and handed hospital gowns. "Put your street clothes in that," the nurse said, pointing to an orange biohazard waste bag hung in a wire frame.

An orderly, also dressed like an astronaut, collected the bags. "These will be given back to you when you leave, but any plastics or manmade fabrics may melt or shrink in the autoclave," he said.

Amanda cried bitterly when they took her blanket away. The orderly put it in a transparent bag and put it on a shelf where Amanda could see it but not retrieve it. "We'll autoclave it when she sleeps, but the bag must remain sealed until she leaves. The blanket can't leave here without going through the autoclave."

Abby was told an investigator from the CDC would visit her in a few minutes to ask about potential contacts. The interviewer would stay on one side of a small table, Abby on the other. This was to protect the interviewer from contamination with the Zürich Virus.

A few minutes later, a short middle-aged woman dressed in white Tyveks named Ethyl introduced herself as the CDC interviewer. She asked Abby how things were going and how Amanda was holding up.

At mention of her name, Amanda crawled into her mother's lap and stayed there. She concentrated on the flower pattern in the hospital gowns, seeming to ignore the conversation. As her mother answered preliminary questions, Amanda burrowed into her mother's hospital gown as though trying to hide.

Ethyl got down to business. "This is unusual because we must track two diseases: the Zürich Virus, which is our primary concern, and chlamydia, an STD. Did you have close contact with anyone after you tested the samples from Nurse Jeager?"

"None, other than Ryan," replied Abby. "And once with a

college student who delivers my groceries. He said he played high-school football."

Abby put Amanda on the floor and pointed to a set of toys in a far corner of the hospital room. "Honey, why don't you try out the toys over there."

Amanda walked to the corner and was soon playing with a doll.

There was a pause in the questions. "Did you have intimate relations with the delivery boy?" the nurse asked.

Abby hesitated a minute. "Yeah. I'd had a hard day and mixed myself a couple of drinks. He was handsome as all get-out, charming, and I was a little buzzed. He's such a nice guy, ya know."

"Ah, do you know the young man's name?"

"No. Ask the manager at the Piggly Wiggly. The guy has black hair, and his nickname is, ah . . ." Abby felt herself blush. "His nickname is 'Stud.'"

The lady seemed to take a deep breath. "Did you shop at other stores yourself?"

"I went to the Tomah Ace Hardware store a few days after I, ah, I worked with Nurse Jeager's samples."

"If it was only a couple of days after you handled her samples, it is unlikely you could spread Zürich Virus that rapidly, but we'll test the personnel at the store. And the only sexual contacts you had were 'Stud' and Ryan, correct?"

Abby took a minute to think the question over. "Correct," she said.

Ethyl gave her an odd look as though she didn't believe her.

"Look, I'm not one of those women who sleeps around," Abby insisted.

"I don't make judgments, but I need the truth," Ethyl said. "Everyone who had even casual contact with Ryan, Stud, or the people at Ace will have to be tested for the Zürich Virus."

"Understood. I sure hope you nail that bed-hopping bastard,

Ryan. I asked him if he's slept with other women. He said, 'No,' but he had to think about it for a while. He's probably been shacked up with any skirt who'd spread their legs for him."

"I'll be talking to—"

"Can you let me know who else he slept with?"

"All communication is privileged. Nothing you say will be released to anyone else, and nothing Ryan says will be released to you."

"Then I'll have to get it out of the creep myself."

Tuesday, January 30, 2018
Fort McCoy Hospital
11:00 a.m. CST

Ryan felt weird. He was used to working on diagnostic tests for other people. Hell, he'd never even been a patient in a hospital before, and now he was in an isolation unit with biosecurity tighter than anything he'd ever seen. He shed his street clothes and tried to decide whether he should put his wallet and ID in the biohazard bag. When Ethyl walked in, he saw her CDC name tag, looked at his wallet, and glanced at her with his eyebrows raised. She nodded, and he dumped the wallet in the biohazard bag.

"Good choice," she said. Ethyl sat at a small table and gestured toward a chair on the other side. "Put on the surgical mask and have a seat." She adjusted her own mask. "To allay any concerns, this conversation is private and will remain so. You'll only be identified by a code number. Do you have any questions before we start?"

Ryan shook his head.

"Do you have any idea where you may have picked up the Zürich Virus?"

"Sure. Abby was under the hood, pipetting samples from Nurse Jeager."

"By under the hood, you mean her hands were in the biosafety hood?"

"Yeah. She wore gloves like she was supposed to, but she, ah, touched me without taking her gloves off. She shouldn't have done that—touched me like that—but if you know Abby, you know she's impulsive at times. We ended up . . ." Ryan started to sweat. He could be in a world of trouble. "You said this conversation is private, right?" he asked.

Ethyl nodded.

"Okay, then. We stepped into the lab stockroom and had sex."

Ethyl snapped her head up and turned a recorder on. "Would you please repeat that?"

"She shouldn't have done that."

"No. Repeat your description of the, ah, of the foreplay Abby engaged in while working at the biosafety cabinet, and what happened afterward."

Ryan did as requested. "She reached around, unzipped my fly, and grabbed my erection. Those gloves are supposed to be stripped off and tossed in the biohazard bag as soon as you bring your hands out of the cabinet," he added.

"Have you had intimate relations with any other women—or men—since that happened?"

Ryan paused before answering. "Yes," he finally said. "I don't claim to be an angel."

Ethyl pushed the microphone a bit closer to him. "Can you give me the names and addresses, please? How many were there?" Ryan crossed his arms over his chest. God, he hoped Ethyl kept her promise that this would be kept confidential. "There were only two women, ladies I met while barhopping a couple of times."

Ethyl nodded and asked for their names, phone numbers, and addresses. Ryan gave their names and struggled to remember what streets they lived on. Ethyl said that would be close enough for her to track them down. Then she asked, "Are there any places, classes, shopping trips, or other functions in which you were put in close contact with other people?"

"Bowling and curling. I've got the names, phone numbers, and addresses of the people here." He handed her a piece of paper.

"Thank you. I can't touch paper you've handled, but you can read the information to me. It will be recorded."

He read the information. Ethyl continued, "Tell me, did you have sexual relations with anyone other than Abby in the two weeks prior to your, ah, tryst in the lab stockroom?"

"Yeah. I spent a night with my ex-wife, but it was before the stuff in the lab. It was one of those for-old-times'-sake things. We're still on good terms. Every now and then we talk about getting back together, but something always comes up."

"You were with no one else?"

"You mean a threesome? We talked about it once, but it never went anywhere."

Ethyl shuddered. "No, no. Not that." She shook her head to rid her mind of the image. "Other than your ex-wife and the two women you picked up in the bars, have you had any other sexual partners in the last, oh, three weeks?"

Ryan shook his head again. "The Zürich Virus shouldn't make my dick itch, should it?"

Ethyl paused and thought a moment. She didn't believe the virus would do that, but they were all still on a learning curve with it. "You are positive for the Zürich Virus. There haven't been any reports indicating it's a venereal disease." She hesitated. "Have you been checked for STDs?"

"No. Abby suggested it, but like I said, I've been busy and haven't gotten around to it."

"Then we'll check you for common STDs. The presence of an infection like the Zürich Virus doesn't mean you don't have something else, something more common."

"If I have an STD, will you tell me where I got it?" Ryan asked.

Ethyl started to put her recorder away. "We can't tell you that. All information we get is confidential. How often do you use a condom?"

"Always. But Abby and I didn't have one in the stockroom that day. That was stupid of us."

"That was probably the least of the mistakes you made that day," Ethyl said as she stood to leave. "I hope you don't develop Zürich Fever, but the treatments do seem to be working on cases that are caught early. With luck, you'll be able to look back on this as a learning experience."

From the commissary, Ethyl called the nurses' station on the second floor of the base hospital after lunch. She introduced herself to the nurse who answered and asked, "I hear you have another new patient for me to talk to." She looked at her clipboard. "His name is Jeb Brown."

"Jeb?" the nurse said. "Yes, that would be 'Stud,'" she chuckled. "We have him here in the old infectious disease section."

Ethyl paused, a little confused. "Why isn't he in the isolation ward?"

"So far we only know that he might have been exposed to the Zürich Virus. We don't have PCR results on him yet. He was positive for chlamydia."

"I'm amazed they located him so quickly," Ethyl said. "From what I understand, they only had a description and a nickname for him."

"Tomah is a small town, and this guy"—the nurse paused, as though looking for words—"this young man has a reputation. He's handsome, intelligent, and he can be unbelievably charming. I assigned a male nurse to him. No point in taking chances."

Ethyl thought about this next interview as she walked back to the hospital. It would be interesting to see if "Stud" turned his reported charm on her. Not much chance of that. Old enough to retire, barely five feet tall, and forty pounds overweight, she doubted if he'd think she was his type.

A half hour later, dressed in her protective gear, she took a seat across a small table from Jeb, a handsome dark-haired young man.

"I gather you had sexual relations with Ms. Abby Peterson after delivering groceries?" Ethyl said.

"Do I have to answer these questions?"

Ethyl stared him in the eye until he looked away. "You don't have to answer, young man, but that would not be advisable. We would have to increase the time you spend with us, and we would ask your employer, friends, and family questions you would find embarrassing. Answer my questions truthfully and no one else will be told what you said. Now, did you have sex with Ms. Peterson?"

"Yes. She'd apparently had a few drinks the first time I delivered groceries. She said she didn't have change for a tip and we ended up in the sack."

"How often has this happened?"

"Two, maybe three times in the last three weeks."

Ethyl shook her head and rested it in one hand. She kept her eyes on the form in front of her. "Have you recently had sexual relations with anyone else?"

"There's a woman named Melody who did the same no-money-for-a-tip story. Her husband walked out on her a couple of years ago. She's kind of homely and I gather she's lonesome, but goddamn, when she gets turned on she's a tiger in bed. She dug her fingernails in my butt so—"

"I don't need a blow-by-blow account."

"Blow? No, she hasn't done that for me."

Ethyl set down her pencil, took a deep breath, and examined what she had already written. "What I meant was that you don't have to describe the activity. Just tell me if you had sex. Okay?"

"Okay."

"Now, did you have sexual contacts other than Melody and Abby?"

"Well, I have a girlfriend too. We have a normal sex life."

Ethyl sighed and ran her fingers over the disposable surgical cap she was wearing. Talking to amoral young men and women depressed her. Retirement couldn't come soon enough. "So, I am to understand you've been having regular and frequent sexual relations with three women?"

"Uh-huh. Sex is the only sport I can afford in the winter. The ladies are happy as clams so long as they think they're the only ones. I suppose you want their addresses and phone numbers?"

"That would be a great help. If you could recite the names, phone numbers, and addresses, I'll record—"

"What about the girl I picked up at the bar last night?"

Ethyl cringed and wondered if this young man thought of anything but sex. "Yes, please include her name and address if you have it. Have you been using protection?"

"Sometimes. I'm very careful."

"Sometimes?" Ethyl tried not to roll her eyes. "With your consent, we'll order tests for STDs as well as the Zürich Virus. All the people you've worked with at Piggly Wiggly will have to be tested for the Zürich Virus. What about any close associates in your classes? Do you sit close to any other students?"

"Classes? What classes?"

Ethyl was perplexed. "Aren't you a college student?"

Jeb waved a hand and laughed. "Oh hell, I tell all the women I'm a college student. Who'd be interested in a grocery boy?"

Wednesday, January 31, 2018
Sioux Falls, South Dakota
8:00 a.m. CST

The sun shone through the motel's ratty drapes and woke Frank. With the ibuprofen, stolen drugs, and a good night's sleep, he felt pretty good. At least better than he had for the past couple of days. Maybe there was something to Grant's virus story.

He had breakfast at the same broken-down diner he'd walked to yesterday. They served great food, but the interstate had turned what had once been a great location for a diner into a disaster. He took a booth as far away from the few other customers as possible, picked up a paper, and checked to see what it had to say about him.

His name had been on the radio and his picture on television so frequently he avoided using either. He was growing a beard, but that would take time. His picture wasn't on the front page anymore. That was an improvement, but he nearly crapped his pants when he turned to the second section. A banner headline on the first page of the section declared "$100,000 Reward." Under it was his picture and a warning that he was armed, dangerous, infectious, and a killer.

Killer? He never would have thought of himself as that. Tony was the guy who'd offed Louie. All he'd done was okay it. *Cripes!*

Next, they'd say he stole candy from children and purses from old ladies. Maybe he should write a letter to the editor about how loosely they'd used the word "killer," but he'd have to wait until he was a long way out of town.

He looked around to make sure no one was reading over his shoulder before he turned the page. His jaw dropped and he had trouble taking a breath. A picture of the car, or one just like it, was on the second page, and the license number was presented in big print. They weren't playing fair. This was more publicity than any crook could handle. How the hell did they expect a guy to make a living? Politicians never had to put up with this stuff, and they killed people by the hundreds, sometimes by the thousands in their undeclared wars.

He surreptitiously removed the interior pages and slipped them under the coat he'd liberated from the SleepyTime Motel after duct-taping Bob. He was pretty sure Bob wasn't worried about the coat.

He finished the paper, wolfed down the rest of his breakfast, and paid at the counter. Fifteen percent for the tip, not low enough or high enough to draw attention. Thank God he'd walked to the diner. A late-model Lexus would draw attention here. Once he was back at the motel, he stole the second section of the paper from the copy in the office and hurried back to his room. He packed and put his suitcase by the door. He would have left even though he had two more nights paid for, but he needed a nap. He was tired, his headache was breaking through the ibuprofen, and he had a hell of a nosebleed.

CHAPTER 28

THE NET CLOSES

Wednesday, January 31, 2018
Wilderness Motel, Tomah, Wisconsin
8:00 a.m. CST

Sybil received a text from the CDC that Frank had been sighted filling up the Lexus on the outskirts of Albert Lee, MN. She shook Tom awake.

"Hey, wake up. They've got a lead. Frank was in southcentral Minnesota a couple of days ago and is thought to be in South Dakota. They don't think he's gone far from the border. We should get ready."

"I doubt if there's a rush," Tom said. "If it was two days ago, he could be a thousand miles away from there by now." He brushed hair from her face and gave her a long and deep kiss. "I can think of something that would be more fun."

He ran a hand from her buttocks to a breast and kissed it. He cuddled close against her.

She closed her eyes, pulled his head tighter to her, and pressed against him. "Oh, you are a sweet talker. Tell me what you had in mind."

"I'm going to turn you into a quivering bowl of jelly," he whispered in her ear. "And then I'm going to make love to you until you scream with pleasure." He grinned and kissed her from jaw to shoulder.

"So, what's stopping you?" she asked. "Better get a raincoat on Mr. Big."

"Oh, crap. We used the last one last night." He returned to kissing her. "I'm game for a round of Richard's Roulette."

"What's that?"

"You're a doctor and you don't know what that is? How did you ever get out of high school? We make love, you get pregnant, and we win. We get married, repeat the game every night, and think up baby names."

This is the craziest, most bizarre marriage proposal ever made. I don't know whether to be insulted or pleased. "And what if I don't get pregnant?"

"We play the game harder and more often."

"Hmm. That sounds like fun." Sybil had worried about her age and biological clock. When her fiancé dumped her, she'd given up serious thoughts of having a family. She didn't admit it, even to herself, but she'd been thinking of Tom in terms of father material. "I have to ask you a big question first. Think you can handle it now?"

"Try me."

"Can you cook, wash dishes, and vacuum?"

"I'll make dinner for you soon. I know my way around a kitchen."

"Just remember that. When I have a twelve- to fourteen-hour day, I don't cook, I don't clean, and I don't do housework."

"No one's asking you to."

She pulled his head up and looked him in the eyes. "You'd better remember that."

"Oh, I will. I will."

"Well, then," she said. "Do you think you can play this roulette? So far, you're all talk, Mr. Big Shot. Let's see some action."

He kissed her again and let his hands roam. She caught her breath.

He whispered, "I should warn you, I'm a stiff competitor."

"There ought to be serious jail time for bad puns."

"But only for bad ones. Mine are good," he replied and returned to kissing her.

She pulled his head up, his lips to hers, and kissed him. "Your books better sell, buster."

An hour later, Sybil woke him again. "We need to get moving or we'll have to pay for a second day."

He yawned. "Okay, I'll get up. But I'm keeping the room in case they don't find him."

"Keeping the room?"

"Where were we going to sleep tonight if they don't find him?" He kissed her deeply. "I'm warning you, when I play a game, I play to win. You might as well sign up for maternity leave."

"I'm all for it." She looked him in the eye. "You'd better not change your mind."

"Oh, I won't," Tom promised. "Have I told you how crazy I am about you?" and he kissed her again. He stroked her hair and looked at his hand. "What kind of ring are you going to get me?"

"Cheap. I know a good woodcarver, but he can work in soap or plastic too. What were you thinking of getting me?"

"I'm a starving artist. Besides, doctors shouldn't wear rings. Rings will interfere with exams and carry contaminants from one patient to another."

They showered together and took their time. They packed their bags in his car in case the cops located Frank, left the motel, and drove to the Fort McCoy hospital. Sybil collected IV packs with liquid forms of the medications Frank had been on and loaded them in the plane. Tom and Grant joined her a few minutes later with the biosafety gear they'd need to handle Frank. They returned to Grant's office at nine o'clock to wait for news.

A few minutes later, they were told Homeland Security had spotted Colonel Williams's Lexus in Sioux Falls. Neither he nor his car had been seen leaving town. Sybil and her crew were ordered to fly immediately to Sioux Falls.

"I think they may be doing more than looking at license plates with their cameras," Sybil said. "They might have facial recognition software on some of them."

Fort McCoy
9:00 a.m. CST

Grant was disappointed. Seating in the plane was as tight as flying coach, and there was barely any space for the equipment they were taking. Grant took a seat across the aisle from Sybil. It was hard to hear each other over the sound of the engine, but he asked her about Abby and Ryan's contacts.

Sybil shook her head. "We're testing Abby's daughter, her daughter's contacts at preschool, and a group of Ryan's drinking buddies. They both have 'friends' we're testing, along with all of their contacts. This will be a major mess if even a few of these people come up positive."

"Great. How do two relatively small organs routinely get so many people in so much trouble?" Grant asked. "Abby's a lab tech. She's been trained in pathogenic microbiology. If anybody should have known better, it was her."

Sybil snorted. "Knowledge had nothing to do with it. Odds are, the men exposed—"

"Men, pleural?" Grant asked.

"Let's just say that Abby is a woman of few gifts, but she's generous with those. Ryan is worse. Their friends, their contacts, and their contacts' contacts might fill the Fort McCoy hospital if all of them are similarly generous. I need to contact the University of Wisconsin hospital to see if they have isolation facilities to handle the overflow if any of these knuckleheads are positive for Zürich."

"Have you heard the latest from Kirby?" Sybil asked.

Grant shook his head.

"Tony died last night. Sam called me and said they've had several more deaths in Zürich among people they were treating. The people who died either had complications from comorbidities or weren't started on the three-drug treatment until after they'd had nosebleeds for a couple of days. If we're not careful, this thing could still turn into a major killer."

Grant turned pensive. A few horny morons were making hash of their efforts to contain the virus. *The Horny Morons—it sounds like a bowling team.* "Next chance you get, ask Sam if they can announce that the Zürich Virus might be passed by kissing and sex. Maybe that will slow it down."

"That would be an outright lie, wouldn't it?"

"Not really," Grant said. "It's hard to engage in sex without getting close and breathing on each other."

"A statement like that would triple the number of samples we'd have to test," Sybil said.

"It would be worth it if it prevented an epidemic."

Sybil nodded. Grant took that as agreement. They were joking, but the truth in it depressed him. Turbulence and engine noise ended the conversation.

The words he used hadn't quite fit though. *Horny moron? Randy fool?* No. That wasn't it. Grant didn't know the right word, or even if English had a word for it. What he needed was a word for people who grabbed low-hanging fruit and easy substitutes for the more complex and satisfying things they really wanted. What do you call people who mistook sex for love, bling and wealth for character and accomplishment, and notoriety or celebrity for distinction or prestige? He wouldn't even know how to do a search for a word that described that kind of mistake.

There'd been notable exceptions, but that type of personality trait was generally lacking in people in science. Grant had met scientists who were famous in their fields. Most had been friendly and helpful to a struggling graduate student. Many had privately been as critical of their own work as they were of the results and hypotheses of others. They were more interested in truth and the search for it than they were in the titles and honors they'd received.

He thought of his own progress as a student. At one time, he had looked forward to being "Dr. Farnsworth." Now he was a veterinarian with a PhD—a "double doc" with a record of damned good guesses. He rarely used the title "Doctor" and, frankly, didn't care what people called him, although he preferred "Grant."

I guess that's what makes the difference—to recognize what's important in work, and in life, and to focus on that. On the other hand, "Moron" had a ring to it. For now, he'd use that, even if intelligent but misguided people often fit the bill.

CHAPTER 29

GREAT BALLS 'O FIRE

Wednesday, January 31, 2018
Sioux Falls, South Dakota
9:00 a.m. CST

Officer Geof Gillam, twenty years on the force with a four-doughnut-a-day habit holding his pants up, wasn't happy. His lieutenant called everyone together, handed out pictures of a chubby bald guy, and told them they were to canvass every motel, hotel, bed and breakfast, and campground in the area.

"Call it in as soon as you catch sight of him," said the lieutenant. "He was last reported driving a black late-model Lexus. This guy is a murderer infected with a fatal virus. *Do not* approach him. Don't even get within ten feet of him, or anybody with him. *Do not* attempt to apprehend. This order has precedence over all but essential jobs."

Gillam didn't mind the orders. What ticked him off was the area they sent him to investigate. He had three cheap motels to check, a flophouse, and a hobo camp. The Hampton Inn, the Hilton, and the Sheraton went to the suck-ups.

He checked under the bridge first, before the homeless guys spread out looking for free or cheap breakfasts. Two guys said they'd seen the suspect, but when he showed them a picture of

Brad Pitt, they'd seen him too. For $10 they offered to tell him where Frank and Pitt were holed up. He took a pass on it.

It took forty minutes to go through the flophouse, banging on doors, showing people pictures of Frank Amorti. All a big zilch. By ten o'clock he had the worst of his assignments out of the way and started on the three cheap motels. A clerk at Motel Six said the guy was in room 106. Gillam asked the clerk to call "Mr. Smith" and ask him to come to the desk to straighten something out.

"What should I say is wrong?" the clerk asked.

"I don't care," Gillam told him. "All I want is a chance to see the guy, preferably from some place he can't see me."

Mr. Smith walked up to the desk a couple of minutes later. His dress shirt was untucked, the top two buttons weren't fastened, one shoe wasn't tied, and his hair looked uncombed. He stepped up to the counter and asked what the problem was. Gillam stood behind a door in back of the clerk. The door was open an inch, and Gillam watched the proceedings through that.

"My manager asked me to check your identification," the clerk explained. "I hate to impose, but could you show me your driver's license?"

Mr. Smith rocked back on his heels. "I, ah, I don't have it on me. It's back in the room with . . . Mrs. Smith. Mrs. Smith is . . . she's a well-known elected representative, and she'd rather not have my—er, our—names in your records." He took a hand from his pocket and slid a $50 bill across the counter to the clerk. "I'm sure you understand."

The clerk swept up the fifty and assured Mr. Smith he understood.

"Not our guy," Gillam said after the man had left the office. "Close, but not him. Thanks, though."

"Glad to be of assistance any time I can help our men in blue," the clerk said and stroked the fifty.

The next motel on Gillam's list was on an old highway at the edge of town. The tall, skinny manager of the Rest Inn looked like a weasel. He glanced at the picture and put it down. "What's he wanted for?"

"Murder. He's also infected with that Zürich Virus that's on the news. He might be real sick by now. Last we knew, he was driving a black Lexus."

The manager turned white and ran for the toilet. Gillam heard him getting rid of his breakfast. He reappeared wiping his mouth. "He's . . . he's in room 119." The manager put his hands on the counter and looked like he might vomit again. "He usually walks down to the—"

"Any chance I could get a look at him?"

"He got in real late. Our security cameras were on. You can look at the tapes in my office."

The manager led Officer Gillam to a back office. The manager's hands shook as he opened the office door. He booted the computer, tapped a few keys, and moments later Frank's tired visage appeared on the screen.

Gillam's heart rate shot up. He looked at the screen, backed the tape up, ran it a second time, and stopped it when it came to a good shot of Frank. He compared that shot to the picture in his hands. *Holy shit, he is here.* Gillam went back to the lobby, looked through the office window, and out into the nearly empty parking lot. A black Lexus, parked at the end of the row of rooms, was half hidden by shrubbery. Gillam became aware the motel manager was still talking. "Repeat that, please."

"Ah, yeah. He generally walks to the diner down the road. Doesn't like our complimentary breakfast. Probably at the diner now."

Gillam glanced out the window again. This time he looked toward the road, but trees and the thick brush of old lilac bushes blocked his view. He pulled his gun just in case, left the office, and peeked around the shrubbery. The road and sidewalk were empty. He went to his cruiser and radioed in his report. A moment later, the lieutenant called on his cell phone.

"Gillam. You said the perp is reported to be at a diner down the street?"

"Affirmative. The motel manager said he walks there every day."

"Good. Go down there, buy a cup of coffee to go, and see if he's still there. Let me know what you see."

The lieutenant wanted him to walk into a room with an infected killer, look around, and turn his back on the guy? Retirement couldn't come soon enough. Gillam went back to the motel office to talk to the manager.

"I'm going to get my car out of here so it doesn't spook him, but this place will be crawling with unmarked cars in a couple of minutes. You and your family should leave or lock yourselves in your apartment." The manager nodded, and Gillam ran to his car and drove to the diner.

There were only a couple of other patrons at the diner. Frank was in a booth at the back. Gillam stopped at the cash register and got a waitress's attention. He was sure Frank could see him shaking as he turned his back to the killer and ordered a coffee and roll to go. Any second he expected to feel a bullet in his back or a knife in his ribs as he waited for his order. It took less than a minute, but it felt like an hour as his imagination ran riot.

Sweat beaded his forehead as he walked to his car. Thank God the coffee had a lid, or his shaking hands would have spilled most of it before he got outside. He drove a block and turned into a driveway where he radioed his office again. "Frank Amorti is still in the diner. I can see the diner entrance from where I'm parked."

"You're positive it's him?" the lieutenant asked.

That infuriated Gillam. He still felt clammy from the scared-stiff sweat. Did they think he ran around guessing whether people fit a picture? "Yeah, it's him. He's in a back booth. I pretended not to notice him, and he did the same for me."

The front door of the diner opened, and Gillam saw Frank come out and walk back toward the motel. "Wait. Frank just left the diner and he's headed toward the motel. It'll take him five, maybe ten minutes to get there."

"Make sure you're out of sight and stay put."

Gillam looked at his watch. It was 10:20.

Wednesday, January 31, 2018
Airplane over western Minnesota
10:30 a.m. CST

Grant heard the click as their pilot put his radio on speaker mode. They were fifteen minutes from the Sioux Falls airport. A male voice identified himself as Agent Dorfner and said he'd have a full-size van waiting for them and their equipment at the airport. Other agents had staked out the motel and were staying out of sight until Sybil and Grant arrived.

As the Cessna descended, Grant saw Sybil close her eyes and her fingers tighten into a death grip on her arm rest. He understood. Landing in small planes always seemed weird. Because of a mild breeze today, the plane was pointed several degrees north of where it was heading. He closed his eyes too.

Agent Dorfner's van stopped next to the plane as soon as it rolled to a halt. He was an intense, thin man with a sharply defined chin and nose, eyes that bored through you, and a manner that seemed abrupt and dictatorial. Dorfner told them Frank Amorti had returned from the diner and was back in his room. He helped

Tom, Grant, and Sybil transfer the equipment to the van. The three from Fort McCoy opened one equipment box and dressed in Tyveks and boots before they got in the van. Grant handed out gloves, goggles, and faceplates as Dorfner drove toward the motel.

A state patrol waved them through a roadblock a couple hundred yards from the motel's driveway. Dorfner pulled to the side of the road and parked near a tall arborvitae hedge fifty yards from the motel's entrance. As Tom, Sybil, and Grant climbed out of the van, Dorfner looked at the bright white Tyveks and shook his head. "Frank is armed, right?"

Sybil nodded. "As far as we know, he has a cop's service revolver."

He pointed at Grant, who was putting on a second pair of Tyveks over the first. "My men can't sneak up on Frank in those getups. Those things are so bright they almost blind me, and every time you take a step, the legs rub together and make a swishing sound. Frank hears that swishing or peeks outside of his room and sees the glare from that bright white, and he could start shooting."

Grant's hopes for an easy takedown of Frank vanished. "But anybody who gets close to Frank without being dressed in this gear could very likely become infected."

"Then we can't do a normal takedown," said Dorfner. "The manager said he walks to the local diner around one. He probably times it to avoid being seen by the diner's lunch crowd. We'll take him in the parking lot when he comes out of his room. Unless he's suicidal, he'll put down his gun and let one of you guys handcuff him."

Sybil looked thoughtful. "A patient who may be running a high fever could be in delirium or close to it. You can't assume Frank will make rational decisions. He could go for suicide by cop or try to shoot his way out of this."

"Do you want to tell me how I should do my job?" Dorfner asked, an icy edge to his voice.

Sybil didn't catch on. "Whoever goes up to cuff him should wear a bulletproof vest over their Tyveks, and we don't approach him until he throws his gun away."

"Gee. I would never have thought of that myself," Dorfner said sarcastically. "My men will all wear bulletproof vests. They'll stay out of sight until Frank leaves his room. When he gets to the center of the parking lot, we tell him to hold it, drop his gun, and put up his hands. If he tries to run, we shoot. If—"

Grant thought he was going to be sick. "Can you shoot him in the leg or something?"

"When we fire a gun, we shoot to kill," Dorfner snarled. He looked angry enough to bite Grant's head off.

"Look, I really don't give a shit what happens to Frank," Grant said. "Except that right now his blood is valuable for diagnostic tests and for treatments. He has an astounding amount of antibody to the Zürich Virus in his blood. The antibodies may not cure him, but we can use them to aid in the treatment of others. We also need to talk to Frank about where he stopped and who he's been in contact with."

Dorfner threw his hands into the air. "I give up. What the hell are we supposed to do? Give him a ride to the diner and ask politely if we can put him in handcuffs?"

Sybil asked Dorfner to show her the motel, and the two set off down the road. Grant couldn't see what they did, or hear what they said, but when they came back ten minutes later they were in good spirits. Dorfner apologized to Grant for losing his temper. He motioned for three men standing near another car to join them.

"This is what we're going to do. The door to room 118 is the closest door to Amorti's door. Two men will be put in that room.

The door to room 120 is a little farther away. We'll have one man in that room. The men in 118 will wear bulletproof vests under their Tyveks. Cars will be parked in front of those rooms to hem Frank in when he comes out. We only let him get a few feet out of the room before I step out from behind the shrubbery in front of Frank and tell him to put his gun down."

Dorfner pointed at one of his men. "I'll be a distraction. When I've got Frank's attention, you come piling out of rooms 118 and 120 and grab him before he can get his gun out."

"What about the noise these damned suits make when we walk?"

"Duct tape," Dorfner said. "The sound comes from the plastic rubbing on plastic. A couple rounds of duct tape around your legs will pull it tight to your legs and silence them."

"Where do you want us?" Grant asked.

"Stay in room 120. Dr. Erypet should be ready to take care of Amorti or my men if anyone gets shot. Grant, you should have whatever you need to maintain biosecurity and help Erypet. Corporal Jones, you'll stand by to help Dr. Erypet or Dr. Farnsworth, whoever needs it."

Dorfner looked at each of the people gathered around him. He told his men to have Grant show them how to suit up and describe how they'd have to disinfect and remove the Tyveks. They'd carry the Tyveks into room 118 in a bag and dress there. Everyone going into room 120 would take their Tyveks off until they were in the room. Frank wouldn't see the white Tyveks until the agents jumped him.

The two FBI cars were parked in front of rooms 118 and 120, and everyone was suited up, had reviewed the plan, and was in position by twelve-thirty. Grant and Sybil set first-aid packs out, just in case. The waiting began. Sybil and Tom sat on the bed and held hands. Grant sat in a chair next to them and voiced his concerns. "Man, I hope this goes as smoothly as Dorfner planned," he said. "I got the feeling there might be more than a little wishful thinking going on."

Sybil nodded. "The guys in room 118 will have to be fast and quiet. They've never worn the biosecurity equipment before. I can just picture them tripping over something or their faceplates fogging."

"They've got bulletproof vests," Grant said. "At least they'll be safe—unless they're shot in the head."

Tom put his hand on Sybil's knee. "Stay here unless someone needs help. Don't poke your head out of the door unless somebody calls for a medic. Even then, don't go out until Frank's gun is in our control."

"Yes, Mother."

"I'm serious. Promise me that much."

"I promise."

CHAPTER 30

THE SHOOTING GALLERY

Wednesday, January 31, 2018
Sunset Motel, Room 119
12:50 p.m. CST

Frank lay on his bed and watched the clock. He felt lousy. His head hurt and the nosebleed still seeped. So much for the meds he'd stolen. He tried thinking about sex. That had always taken his mind off his problems before. This time he couldn't even keep his mind on that. Maybe if he checked out the waitress at the diner he could get his mind off his headache.

When he moved his head, he felt something wet. He stood and looked at his pillow. *Aw, shit.*

Blood.

He felt a trickling sensation down the side of his head. Wiping at it with a tissue, it came away bright red. In the mirror above the dresser, he saw a trail of red coming from his right ear. *Jesus.* He was going the way Tony had. No wonder he felt like shit.

His forehead felt hot, so he took more ibuprofen. It was almost one o'clock. Time to go to the diner, even though he wasn't hungry. Maybe he'd get an appetite after the walk. Try some soup if nothing else. Mom had always given him chicken soup for everything. That would help. But what if the cops stopped him? The fat cop at the diner this morning hadn't paid any attention to him, or maybe it had been an act. He'd be damned if he went like like Tony, moaning all night, tubes sticking in every hole, and bleeding out of his ass.

He stood, put on his coat, and stuffed his gun in his waistband. A quick look in the mirror verified the coat covered his gun. If the cops stopped him, he'd go down shooting. Better a cop killing him quick than the virus taking him by inches.

Wednesday, January 31, 2018
Sunset Motel, Room 120
12:55 p.m. CST

Grant heard the door of 119 open from the next room. The FBI agent quietly turned the knob on their own door and opened it a crack to watch for Frank. Grant peeked through the curtains of the front window. The sun glinted off the blacktop in the two parking places between the FBI cars. That was where Frank would walk out, and the blacktop the FBI agents would have to rush across to get to Frank. Grant's stomach turned into a knot. *Patches of black ice.* The temp was up to twenty degrees today. The ice would be slippery.

Frank stepped out of his room, glanced at the new cars parked to either side, and sauntered through the empty space between them. Grant wished the FBI had used old Chevys with a little rust on them. They'd fit this motel better.

The ice didn't seem to bother Frank. He'd gone about ten feet when Dorfner stepped out of the shrubbery thirty feet in front of him. "Frank, Frank Amorti. This is the FBI. You are surrounded. Drop your gun and put your hands up. Now!"

Justin, the agent in Grant's room, quietly rushed through the door and charged toward Frank's back. Grant and Sybil stood in the door until Tom moved Sybil to the side and watched. The

agents from room 118 were a couple of steps ahead of Justin. They
hit the ice on the sidewalk and their legs shot out from under
them. The disposable boots Grant had insisted they wear provided
no traction, and the two agents fell in a pile of arms and legs and
slid toward Frank. Justin flopped on top of the pile and made it
slide faster. Frank drew his gun and turned toward them, only to
be bowled over by the oncoming mass of bodies.

Frank dropped his gun when he hit the ice. The agents' guns
beyond reach inside their Tyveks, they scrambled on hands and
knees to get behind the only cover available: the front ends of
their cars. Frank came up with his gun, but his footing wasn't great
and he looked a little shaky. He fired once at the agents' butts as
they disappeared around the fenders but missed. He turned his
fire toward the open door of room 120. A shot splintered the
doorframe next to Sybil. A piece of wood struck her on the side of
the face, drawing blood.

"That was close." Sybil felt the wound, drew out the splinter,
and tossed it behind her.

Tom looked at Sybil, reached up to touch the blood, and
charged after Frank. Grant didn't see where he'd gotten it, but
Tom raised a gun. Frank fired. An ugly red blotch appeared
against the white Tyvek high on Tom's left shoulder. He staggered
backward toward the motel room and fell. One of the agents
reached out, grabbed him, and dragged him behind the cover of
the car.

Dorfner stood, mouth agape. He lowered his gun from his
aim at Frank and lapsed into what sounded like a long string of
expletives, but he wasn't loud enough for Grant to hear more than
a growl from where he crouched by the door.

Paying no attention to Frank, Sybil rushed to Tom, lifted his
head, and quickly checked his wound. Grant ducked behind the
front of the car with Sybil as tears coursed down her cheeks.

He heard her say, "Thank God. It's just a flesh wound, nothing serious." She took a gauze pledget out of a first-aid kit and placed it on Tom's wound. She turned to Grant. "Put light pressure on the pledget and make him comfortable. I'll be back."

Frank advanced toward Dorfner, firing two shots. Grant saw that Dorfner couldn't return fire. His men, in their panic to get away, had moved so they'd be in his line of fire. It was now a circular firing squad with Frank in the center. Any shot at Frank would imperil FBI agents. Dorfner dodged out of sight behind the thick, leafless lilac shrubbery.

"You son of a bitch!" Sybil screamed. She grabbed Tom's gun and fired at Frank. Oblivious to her own safety, she advanced toward Frank, continued to scream, and opened sustained fire.

Grant watched her first shot fracture the back window of one FBI car. The next shot blew out a rear tire of the other car. The head of a garden gnome exploded on Frank's left, and the branches of the lilacs concealing Dorfner splintered. Grant ducked below the car's hood. As wild as her aim was, he'd be lucky if she didn't hurt him.

Frank turned toward her in a partial squat and took aim. Sybil fired again. Frank gasped, dropped his gun, and fell to the pavement.

"There," Sybil screamed. "You motherfucking bastard. You got what you deserved, damn you."

She rushed back to Tom and tore off his Tyveks to get a better look at the wound. She looked at Grant and pointed toward Frank. "See what damage I did to that filthy lowlife. I'll take care of Tommy."

Tommy, now, is it? Grant approached Frank, who lay moaning on the blacktop of the parking lot. Blood seeped through his pants below the zipper of his fly. Grant kicked Frank's gun away, lifted him up, unbuckled his pants, and pulled them halfway down his thighs. Frank came to and gasped as his butt hit the ice-cold pavement. The front of his white briefs was torn and bright red. Blood clotted on the cloth and pulsed beneath and around it. Grant pulled the briefs down, eliciting a louder groan from Frank.

Clearing the blood away with a gauze pledget, he saw blood shoot in pulses from Frank's scrotum. He pulled out a fresh pledget and put mild pressure on the wound. The bleeding didn't slow. The spurting blood indicated arterial bleeding. Examining more closely, he saw that most of one testicle had been shot away. The other testicle had been nicked. First aid to control the bleeding would be difficult and possibly destroy what was left of Frank's testicles.

Grant remembered what he'd seen in vet school. Some animals bled to death from damage to the testicles—in pigs and steers, it occurred most frequently from a botched castration performed by a farmer.

Frank emitted loud groans. Grant had three options. He could wait until a physician could look at Frank, but the nearest physician was Sybil. Having her treat Frank would not be wise, he decided. The other choice was to grasp Frank's testicles high on the spermatic cord and pull the testicles off. The arteries would snap back into the inguinal canal, and the pressure of the muscles around the canal would close the arteries and stop the bleeding. It was the standard treatment for a bull calf or pig. He'd never heard of it being done to a man.

As disagreeable as Frank could be, Grant thought he'd probably object to that treatment. Lawsuits would follow, and as a veterinarian treating a person, he could only use standard first aid. Doing the testicle tug wouldn't give him a leg to stand on in court.

The third option would be to put a tourniquet high on Frank's scrotum. That should work. It was an accepted first-aid procedure—if not on the testicles, on other parts of the body—and seemed the least likely to get Grant or Sybil into a malpractice lawsuit. He untied one of Frank's shoes and removed the lace. Wrapping the lace twice around the scrotum, he cinched the knot down until blood stopped pouring from the testicles.

Frank's eyes opened wide. His scream sounded like a freight train suddenly applying the brakes, or the time Grant had put a big spider in his older sister's bed. Grant hadn't thought a man could hit notes that high. It broke off in mid-scream as Frank fainted again.

Grant checked the bleeding to make sure it had stopped before he looked for Dorfner. He found the agent sitting behind the shrubbery, nursing a wound in his thigh. "How serious is it?" Grant asked.

"Flesh wound. Just broke the skin."

"Frank shoot you?"

"No. Erypet did," Dorfner said. "From what I can tell, she got two Chevys, a garden gnome, me, the FBI agent in charge, and Frank, all because her boyfriend got nicked. That woman hit something every time she pulled the trigger."

"If it makes you feel better, she hit Frank in the nuts."

"Good Lord. Was it deliberate?"

"She said she was aiming for his heart. That's what she was aiming at when she hit the garden gnome and the Chevys too."

"What did you do for him?"

Grant described the tourniquet.

Dorfner looked at Grant and shook his head. "This is the first time I've ever felt sorry for a murderer." He chuckled. "Your sidekick Dr. Erypet will have a mountain of paperwork to fill out on the shootings. I'm not even sure what her legal status is—she's not really law enforcement, but she was here as part of our team."

"Don't bother bringing up the paperwork issue until she's back in Kirby. There'll be paperwork to even allow her to fill out the paperwork you want. Any paperwork she completes will have to be autoclaved until we can prove she isn't infected."

CHAPTER 31

BACK TO MCCOY

At the nearest hospital, Sybil and Grant cleaned up and disinfected each other in a little-used room. They stepped out of the room, put on fresh Tyveks, and a crew disinfected and sealed the room. Dorfner and Tom were treated as outpatients.

The problem was Frank.

The hospital administrator asked Grant and Sibyl to step into his office. "Our lawyers tell me I have to be careful how I phrase this," he said, "but it wouldn't be wise for us to admit Frank for surgery and post-op care. It would expose the hospital, our staff, and our patients to the Zürich Virus. We aren't set up to properly quarantine Frank. A specialized university hospital might be able to handle it."

Sybil snorted. "The CDC doesn't want him here, either. There may not be a hospital in South Dakota capable of handling the Zürich Virus. We believe it's spread by aerosol, which makes handling patients even more dangerous than Ebola. There are only a handful of hospitals in the US capable of safely treating Ebola patients. Fortunately, we have a treatment for the Zürich

Virus, but I don't want Frank to take a step out of the ambulance until he's back at Kirby."

Grant cringed as he thought of his tourniquet being on Frank's scrotum for the five-hour ambulance ride to Kirby. "What about the University of Nebraska Medical Center in Omaha? It took care of Ebola patients successfully. They have a helicopter pad. Frank could be there in minutes."

Sybil glared at Grant. "UNMC had weeks of warning before the Ebola patient arrived, and Ebola is spread by contact, not by aerosol and the respiratory route. We'd be dropping a killer on them without warning, and a virus with a method of spread that's much more difficult to control than Ebola. I want Frank in a medical facility with armed guards *in* and *surrounding* the facility, and one that we've set up to handle a respiratory disease. That's Kirby."

"Is he healthy enough to make the trip?" Grant asked.

"I believe so. He's asked for something to eat. An hour ago, he planned to walk a quarter mile for lunch, *and* he held four FBI agents at bay. He's being given fluids, supportive therapy, and the correct anti-RNA viral drugs as we speak. Two medics are on their way to ride back to Kirby with him."

"But—"

"Grant, I have a responsibility to treat Frank, but I work for the CDC as an epidemiologist. My primary responsibility is to protect the population of the United States. I cannot risk starting an epidemic to give Frank a modest improvement in treatment."

After that meeting broke up, Grant wandered down the hall. A urologist coming out of surgery stopped him and asked where Frank was and how he was doing. They turned into a small surgical waiting room. The walls were painted a cheerful yellow. Particularly appropriate for urologists, Grant mused. Outdated magazines and a couple copies of the local newspaper were on an end table between plastic chairs. The doctor dropped into a chair and motioned Grant to take the one across the table from him.

"I'm asking about Frank because I seem to be the only urologist here without an ironclad excuse for avoiding his case."

Grant explained Frank's injuries and how he'd applied the tourniquet.

The doctor gave him a nasty look, turned, wadded up a piece of paper, and threw it into a wastebasket. "Damn. You know what this means, don't you?"

"Sorry," Grant said, "but I have no idea what you're referring to."

"We've got a patient who has lost one testicle and will probably lose the other, and he's shedding copious amounts of the Zürich Virus. Because we don't want him contaminating the surgeries, I'll have to operate in the ambulance with hardly enough room to move, and inhale the virus with every breath I take. After that, all of my appointments and surgeries will have to be rescheduled because I'll be quarantined for two weeks or longer. I'll probably have to take vacation time to cover that."

Grant realized there was a chance to treat Frank and remove the tourniquet soon. "I—"

"But it gets better. He's a killer who will be sitting in prison for the rest of his life with nothing to do for recreation but bring lawsuits. I'll be spending one day a week in court for the rest of Frank's life as he tries to sue *my* balls off for malpractice."

"I take it that's a 'no,' then," Grant said. He'd only given Frank first aid. He couldn't be sued for that, he hoped.

"It's too bad Dr. Erypet couldn't take a few more shots at him," the urologist said. He glanced at another note from his pocket and tossed that in the wastebasket too. "Sooner or later, she'd have had to hit something vital—preferably in Frank." He sighed, leaned back in his chair, and turned toward Grant. "No chance Frank could make a break for it, is there?"

Grant shook his head. The question hadn't sounded serious anyway. "He's cuffed to the gurney and the ambulance."

"Have you thought about finding an army surgeon? If the surgery were done in Kirby or at Fort McCoy, you wouldn't be closing a hospital because of the Zürich Virus. Those hospitals are already contaminated, and any liability will be the US Army's. I don't think Frank can sue them unless the government gives its permission. They've given soldiers on duty that permission, but they might be less likely to give it to a convicted drug mule and murderer with no service record."

"He'll lose both testicles if the tourniquet has to stay on long enough to get him to the Kirby hospital," Grant whined.

"So? It's not like he's going to be fathering a family. He's a killer. His ass is going to be in jail for the rest of his life. He can be treated with testosterone to maintain muscle mass and sex drive if that's an issue. I'd love to hear his argument to a court on why he should be compensated for low libido as he sits in prison."

Grant knew when he was beaten. At least Frank was already handcuffed to the ambulance cot and prepared to be shipped back to Fort McCoy. The antiviral drugs he'd stolen had bought him some time, but they hadn't been the optimal ones. Sybil had established IVs and had him on the correct drugs now.

Grant, Sybil, and Tom wore fresh Tyveks in the airplane for the flight back to Fort McCoy to keep the plane and pilot free of contamination. On landing, they were put in quarantine in the field hospital. Tom nursed his shoulder, putting on what Grant thought was one hell of an act to keep Sybil's sympathy. Grant was glad to be back at McCoy and wondered how long before he could go home to Sarah.

Friday, February 2, 2018
Fort McCoy
10:00 a.m. CST

Sybil kept busy organizing the armada of public health nurses needed to track down the people who'd had contact with Frank, Abby, Ryan, Stud, and Melody, and the contacts their contacts had. She told Grant and anyone else who would listen that it was a "rolling nightmare, a succession of dominos falling in all directions. How did mankind survive this long with so many horny morons?"

Five days after the debacle in Sioux Falls, nasal swabs were collected from everyone and tested for the Zürich Virus. Only Frank was positive.

Tom got out of the hospital the same day Sybil got out of quarantine. She picked him up in his car and headed off base.

"I thought you were taking me back to the barracks," he said. "Where are we going?"

"Your surgeon says you're excused from any work for at least another week. We're taking a couple of days off."

"And your work?"

Sybil turned to him and smiled. "I can work from anywhere as long as I have my phone."

"You still haven't told me where we're going."

"There's a motel in Sparta with a pool and hot tub."

"But I don't have any clothes with me. We'll have to stop at my—"

"You won't need clothes for what we'll be doing. Now sit back and relax. You'll need your energy."

Half an hour later, Sybil was helping Tom undress. His

shoulder was still stiff and sore, and there was a bandage over the wound. As she undressed and Tom gingerly rolled into bed, she remembered when Tom was hit in the shootout. "I still can't believe I grabbed your gun and shot Frank," she said, "but every time I look at you, I know it was worth it."

Tom kissed her. "It's nice to be appreciated."

After they made love, she picked up her phone and made a call. "Sam, I'm up to my earlobes in work chasing down contacts, and I've got local cops asking me to fill out a pile of paperwork on the gunfight at Sioux Falls. I can take a day off and fill out the paperwork or I can stay on the contacts. Which do you want me to do?"

"Stay on the contacts and I'll make some phone calls. This really is a matter of national security."

"When this settles down, I'm getting married."

She looked at Tom. He smiled and nodded as she continued. "You're invited, but our honeymoon is ours. I won't be taking any emergency jobs for a month after that, and by next year I'd like a desk job. We'll need time for a family."

"Congratulations. I'm looking forward to meeting Tom. I'll do what I can to—"

"This isn't a request, Sam. It's what I need and I'm going to have it. I'll spend six months or so to train in my replacement, but these changes aren't negotiable."

"I'll see what I can do, but our budget—"

"With the Zürich Virus still a problem in Europe, your budget will be just fine. I can help on that front too. Tom has already started outlining a new book. The tentative title is 'Zürich Virus in the United States.' It should hit the stands three or four months after we have things cleaned up if he can have access to CDC documents. I guarantee the manuscript will make the CDC look awesome."

Monday, February 5, 2018
Fort McCoy
11:00 a.m. CST

Grant knocked on the door to Sybil's office. It was a small room painted a drab pale green. Her metal, government-issue desk wasn't big but it filled a large part of the room. That and two metal filing cabinets left only enough room for Sybil's chair and a chair for visitors.

Grant plopped into the visitor's chair across from her. "How's it going?" he asked.

Sybil put down her pen and took off her reading glasses. "Busy. And with you? What is your lab working on now?"

Grant gave a nod. "Busy here too. The nasal spray targeted with Frank's antibodies appears to have cleared Mrs. Anderson's infection. She's going home tomorrow, but we'll monitor her weekly for the next month." His expression intense, Grant leaned forward in his chair. "Do you know if Frank will donate more antibodies if we need them?"

"He'd darn well better. We've agreed to pin Professor Antoine's murder on Tony and reduce the charges against Frank to being an accessory." Sybil leaned back in her chair. "He'll be in the witness protection program if he testifies about his work as a drug mule. The deal is, he'll get protection in prison and early parole, but he has to provide us everything we want."

"Sounds equitable," Grant said. "We're working on an ELISA to detect the virus, and another to measure antibody levels to it. Progress has been slow. We don't even know yet whether the antibody response is protective or dangerous to the patient."

Sybil shuddered. "Yeah. The ghost of the Dengue Fever vaccine debacle. When is Sarah due?"

"Tomorrow. I'd like to leave for home this afternoon. Randy in the lab knows more than I do about the development of ELISAs. He can continue that work."

"Good. Go home. Spend a couple of weeks with your wife and Jimmy. Remember to check back with Sam Barker and me when Sarah's got Jimmy and the baby under control. We'll have an offer for you."

Grant fidgeted in his chair. "Offer?"

"We've been impressed with your work, Grant. The head of the Appropriations Committee in the House is from Wisconsin. He's responsible for budget cuts we've suffered during the last few years." She grinned. "Now he's scared witless it'll come back to bite him. For the first time in years, we'll have the money we need to do public health properly, and I can guarantee you there'll be an opening for a man like you."

"I'd hate to leave Ron hanging . . ."

Sybil's eyebrows rose briefly. She wrote a figure on a piece of paper, slid it across her small desk, and watched him expectantly. Grant picked it up and looked at it. His eyebrows shot up. "Really? This would be my starting salary?"

Sybil nodded. "I believe that's many times what you're making as a postdoc."

Grant didn't trust himself to do more than nod. Bus drivers made more than he did as a postdoc. Ron had better get used to working without him.

"Give me a call when things are settled at home. And don't rush. Sarah needs you." She stood and shook Grant's hand as he rose to leave.

Monday, February 5, 2018
I-94 north of Tomah, Wisconsin
Noon CST

Grant didn't trust himself to stick to the speed limit, and he knew the Wisconsin State Patrol wasn't as forgiving as their Minnesota brethren. To be safe, he put the SUV on cruise control. He made it back to St. Paul late that afternoon. Sarah was still home, but her contractions were only two hours apart.

They put Sarah's suitcase in the SUV. Grant played with Jimmy and wore him out, and they both took naps. Sarah woke Grant at 2:00 a.m. and told him they'd better head to the hospital. Her contractions were five minutes apart and rapidly getting closer. It took longer than they'd planned to drop Jimmy off at the neighbor's house, and the contractions were only a couple of minutes apart when they arrived at the hospital. Sarah's water broke as she was being wheeled up to her room. She gave birth to Ariana an hour later.

Sarah was exhausted. Grant was thrilled and happy to call relatives and friends with the news. Not all were happy to get a call from an excited and voluble new father at 4:00 a.m. He slept until noon, talked to the neighbor who was taking care of Jimmy, and visited Ariana and Sarah in the hospital. Late that afternoon, Sarah asked Grant how things had gone in Wisconsin and if the threat of an epidemic was over.

Grant shook his head. "The public health nurses and counselors will be going nuts for the next couple of months as they track down infected people, but the threat of an epidemic that kills hundreds of thousands is over."

Sarah looked relieved. "I was so afraid you'd become infected."

He held her hand as Ariana nursed and the radio in Sarah's

room played in the background. "So, what did you learn working on Ron's unbelievable fuckup?" she asked.

Grant paused. The radio was tuned to NPR. Playing was a recording of Liz Taylor singing "Send in the Clowns" from *A Little Night Music,* a bewitching old Stephen Sondheim musical. He remembered the hope and fear he'd felt when Ron first told him of his new project, the horny morons, and the blind fools he'd encountered. *Holy shit,* he thought. He'd danced with death and destruction, alternately thrilled and terrified. It had been the most exciting, frightening, and rewarding thing he'd ever done. And now it would be his profession.

He looked at Sarah's contented expression and the baby nursing at her breast. *How much do I dare tell her?* He gently squeezed her hand and looked in her eyes. "I learned that you and the kids are the most important thing in my life."

ABOUT THE AUTHOR

Gary F. Jones is a retired veterinarian with a PhD in microbiology and an interest in history. He'd heard of outbreaks of hemorrhagic viral diseases in Europe during the Dark Ages. The victims and epidemics died out quickly, and their causes remain unknown.

Enter the Iceman, the five-thousand-year-old mummified corpse discovered in the Alps. What if another Iceman, one from around 800 AD, were discovered, an Iceman who had died of a hemorrhagic virus? Combine that with the eccentricities of people Jones met in his small-town veterinary practice, and he recognized a story waiting to be told.

OTHER BOOKS BY GARY F. JONES

When Wisconsin veterinarian Doc dies, his family learns that to inherit his fortune, they must decipher the cryptic codicil he added to his will: "Take Doofus squirrel-fishing." They can only do that by talking to Doc's friends, reading the memoir Doc wrote of a Christmas season decades earlier, and searching through Doc's correspondences. Humor abounds as this mismatched lot tries to find time in their hectic lives to work together to solve the puzzle. In the end, will they realize that fortune comes in many guises?

Doc's Codicil is a mystery told with abundant humor where a veterinarian teaches his heirs a lesson from the grave.

Veterinary virologist Jason Mitchell can't keep his mouth shut, lie convincingly, or follow orders. He's an unlikely candidate to help the CIA locate and destroy a deadly hybrid virus stolen from Jason's lab at the University of Minnesota. From Washington to Djibouti, From Minneapolis to Yemen, Marines cringe, Senators turn livid, and CIA agents shudder as Jason struggles to prevent the virus from becoming a biological weapon in the hands of insurgents.

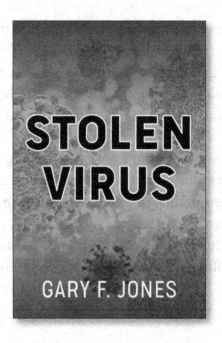

Veterinary virologist Jason Mitchell can't keep his mouth shut, can't lie convincingly, and can't follow orders. He's an unlikely candidate to help the CIA locate and destroy a deadly hybrid virus stolen from Jason's lab at the University of Minnesota.

From Washington to Djibouti, From Minneapolis to Yemen, Marines cringe, Senators turn livid, and CIA agents shudder as Jason struggles to prevent the virus from becoming a biological weapon in the hands of insurgents..

Jason and Ann Hartman, veterinarians, lovers, and graduate students, conduct a study of BCV in calves, a common virus that causes diarrhea in cattle. A recently arrived Chinese student accidentally exposes the calves to the SARS virus, a close relative of BCV. The calves and the Chinese student develop a severe and puzzling pneumonia. The Center for Disease Control (CDC) isolates a hybrid BCV-SARS virus from the Chinese student and the calves. The FBI is notified of the new and dangerous virus.

Meanwhile, Ahmed, more con man than graduate student,

discovers samples of Jason's that contain the virus. He steals them and flees to Yemen where he pretends to be a devout Muslim to get funding from a terrorist group that believes the virus will be valuable as a biological weapon and as bait to lure the CIA into military action that will kill innocent civilians and increase hatred of the US.

In a very serious situation with a bumbling hero and unexpected situations, Jason and an unconventional CIA agent redefine "thinking outside the box" as they con Ahmed, dodge bullets, and thwart the bad guys.

"A medical thriller that will keep you guessing and engaged while offering subtle humor as the good guys triumph.